DOUBLE EXPOSURE

A photographer is blown to bits while staking out a private royal visit. Vernon Summers was no ordinary paparazzo. In his scrapbook is a Gulf War photo which suggests he was about to expose a multi-million pound arms scandal. Detective Inspector 'Jacko' Jackson suspects the cameraman was tracking the royals as cover to collect evidence against a well-connected family. As he pursues his enquiries, Jackson treads through a minefield of sanctions busting, sex smears, blackmail and a Whitehall wall of silence...

For SYD and JACKIE

DOUBLE EXPOSURE

by
Frank Palmer

Dales Large Print Books
Long Preston, North Yorkshire,
England.

British Library Cataloguing in Publication Data.

Palmer, Frank
  Double exposure.

  A catalogue record for this book is
  available from the British Library

  ISBN 1-85389-612-8 pbk

First published in Great Britain by Constable & Company
Ltd., 1995

Published in Large Print April, 1996 by arrangement with
Constable & Company Ltd.

Dales Large Print is an imprint of
Library Magna Books Ltd.
Printed and bound in Great Britain by
T.J. Press (Padstow) Ltd., Cornwall, PL28 8RW.

Special thanks to Keith Graves for background on the arms trade.

The lines from 'Have a drink on me' (Huddie Ledbetter: John Lomax: Alan Lomax: Lonnie Donegan: Peter Buchanan —© 1961 Folkways Music Publishers Inc., USA) are published by arrangement with Cromwell Music Ltd, Suite 2.07, Plaza 535 Kings Road, London SW10 OSZ.

The East Midlands Combined Constabulary, its characters and its cases are fictional. So, too, is the island, its inhabitants and all the events in this story.

1

Zero hour minus fifteen minutes

His good hand squeezed his unshaven chin, palm prickled by black bristles. A dark grizzle always made him look hard, feel tough.

Yous're tough, he told himself; hard. Now concentrate.

In a subconscious display of self-discipline, his eyes dropped to his black waterproof watch: fifteen minutes to go. They returned to his binoculars. With right finger and thumb, he adjusted the dial in front of his nose. The island came closer.

He breathed in the cold air. Right then, Starling. Formally he called himself a name he seldom answered to these days. Right then, check off.

In a kneeling position, sitting back on the rubber heels of his combat boots, he moved his upper body slightly to his right. His eyes stopped at the railed wooden bridge which linked the peninsula to the island.

The newsboy on his bike and the milkman in his trolley had been and gone. No other regulars, according to the brief. Check? Check.

Over that bridge, in a quarter of an hour, fractionally less now, would come the convertible—white with a black top. Check? Check.

His head moved left. His arms, pinned to his midriff by the elbows went with it. All movement stopped again as he studied the willow tree, leafless branches bent double at the edge of the choppy water.

Behind the tree, out of view, he knew that the narrow road forked. Straight on round a sweeping curve that followed the bank stood a big white house overlooking the lake. A dirt track climbed north behind the tree up a wooded hill to the stables.

The island, he'd been relieved to discover, had sandy subsoil. With no overnight frost to harden the track, it had taken only a few minutes to dig the hole for the mine.

In the darkness, two hours earlier, he hadn't really noticed the stables. Now he could see they were clad in white stucco, like the house, with a dark tiled roof below a spire with a weather vane.

When the target's behind the tree, detonate, check? Check.

But would it work? Would it?

If it doesn't, it's no my soddin' fault, he answered himself angrily. Thirty-six hours to plan an operation like this, to study the maps, carry out the recce, make the bomb.

He'd never used remote control before; always wire. What if some kid and his dad were flying a plane or sailing a boat? Could they trigger it?

He lowered his rubber-armoured binoculars. With naked eyes, he scanned the wide, silvery blue waters. Just one yacht with a white sail was in vision.

Relax. Who'd be sailing a model boat or flying a plane on a murky, raw morning like this? Even if it went up by mistake, his escape route was secure. He'd have liked to have been closer; on the peninsula, for preference, but it was too easily blocked off. No, this position's perfect.

He touched, careful not to pat, a pocket in fatigues that hung loose around a bodybuilder's frame, gently feeling the box that contained the transmitter.

The battledress was black, a last-minute decision. Had it been white with snow, he'd have worn his arctic gear. Black had been right in the frost-free darkness two hours earlier. Now the sky was lightening into greys, he wondered if brown and olive might have been better.

His eyes went back to the island. Without bins he could still make out the big willow with the mine behind it.

Thoughts lapped in and out of his mind like the white-topped waves beating against the stony causeway where he knelt.

The assignment had shocked him, scared him a bit, but he needed the cash; to get away, right away. He was sure, positive, that the reason for the mission was bullshit.

'Cutting the enemy's supply line,' he'd said last time, but it had been his mate who ended up with his windpipe cut.

'Striking a blow for Queen and country,' he'd called it this time. More bullshit. What could the real motive be? A woman? Money? More arms smuggling? An insurance job?

Ours is not to reason why; ours is but to do and let the other poor bastard die.

He raised his binoculars again, focusing

on the wooden bridge. Behind them he put on a poker face, denying himself permission for a grim smile.

Keep concentrating, he ordered himself. Watch and wait for your target.

2

Zero hour

He was on his haunches now, sheltered from the wind by the pillars of the church on the causeway.

In his left hand was a black box, no bigger than a cigarette packet. His right held the binoculars to his eyes.

From the east, the vehicle he'd been told to expect. The target. Check? Check.

Downhill from the north, a vehicle entirely unexpected, a dark truck, moving slowly.

Sh... The obscenity died on his lips as his face creased into a confused mixture of puzzlement and panic.

On to the driveway from the east.

Down the hill from the north, slower,

but still coming.

Stop. Oh, Christ! Stop.

Fifty yards apart.

Slower from the east. Bad.

Slower still from the north. Better.

Thirty yards apart.

What do I do? Tell me. What the fuck do I do? He should have been here, at my shoulder, making decisions. What did he say? 'Now or never.' His decision, not mine.

Three yards east of the tree now, from the right.

Now. It must be now. It has to be now. If there are other casualties, well...

Now. Check? Check.

He lowered the binoculars to his hip, freed his hand. First two fingers forked, he flicked back two tiny joysticks on the control box.

Initially, from this distance, it was a disappointing explosion for fifteen pounds. Not much louder than a grenade.

Silver waves in semicircles fled in shock from the roots of the willow, dying within a hundred yards or so.

Then he saw the target rising slowly in a grey and yellow cloud, bursting into orange flames and disintegrating, in blazing bits, which fell around the second vehicle.

Involuntarily, a reflex, really, he pulled his bare dark head into his wide shoulders, eyes never straying from a scene that could have come straight out of a 'Nam video.

From across the ruffled water he heard frantic shouting. He could not make out if it came from within the thick black cloud edged with oranges, reds and blues, or from the yachtsman. He didn't strain his ears to find out.

Crouching, the way he'd been trained, he ran down the causeway and across a wide grass bank to his van parked beyond a roadside wood.

He raced through gears, grinding from two to three, and drove too fast, far too fast, almost blindly, for a few hundred yards.

Through his mirror he caught sight of a grey Mercedes turning out of a hotel. He slowed, thinking again and, soon, smiling.

Ma first. Always the hardest. At last. A difficult op but I've done it. Done for him. Must have. Went up right beneath him.

Now all he had to do was pick up the balance in three days' time, when the dust had settled.

He'd hole up, track developments, pack and decide on his destination when he'd got all the money.

In a little over seventy-two hours, he'd collect. And he'd be gone. Away.

3

Four to twelve hours

The numb-faced constable at the road-block, strategically set up at the narrow neck to the peninsula, held a warrant card against a clipboard. His watery eyes were running down a long list of names, seeking DI Jackson.

'Some security,' Jacko said, sympathetically.

Already four hours or so into a boring shift as a sort of uniformed bouncer, the PC's brain seemed to have frozen, too. He said nothing.

'Still,' Jacko went on, musingly answering himself, 'not every day you get an assassination on a royal visit, I suppose.'

The constable looked from Jacko's photo

at him, hard; into a face that had added more creases and lost more hair in the year since it was taken. Even the bifocals had changed—from gold frames to gunmetal. Another year and a bit, Jacko realized, and he'd be handing that card in for good.

Satisfaction, if not recognition, slightly thawed the officer's sullen expression. 'Has to be tight to ward off the vultures.'

He looked sideways, to a lay-by where reporters and cameramen, hordes of them, were kennelled and guarded like wild strays beside a nature reserve where a row of dead, black trees poked out of greenish water. 'One just tried to sneak through on a milk float. White smock, peaked cap, the lot.'

Jacko laughed briefly. He liked most journalists he'd come across, envied their anarchistic attitudes, their bizarre behaviour.

Some were shouting into portable phones. A couple sipped from hip-flasks. Most laughed nosily, oblivious to the cold.

'Smartarses.' The constable clearly didn't share Jacko's on-the-road fellow-feeling. 'You wouldn't think they'd be so bloody cheerful when one of their own has been blown to smithereens.'

'Oh, I don't know,' said Jacko, smiling,

thinking of his own No 1 hate figure, an assistant chief constable. He took his card back and wound up the driver's window, shutting out the cutting wind.

After a couple of miles the road rose, narrowed and zigzagged through a picturesque village too small to merit its own resident bobby.

Now it seemed to be entirely populated by them, knocking on the doors of stone cottages which had thatches or beams or leaded windows or ivy creepers. Or, in the case of the old post office, the lot, plus a clock within a metal shield. Its Roman numerals showed quarter past noon.

He drove on for another mile and saw only sheep in fields that sloped down to vast expanses of water on either side of the road.

By the time he reached the foot of the peninsula, they'd already put the bits and pieces into plastic bags.

'Vernon Summers. Photographer of some sort. Aged thirty-three,' said the coroner's veteran officer when Jacko wound down the window again and let out a cloud of stale cigarette smoke. 'Not official yet,' he added, tapping the side of his nose.

He went on to speculate ghoulishly that when they put all the bags on the mortuary scales his dead weight would be much heavier than when he'd been alive—'but that's what you get with half a car seat blown up your arse.'

Up his smartarse, thought Jacko.

He was in a relaxed mood, among the third wave of reinforcements to hit the beaches of Rutland Water, so he'd missed the headless chicken flap that comes with the early stages of any major incident.

He'd been heading for a court hearing, to give fairly straightforward evidence, when the bomb—and soon his bleep—went off. They'd called him into the witness box first, but a radical defence lawyer had subjected him to a longish cross-examination.

He'd been subjected to a much longer drive—one cigarette between half a dozen M1 exits, three covering the same distance on Leicester's ring road and along a jammed trunk road.

Most of HQ and half of Scotland Yard seemed to have got here before him. Lots were top-rankers, airlifted in, that assistant chief among them, no expense spared on a royal job.

A few stood in a tight knot, in earnest conversation, looking, pointing at a crater, four yards round, in a rough road beyond a wooden plank bridge.

The blackened mangled remains of a car were upside down beside a magnificent old willow tree, with a thick, moss-coloured trunk, sturdy, then slender branches with new green growth fingering the water. Twenty or thirty yards away was a Land Rover, dented and deserted.

Dotted around between the two vehicles were white numbered pegs marking the spots where Vernon Summers had landed.

The air hung heavy with a fishy smell—the smell of spilled blood he knew so well.

The huddled high-flyers ignored him. Come nightfall, he conjectured, cynically, they will fly off again, having ensured they got their names in the papers, so their trendy friends could say at dinner parties: 'I see you were on the royal bomb case.' Bollocks to 'em all, he grumbled to himself, climbing reluctantly out of his warm, silver-grey Cavalier.

He wished he was skiving in a cosy pub with steam railway souvenirs next to that distant court-house, instead of shivering in

18

the wind at a freezing beauty spot without his thermals.

'Ah, Jacko.' From behind him, not out of the huddle, came a woman's voice, southern, warm and welcoming. 'I've a job for you.'

Well, not bollocks to 'em all, he thought, turning, smiling. Sometimes in a vague, spiritual way, he loved this woman, his boss.

OK, you miss the initial panic, but the trouble with turning up late on a big one, in his experience, was that you spend the rest of the day chasing your tail, never really catching up.

He had chased twenty miles south in twenty minutes into the next county where, by royal command, the Queen's Flight helicopter had taken Captain Simon Willis to hospital.

All he knew about him was what his boss had given him to read in the log at the mobile command post:

Age: thirty-four; single. Occupation: Head of Personal Security to Lord Hamb who owned the big white house and stables behind a screen of trees on the island which Jacko had glimpsed as he had driven to the foot of the peninsula.

08.15: Drove Land Rover south out of stables on a rough track. Saw a white VW Golf approaching, recognized its driver as Vernon Summers, professional photographer. Intended to intercept and interrogate. Before his eyes, the car blew up. He stopped his truck, got out, ran to it, saw what was left of Summers was beyond help, received minor burns to face and hands.

'He's not too co-operative,' said a nurse with a lilting Irish accent. 'Indeed, he is not.'

'Why?' asked Jacko, following her down a cream hospital corridor so hot he was glad he wasn't wearing his thermals.

'You'll see.' She nodded her head forward. 'He's occupying a private room.'

'A BUPA patient?' asked Jacko idly.

'A bullshit one, that's for certain.'

He laughed again. He was laughing a lot today, under no pressure. 'It was kind of Prince Charles to give him a lift though, wasn't it?'

She pulled a supercilious face to tell him she was from the republican south.

'Ridiculous.' A light accent, public school

maybe, officers' mess certainly. 'Can't you do something?'

Captain Willis was on his bare white feet. His sharp face had been coated with white balm which made his blue eyes look purple and very feminine.

'About what?' asked Jacko from the opened door.

'Getting me out of here.'

'If you won't go to bed, at least sit down,' said the nurse, gesturing to a deep wing chair.

Willis, in beige cavalry twills and what looked like a white long-sleeved vest, ignored her, addressing Jacko. 'Well?'

'I'm a detective, not a doctor.' He showed him his ID.

'Grief.' Willis sighed, frustrated. 'I spoke to your chap on the phone when I reported it. There's no need...'

'Sit down,' said the nurse, quite sharply.

'I'm perfectly all right. And don't give me any more of this rest and hot sweet tea business.' It came out in a torrent, gracelessly, as if he was unused to speaking to women on equal terms.

Shock, Jacko diagnosed. 'Prince Charles thought otherwise or he wouldn't have brought you in.'

21

'Hmm.' Willis still looked agitated, but at least it stopped him gabbling.

'We need to flesh it out.' Jacko noticed the vest was short sleeved. The skin on his arms and feet had been smeared with the same white balm as his face. A stupid thing to say, he chided himself, so, hurriedly: 'Your statement, I mean.'

'I'm A1.'

'You don't look it.' Jacko nodded at his arms.

'Oh, they slap it on anywhere the heat might have travelled. Had worse sunburn in Cyprus.' A grey shadow crossed his white cloud of a face.

'Sit yourself down,' said the nurse anxiously, but now Willis seemed to be pretending she wasn't even there.

Jacko walked across a maroon carpet to a neatly made bed that hadn't been lain on, never mind slept in. He took off his heavy brown raincoat which didn't really match the grey suit underneath and certainly not the black shoes. He folded the raincoat in two, put it on the floral cover, lowered himself on to the edge of the bed.

Willis sighed again, sat down gingerly in the wing chair, stretching out long legs that came with a lean, six-foot-two body.

'Good,' the nurse declared. 'Tea?'

'No,' said Willis, bluntly, looking at Jacko.

'Please,' said Jacko, smiling at the nurse. 'No sugar.'

He had him on his own for the next hour or so, interrupted only by the nurse's brief returns with his hot cuppa and, later, a second cup and a beef sandwich.

Captain Willis had come out of the Corps of Royal Engineers eighteen months earlier. 'Head-hunted by Lord Hamb,' he added, unsolicited. 'You know him?' He put it in that annoying way Jacko had noticed was used by inconsequential people acquainted with VIPs.

'Only by name.'

Everyone who'd ever read any paper knew of Lord Hamb. The front pages ran his friendships with the royals. The gossip columns ran big pictures—he was too fat for small ones—of him with showbiz personalities who supported his charity for wildlife worldwide.

The back pages fawned over his sponsorship of water sports. The City pages were full of a business empire that seemed to produce and transport by inland waterways half the nation's requirements for stone and sand and gypsum; everything mineable, apart from coal, of course, in which there was no money these days.

It had expanded so fast that he'd taken over a company that made some of the explosives he needed. The surplus was shipped abroad by his own line. Vertical integration, analysts called it.

Media snipers in the gossip columns hinted that he took over Midshires Munitions and Shipping to get his hands on Hamb Island, thirty private acres at the foot of Hambleton Peninsula on Rutland Water, which came into his ownership as part of the multi-million pound deal. When Mrs Thatcher inevitably made him a life peer he'd duly become Lord Hamb of Hamb.

He was an awesomely powerful man, on a different planet to Jacko. 'How did you get to know him?' he asked.

'When I was based with the United Nations in Cyprus.' Hamb had a place in the Troodos Mountains, and another in Chelsea, too, he added.

'What's your job entail?'

'His personal security.'

'Anything to do with any of his businesses?' Jacko had Midshires Munitions, the explosive manufacturing firm, in mind.

Willis shook his head.

'Does he need your level of personal security?'

'There's always a risk for a man in his position,' said Willis, not really answering his question.

Jacko began to suspect Hamb used him more as a commissioned batman than a bodyguard.

'He often has royal guests,' Willis went on. 'At Island Lodge, I mean.'

A humble name, Jacko thought, for a place that, even on the briefest of glances, had looked spacious and imposing.

'Prince Andrew for the water sport, Prince Charles occasionally for hunting or shooting, Prince Philip bird-watching and shooting.'

'Seen their pictures,' said Jacko.

'In that case,' Willis replied bitterly, 'Summers would have taken them.'

'Paparazzi.' Willis actually curled his thin lips in disgust. 'Know 'em?'

Jacko nodded. Photographers who hide in bushes to snatch candid shots of royals off-duty, sunbathing topless for preference, and showbiz personalities leaving nightspots with other people's partners on their arms.

'Caused us a lot of bother.'

'In what way?'

It began a year earlier, he said. By then, royal guests had already started paying regular unreported visits to Island Lodge. 'To relax away from the goldfish bowl, have a bit of enjoyment, a spot of hunting and so on.'

Not a lot of fun for the foxes they chased and the pheasants they shot down, thought Jacko moodily.

He had no strong feelings about blood sports. He ate pheasant without questioning how it got to his table. He'd been anti-fox since he'd seen as a boy what one did to a neighbour's chickens on his allotment.

It was just that he could never reconcile the way the police, his own colleagues, herded soccer fans like cattle on Saturdays, but meekly held up the traffic for hunt followers the rest of the week while their horses shat all over the road. Let a dog do that and it would be its owner who was in the shit. (Jacko was a devoted dog owner, and he accepted that he was biased and growing jaundiced with age.)

'Quite suddenly,' Willis continued, 'Summers started showing up almost every time a royal guest did, dogging their footsteps, following their cars or taking pictures from a hired boat. Most disconcerting. We knew who he was, of course. His name often appeared under the photo in the papers next day.'

'What could you do about it?'

'Try to find the leak.'

Jacko cocked his head, his questioning gesture.

'Stands to reason, doesn't it? He was getting inside gen on their movements.'

'Did you find his contact?'

He shook his head sadly. 'Never got the chance to question him.'

Private royal visits, he went on, were always signalled well in advance, but only confirmed the day before.

On Saturday evening, he'd personally taken the call from Sandringham to say that Prince Charles would be arriving late on Sunday, staying overnight and going hunting next morning. 'He often rides to hounds on a Monday.'

'Who did you inform?' asked Jacko.

Lord Hamb, he replied, just as he was about to set off on a business trip to France, his son, the Honourable Matthew Hamb, and a guest called Toby Blewis. Both had been due to hunt with Charles this morning.

'Why didn't Prince Charles travel here this morning?' asked Jacko.

'Visibility can be dicky for a chopper this time of year.'

'So he came by chopper last night?'

'That came this morning just after dawn. He drove across with his own detective last night. The Wessex came this morning. Landed on the pad on the island.'

'Why?'

'To get him from the island to the meet and straight back home afterwards.'

Jacko had questions about this but put them on hold, wanting the story chronologically, the way he worked.

'Who was at Island Lodge last night?'

'Matthew was in residence,' he replied, rather over-familiarly. 'And Mr Blewis was an overnight guest.'

Jacko asked who he was.

An executive for Midshires Munitions and Shipping, he was told, but not for much longer. 'He's quite a well-known politician, just landed that safe seat down south, you know.'

Jacko didn't, never followed politics. 'Who else?'

'Just me and the regular domestic and stable staff, and the royal detective, of course.'

'No Lord Hamb?'

An impatient headshake. 'Told you. In Paris.'

'What time were you all up this morning?'

'Me? Six. Can't speak for the rest of the house.' He never looked in on royal guests while they were breakfasting and reading the papers, he fussily explained, knowing his place. 'Never saw them until afterwards. I was lying in wait for Summers.'

Jacko fell silent, wondering whether to caution him. His indecision must have shown. In a flurry, that made him sound flustered and girlish, Willis added, 'Only to challenge him, I do assure you.'

Willis drove his Land Rover downhill from the stables. On a previous trip Summers had been spotted sitting in his white car close to the willow tree, binoculars trained on horses going into their boxes.

'Prince Charles has one of his hunters in livery with us, you know. All Summers had to do was follow the horse-box.'

'If he wanted to snap him, couldn't he just turn up at the meet?'

'Oh, no. Prince Charles never goes for stirrup cups. Attracts too much media attention. He always joins the hunt a mile or so away at some pre-arranged spot, a copse or some other landmark.'

'Wouldn't a specialist cameraman like Summers have figured that out?'

'Makes no difference if he had. His Royal Highness could be joining any one of six or so hunts round here. The East Midlands crawls with them.'

'Did you know which hunt he was joining today?'

A curt nod. 'A meet at Melton. The Veterinary Corps HQ. I have to know so I can tell the stablehand who drives the box where to go. Security's that tight.' He looked rather pleased with himself.

'So,' said Jacko, double-checking, 'the only way for Summers to know was to have been tipped off that Charles was here and then follow the right horse-box?'

'Exactly.'

30

'And Prince Charles flies from the island by chopper to the rendezvous with the horse?'

'Correct.'

Jacko had it clear in his mind now. 'So there you were, eyes peeled. What happened?'

'I spotted Summers' white car approaching the bridge from the peninsula road. I started up, but drove very slowly.'

'Why?'

'To let him get on to private land, our land, on the island, so I could tackle him for trespass.'

'Were you planning to call us out?' Jacko was so seedy-looking in specs and off-the-peg clothing that fitted where it touched that few people ever took him for a detective, so he added, 'The police, I mean.'

'Trespass is a civil matter, is it not?' Willis gave him a clever smile, a touch effete.

'What was your intention then?'

'To stop him, nose-to-nose, and confront him.'

'About what?'

'Where he was getting all the gen, his tips. To root out the leak. To give

31

him a stiff rocket...' A crass phrase, acknowledged with a sorrowful face. '...to warn him off.'

He sped on. 'I approached at no more than ten miles an hour. When he was, what, a cricket pitch and a half a way from me...'

'About thirty yards,' Jacko interjected expertly.

'...and boom.'

Plonker, thought Jacko, angrily.

He had an old soldier's critical view on certain officers. Some he'd clerked for in his teenage years, staff officers, had quick minds capable of earning big salaries in industry, and serving out of love and loyalty to their country, a feeling Jacko didn't always share. The rest were barrack square material, bullshit baffles brain. That Irish nurse had read Willis right. He placed him in the latter category.

'His car shot straight in the air,' Willis continued. 'It was in flames by the time it hit the ground. Got out, naturally, ran as close as I could...' He looked at his arms. '...a bit too close, it seems, but he was a goner. I know one when I see one.'

'Did you realize what it was?'

'Seen enough in Ulster.'

'Give us your expert view then.'

'From under the car upwards.'

'A land mine?'

'Or a device attached to the underside. Don't your boffins know yet?'

Jacko knew little about explosives and didn't want to know more. As a boy he had seen a French film, *The Wages of Fear*. Two hard-up lorry drivers hired to ferry truckloads of nitroglycerine over bumpy terrain. One stopped to roll a cigarette. A gust of wind took the tobacco off the paper, telling him that his mate had been blown away. He'd never even thought about joining the bomb squad in either his army or police service.

All he said was: 'They were still at the scene when I left.'

Willis described how he abandoned his damaged vehicle, ran back to the Lodge, and dialled 999. Then, despite protesting 'It's only a scorch,' he was ordered by the royal detective into the helicopter, which Prince Charles piloted and landed on a sports field close to the hospital.

Without a knock, the door burst open.

'Boom, boom,' bellowed a beaming giant figure in a giant voice.

4

The room was suddenly overcrowded, filled by the very presence of Lord Hamb. He was twenty stone and six foot, but it was much more than physical. He radiated overwhelming persona and power; full of himself, and there was a lot to fill.

Sixtyish, in a dark pin-striped suit, he didn't enter the room as much as storm it and capture it single-handed.

Still beaming, he asked, very loudly, 'What happen, Cap'n?' He emphasized the 'p's in happen and captain, put on a transatlantic voice, and Jacko guessed it was some sort of regular soldiers' greeting, an old joke.

Willis sat proudly, beginning to come to attention and said, 'Good of you to come, sir.' Jacko surprised and annoyed himself by slipping upright off the bed.

In three or four paces, Hamb reached the wing chair. He grabbed Willis' right hand, oblivious to the white ointment, and pumped it vigorously. Left hand to shoulder, he pushed Willis back into his seat as he attempted to stand. 'Bad business. Thoroughly bad.'

'Yes, sir,' agreed Willis, eyes fixed on him, like an obedient dog. 'I tried to reach you from the Lodge. They said you were in a working breakfast and couldn't be disturbed.'

'Fucking Frogs.' An angry growl accompanied a dramatic, dismissive wave. 'Came as soon as I heard, old man.'

Willis looked at Jacko, still standing. 'He was in Paris, you know.'

Jacko said he knew.

Hamb acknowledged him for the first time. 'And who might you be?' When he spoke normally his accent was neutral and hard to place.

Jacko told him who he was.

'A Johnny-come-lately, aren't you? Talk about shutting the stable door. Good lord.' He guffawed so hugely, brimming with such bonhomie, that Jacko knew he was not being reprimanded for not being around to be blown up, too.

Hamb switched back to Willis. 'How's his horse?'

'Fine,' said Willis. Jacko assumed he was talking about the royal horse, unridden

35

that morning, and could tell that the captain didn't really know, the last thing on his mind.

'Now...' Hamb marched past Jacko, turned and lowered himself lightly on to the bed, which sagged slightly under his weight. The welts of his polished black shoes were streaked with wet mud. That didn't stop him swinging his legs on to the floral cover.

He half hitched, half hunched himself up and backwards, a mighty effort. The bed seemed to bow. He ripped the pillows from beneath their cover, pounding them together against the bed-head, pulled himself further up so they became a backrest. 'What happened?'

Willis ran through the story again. Hamb nodding heavily here and there.

The only place for Jacko to sit was a square, brown plastic stool which made him feel like Gulliver at the great man's feet.

'And HRH saw nothing of this?'

'No, sir.'

A satisfied nod. 'Don't like my guests disturbed.'

'He was very good to me.'

'Would be. Sound chap. What...' He

looked round and down. '...what do you make of it, Mr Johnson?' He didn't wait for a correction or an answer. 'Someone clearly wanted Summers dead. Not surprised. Turned out to be a bad apple.'

'Or Captain Willis,' Jacko replied quietly. His eyes went to the chair and he imagined the captain going a whiter shade beneath his balm.

'But not Prince Charles?' said Hamb. A future king clearly concerned him more than any flunkey.

'On previous occasions,' Jacko asked, 'did he always fly to hunt meets from your chopper pad on the island?'

Hamb looked at Willis, who said, 'Always.'

'Never drove down that road from your Lodge?'

'Never.' Willis again.

Hamb gave this a second or two of thought. Then, an almost delighted, 'Good.'

'Why me?' Willis's tone wasn't so happy.

'Did you often use that track?'

'Most mornings. Just for a recce. Looking for fishermen, mainly, trespassing. Or poachers.'

'Well, if it was a land mine rather than a car bomb, we can't rule you out as the target, can we?'

Willis seemed to go paler still.

'You're sure they weren't after Charles?' asked Hamb, who appeared to have missed the whole exchange.

'On the face of it,' said Jacko, guardedly.

A woman, middle-aged, sharp-suited, walked in. 'No go,' she said.

'Shit,' said Hamb in his clipped, neutral accent.

'Gremlins. Don't ask me what.' The woman displayed no fear of Hamb, and Jacko guessed she was a travelling secretary.

She looked at Willis. 'All right, Simon?'

'F-fine. Th-thank you.' His reply was a stammer.

She turned back to Hamb. 'He won't take off.'

'Fucking Frog.'

Jacko had Hamb pegged now as one of the Chelsea set (*circa* late fifties/early sixties) who used bad language in order to shock, a bit old-fashioned really. Not that he was personally opposed to obscenities; he'd peppered them aplenty about his words and thoughts since his army days, but that was the Aldershot in him, not Chelsea.

'I'll order transport down from the Lodge,' the secretary offered.

'No.' He pulled his massive frame off the bed. 'Right, Willis. Bed rest.' He pointed to it, aggressively.

'B-but—'

'Bed.' A firmer voice, a harder stab with his finger. 'Now.' Willis got up, walked to the bed and sat on the edge.

'Off with your trousers.' Willis stood again, did as he was told, colouring at the neck through the balm, eyes deeply dismayed and embarrassed. The secretary smiled and looked away.

'In.' Willis, in vest and white boxer shorts, followed his orders, a sent-to-bed public schoolboy, not quite tucking the top white sheet beneath his white chin.

'Good.' Beaming, Hamb turned to Jacko. 'You. With me.'

Jacko got up and followed him and the woman out, dragged along in the wake this whale of a man left behind him.

Walking back down interminable corridors through interminable double doors, the obligatory two paces behind, the woman explained that the helicopter hired in Paris had developed technical difficulties. They'd landed safely outside the hospital but the French pilot was refusing to fly on the last leg to the island off the peninsula.

'What's he want with me?' asked Jacko, a touch overawed.

'Your car, I expect.' She smiled. 'Once, when his Rolls was late, stuck in a jam in a side street, he marched into Kensington High, held up his hand to stop the first vehicle that came alone, a dustcart as it happened, and demanded a lift to the Savoy.'

Hamb heard all of this and laughed happily ahead of him. 'Got it, too.'

'And once his chauffeur got so fed up with his hectoring he stopped the car, got out and said: "Drive the bloody thing yourself. I quit." '

Hamb laughed again, even louder. 'Like a bit of spirit.'

'Did he get his job back?' asked Jacko.

'No,' Hamb said firmly, not looking over his shoulder. 'Plenty where he came from.'

He stopped in the foyer at the end of the corridor at a shop with a news-stand. Both the *Evening Telegraph* and the *Chronicle and*

Echo had cleared their front pages of all other news. 'Get 'em, will you?' he said to Jacko. He ran his hands down his chest above his waistcoat. A trace of the white balm was transferred to his wide lapels. 'No change.'

'He never carries money,' said the secretary.

Jacko handed over fifty pence, helped himself to a copy of each paper, privately fuming: Thinks he's bloody royalty, too.

Jacko knelt with one knee on the driver's seat to unlock the nearside passenger doors, front and back. He picked up a portable phone in a black leather case which the collator at the command post had given him.

Hamb surprised him by heaving himself into its place. It was such a tight fit that he screwed the seat back for more leg room. He didn't put on the seat belt. He held out a hand for the papers, which he placed across his tree trunk thighs.

Jacko decided to break the law by not ordering him to strap up. He doubted that the belt would reach round him anyway.

The woman got in the back and immediately started punching a number

41

into the phone which Jacko had handed her. 'Engaged,' she said.

'Bloody press,' said Hamb, but not unpleasantly.

Jacko drove out of the grounds of the hospital, as big as a university campus. Confused by a new road layout in a town he didn't know very well, he missed a sign at a roundabout and headed for the centre of Kettering.

Hamb snorted. 'Next left.'

Too late Jacko saw the red 'No Entry' notice. He braked and looked over his shoulder.

'What the hell you doing?' asked Hamb, an edge to his deep voice.

'Backing out, aren't I?' Jacko snapped.

He waved a dismissive hand. 'Ignore that.'

'But—'

'This is an emergency, is it not, the defence of the realm and all that, and you are the law, are you not? It's much quicker.' Then mysteriously: 'Do as the Queen's representative commands.' A menacing pause. 'Now.'

For the second time within minutes, Jacko broke the law, driving the wrong way up a one-way street, incurring the wrath of a van driver who waved a fist and shouted towards the nearside, 'Fat bastard.'

From the passenger seat came a royal wave back.

Hamb talked as he scanned the front pages. He wanted to know if the car belonged to the police. 'Mine,' said Jacko, wondering why he wasn't telling him to mind his own business.

He asked, nosy to the point of rudeness, about Jacko's private life. Tell him to piss off, the rebel within demanded. Think of your pension and be polite, the conformist cautioned. 'A wife, a kid and a dog,' he replied politely.

'Length of service?' he asked, quite pleasantly.

'Coming up to thirty.'

'No need to drive at it, though,' Hamb said with a sudden rasp. He rested the papers on his knees. 'Put your foot down.'

Jacko picked up speed, feeling cowed and disgusted with himself.

The secretary tried the number again and tutted.

Head down, Hamb read the papers, some

extracts out loud for the benefit of his secretary.

Jacko drove by a soccer stadium and out of town in silence, listening, not learning much.

After six or so miles of dual carriageway, northbound on the A6003, he saw another stadium. Its grandstand had red seats with white lettering which formed the words: 'Corby Works'.

Not strictly true a decade ago when they closed most of the steelworks and dumped thirteen thousand on the dole, Jacko recalled. He wondered if they'd found jobs. He worried about unemployment. He blamed it for the ever-rising crime figures, but it was more personal than professional.

His own father and both grandfathers had been out of work in the thirties. As a boy, he heard their stories of soup kitchens and bread queues and bastard bosses like Hamb. He'd always feared losing his own job. It made him work hard and carefully to try to make sure that he didn't.

Soon after a roadside sign announced their return to Rutland, Hamb finished reading and looked up.

He gave a wave as they sped by vast

gravel pits with a big board on a grass bank that said: 'Hamb Aggregates'. 'Half a million ton output to the year's end.'

'How much profit?' Jacko asked, sourly.

'Same.'

Jacko glanced left on to a large lagoon with a rough banked-up road running round it. Across the water was what looked like a giant Heath Robinson contraption—ramshackle buildings with green conveyor belts, pipes on platforms, square wooden hoppers in black steel frames and mountainous heaps of brown sand. 'Got many?' he asked.

'Ten or a dozen.' Hamb made the difference between five and six million sound a matter of indifference to him.

'When it's played out there's water and sand and room enough for a golf course,' said Jacko, taking one last glance.

Hamb shook his head. 'Reclamation and in-filling are far too expensive.' He paused. 'No.' Another pause. 'A sailing club, perhaps. Or another wildlife sanctuary.'

Typical, thought Jacko. He gets all this free publicity as a saviour of wildlife and a patron of boating when, really, they're cheap ways of solving the problem of what to do with a pit that he's exploited and exhausted.

He got back to business. 'Do you ride to hounds?'

'Never.'

That's a break for some lucky horse, Jacko thought. 'Shoot and fish, then?'

'Naturally.'

And eats everything he bags and hooks, Jacko privately added, by the size of him.

'Poachers and trespassers, too, but don't worry. I always give them ten yards' start.' He roared with laughter at his own joke.

'Your son, too?' asked Jacko.

Hamb flicked a thumb back towards Corby. The chimneys of its new power station and two flour mills which had replaced the steelworks were just visible on the skyline. 'Should be there, running the show, instead of chasing after foxes.'

Jacko assumed the Honourable Matthew was in charge of one of his many companies based around here. 'Into field sports, then, is he?'

'All three judging from his poor balance sheets, bloody playboy.'

The secretary finally got through. 'Your playboy.' She laughed lightly as she handed the phone over his shoulder.

'At long bloody last, you long-winded waster,' said Hamb, in a jocular tone into the mouthpiece.

A short laugh from the earpiece. From a one-sided conversation Jacko got the impression that the Lodge had been inundated with calls and the press was invading their little island by helicopter and boat. 'Say nothing till I get there. ETA, oh, five mins.'

Some hope, Jacko calculated. They still had ten miles to go and they hadn't got through busy little Uppingham yet.

Gushingly, Hamb let his son know he had virtually taken control of the radio on the helicopter hop across the Channel and had already spoken to the Palace, the heir's secretary, valet, the press officer, detective—everyone but the main man himself.

All seemed to have been told to rest assured that he was flying home to take personal charge of the entire operation, as the old county's Lord Lieutenant-elect.

News, this, to Jacko, though it was well known the present incumbent was on his last legs after years of service as the Queen's local representative, greeting minor royals, foreign dignitaries, sitting on

47

sundry committees and attending various receptions often dressed in black velvet and white breeches. Hamb, he suspected with a smile, would cut a rather Ruritanian figure, who'd have preferred the crown on his head rather than his uniformed shoulder.

Not once in a long conversation was there any mention, much less a word of regret, about Vernon Summers, now scattered in bags about the mortuary in the hospital they'd just left.

Hamb passed the phone back over his broad shoulder.

Jacko got down to business again. 'Did you know Summers?'

'Vaguely.'

'How did you first meet him?'

'In Cyprus, when he was buzzing about the Middle East. My wife lives there all the time, you know.'

'How did you and your wife get on with him?'

'Fine over there. Did a nice feature spread. A very respectable photo-journalist.'

'Why did he come back to do all this peephole photography?'

Hamb went silent and Jacko tried a probing aside. 'Regarded him as a poacher

48

or a trespasser, did you?'

'Both. And an infernal nuisance, most certainly.'

'Why then did he come back from worthwhile assignments in the Middle East to specialize in royals and so on?'

'Search me.' A deep sigh, distracted. 'Ask his colleagues.'

Jacko assumed someone would be doing just that. 'This other house guest, the future MP...'

'Toby Lewis.'

'Blewis.' This time Jacko did correct him. 'A friend of yours?'

'Of my son's. Another playboy. A bimbo on his arm. We inherited him, you know. Unfortunately. When we took over Midshires at Corby. Jetting between Strasbourg and Brussels, at our expense, doing bugger all. Who needs Froggie sand or Kraut stone? Who wants Belgian armaments or foreign flags of convenience sailing the seven seas?'

He spread both arms, expansive, hamming it up. 'Here...' His right interfered with Jacko's line of vision for a dodgy second. '...in this green and pleasant land is where the future lies for this wonderful country of ours, Mr Johnson.'

'Jackson,' said Jacko out of the corner of his mouth.

The road-block at the neck of the peninsula had been removed, swept away, Jacko guessed, by the sheer weight of the media invasion.

He drove through the quaint, tiny hamlet, capital of the parish, where press and radio cars jammed the narrow street round the one village pub. The churchyard opposite was empty.

Journalists and uniformed policemen were elbowing each other to reach doors on their house-to-house inquiries. Two policemen were untangling traffic on the one road.

A sodding shambles, thought Jacko.

A mile further on, surrounded by badly parked cars, more police were making their last stand at the wooden bridge which led to Hamb's island.

Over them, in a thunderous din, a departing police helicopter hovered. From the air, Jacko supposed, the island would look a bit like a miniature Italy with its foot about to drop off.

He stopped. Every car door—and there was a score of them—flew open. Out jumped the hounds, as many women as men. They descended in a pack on the passenger side. The first to arrive tapped sharply on the window and cried above the clattering helicopter: 'Lord Hamb. Give us a word, Lord Hamb.'

He wound down the window, but said nothing until the helicopter snaked away across the water, adding to the wind in the sails of the yachts. It rose up and over an elegant church which stood on what looked to Jacko like a pier jutting out from the southern shore.

Its din became a distant drone, but the noise didn't slacken as, all around him, people were shouting over each other. Their babble filled the car. 'When did you hear?'... 'Is Charles OK?'... 'What can you tell us?'

Hamb waved his hands slowly down in front of his chest, a conductor calling for sotto. 'Lads. Lads. Lads.' He sounded like a northern businessman trying to quell trouble at mill. 'Just arrived. I'm not briefed. Give me a minute or two.' A dozen cameras clicked.

'Give us a minute or two,' a newsman pleaded.

'I'll give you as long as you like.' He

51

withdrew a gold fob watch on a chain from a pocket in his waistcoat. 'At four. In the village hall.' Simultaneously he flicked his thumb back and his head forward. 'On.'

It was like a scene from *Upstairs, Downstairs,* Jacko decided, all the retainers on parade for the return of their lord and master.

Everybody, including a white-coated Asian and a couple dressed like grooms, stood on the wide front steps to the white lodge. Jacko half expected a quick burst from 'The Arrival of the Queen of Sheba'.

Hamb swept past them all, with the briefest of grim nods, into a hall, walking so swiftly that Jacko just had time to take in the oak panelling and a marble staircase.

Everyone trooped after him into a study with a huge desk, topped with red leather, a matching captain's chair and a line of antique high-backed chairs in front of a book-lined wall. Every other wall was plastered with framed photos.

The secretary sat at the desk and made a call on a phone with a conference loudspeaker while Hamb stood and talked generally.

'Willis all right?' asked a dark, thin, tense man, mid-thirties, casually dressed; his playboy son, Jacko guessed.

'Fine.' A dismissive wave.

His father turned to the woman groom. 'His horse all right?'

'Fine,' she said. They talked horses for some while.

Jacko carried on to the opposite wall. All the photos featured Lord Hamb posing alongside various government ministers, celebrities associated with wildlife charities and heads of minor states.

In all he wore his treacly smile, like an amiable drunk. In one, he stood with Prince Charles, in hunting pink. Between them was a bay horse with lots of white on its face. Next to Charles stood Captain Willis, who wore a check hacking jacket.

Other photos were more scenic than social—a string of barges heading into a sunset, Hamb at the helm; sailing boats on an old gravel pit, Hamb in the foreground; a cargo ship, big by comparison, very white against a shanty-town background, but, uniquely in this collection, no Hamb.

Jacko turned, startled, when the secretary spoke from the desk. 'The Chief Constable.' She flicked a switch so the whole room would be able to hear both sides of the conversation.

'Mr Chief,' boomed Hamb.

'Sir,' said the Chief Constable servilely.

'Messy, messy business.'

'Formal identification will be difficult, yes,' the Chief agreed.

'The vultures.'

'Pardon?'

'The press, I mean,' said Hamb. 'Totally besieged, we are. Get rid of 'em, if you will, there's a good chap.'

'Easier said than done, I'm afraid.'

'Give 'em what they want.'

'We are issuing regular bulletins, sir,' the Chief replied in a tight tone.

'Paperwork.' Hamb sorted it. 'A press conference is what they need. A few up-to-date photos and sound bites. Then they'll go. Fix that, will you?'

'I'm not sure we're ready—'

'Four o'clock. In the village hall. Most kind.'

As if acting on some coded phrase, the secretary flicked off the switch. Hamb roared with laughter which his hangers-on joined.

Not Jacko, though. He was fighting off a sinking feeling that always came when he was sailing in deep waters.

One mistake on this job with these people, he thought anxiously, and I could be joining those steelworkers on the dole.

5

Back at the command post, a fancy name for a big grey metal caravan with a communications mast on the roof, Jacko finished briefing his boss with, 'He's part showman, part madman—the Goldfinger of arms and aggregate.'

'Pity you're not James Bond then,' said Chief Superintendent Carole Malloy with a thin smile.

Jacko laughed, but not too brightly. He'd been about to add, 'He sells arms to one side and fills the sandbags for the other,' but her cutting quip had taken the shine off the sardonic aside he'd mentally rehearsed and was going to pass off as impromptu. He wasn't going to bother to top her.

Carole Malloy was a slim, smallish woman, mid-forties, dark-suited, with short, neat red hair, a quiet smile and always tired blue eyes—bedroom eyes, Jacko often thought.

Twelve days earlier, on a mild, bright New Year's Day, Jacko had resolved that he would slow up and wind down in his final year and a bit, keep his nose clean, doing as he was told and no more. He'd run too many risks, been too close too often in his eight years on the Major Crime Squad of the East Midlands Combined Constabulary.

But, he'd also vowed, he would never backslide on Little Velma, as Chief Superintendent Malloy was called throughout the squad.

In the year just ended, she had guided him through two difficult, dangerous assignments. He needed his hand held—by a good boss and trustworthy sidekicks.

He was, he recognized, no brave Bond, no egghead Morse; average, in fact. Having first-rate workmates, mostly women in these more enlightened times, brought out the best in him and, once or twice, launched him on binges of brilliance he'd always thought beyond him.

This private acceptance of his limitations had given him a simple philosophy of life: You deliver for people who have delivered for you. And Little Velma was one of those half-dozen or so whose working relationships had developed into close friendships he'd always treasure. Oh, he loved her all right in his way.

He gave her his concerned chum's look. 'How you gettin' on?'

'Chaos all day,' she sighed. 'Like the Portuguese navy; all admirals and no matelots.'

Velma was sitting in a compartment twice the size of an old phone box, just room for a small fold-down desk, so cramped that she shared a wooden bench with a much younger woman, back to her, backsides touching.

The other woman's shoulders were hunched over a phone at her feet as she brought the conversation to an end. Replacing it, she swivelled round her head and upper body.

Lord, but she's beautiful, he thought, startled. Flawless skin. A wide red mouth with a wide white smile.

Her dark brown hair came down in a deep fringe that ended just above her eyes—hazel eyes which looked warmly at him. She wore a chunky white sweater dotted with black buttons and a dark skirt he couldn't see a lot of.

'Nothing,' she reported to Velma.

'Hazel's...' Velma stopped. 'This is Hazel.'

Well-named, Jacko thought, smiling, nodding.

'...been doing a media ring-round to see if there's been any claims of responsibility,' Velma continued.

Jacko nodded again. He knew that terrorist organizations from both sides in Ulster and other crackpot organizations like animal lib militants loved their publicity.

They like to brag about outrages they commit. So they phone major news outlets—notably the BBC and Press Association, the national wire service in Fleet Street, to claim (proudly or obscenely, depending whose side you're on) responsibility for their bombings or shootings.

So sophisticated have lines of communication became that they prefix their messages with a code, notified in advance, to prove the call is not a hoax.

'It's not got Irish fingerprints on it, that's for sure,' Velma went on.

'You know Lord Hamb's got a factory that makes arms?' said Jacko, certain she did.

'Got a team there,' Velma answered. 'Military stuff, they report. Cluster bombs. Mines, too. But Forensics think this one is a commercial explosive, nitroglycerine-based. From the size of the crater, they fancy a home-made mine more than a car bomb. A bit of drainpipe was used. Very professional, they say, but not associated with anything made at Midshires Munitions. They can't find the wire, though. We've called in the underwater search unit.'

Jacko wasn't sure what she was talking about. Not his problem, he decided. Instead: 'How's the Summers background going?' Had he arrived earlier, this would have been his assignment.

'Slowly.' A suspicious look. 'Why do you ask? Not muscling in, are you?'

'No, no,' Jacko replied quickly, not looking for work. There appeared to be a Cyprus connection between Summers, Hamb and Captain Willis, he explained. 'I was wondering what it was, that's all.'

'The problem is that Summers' agency chief—name of...'

'Larry McAllister of Fine Focus,' Hazel interjected helpfully.

'...got an early call from us as soon as

the national vehicle computer put a name to the registered user of the VW Golf. He tipped off everyone...'

'And beat PA,' said Hazel. 'Must have made a fortune.' She explained at some length how national newspapers paid big money to informants who gave them the first tip on big, breaking stories. Jacko concluded she was Velma's expert on media matters.

'McAllister did a runner from his Fleet Street office after tipping off his clients,' Velma went on. 'He's known Summers man and boy. And Summers' lady...' She looked at Hazel again.

'Marilyn Moore,' said Hazel.

'...she left their flat in Clapham within an hour of us breaking the news. An air hostess, apparently. A longtime love. They were together in the Middle East. We can't find her.'

'Odd,' said Jacko, puzzled.

'Not really,' said Hazel. 'The chances are that McAllister whisked her away and she's now selling her story to one of the tabloids. Happens all the time.'

'Which is why,' said Velma, 'I'd like you to go with your new-found friend Lord Hamb to the press conference. Keep your eyes open for McAllister. He might have come up here, holding court...'

'For another fee,' added Hazel, with a slight shrug, not making a judgement.

'Aren't you going?' asked Jacko, surprised. The CID chief normally chaired major incident press conferences.

'The Chief jocked me off. Wants a higher rank sitting alongside the Lord Lieutenant-to-be. Mr Knight's taking it.'

Sometimes, just a word, one name, and Jacko had an inexplicable feeling of impending doom, a disaster about to happen with nothing in the world that anyone could do about it.

Knight was such a name. He was an assistant chief constable in charge of AT3—the Anti-Terrorist Task Team.

He had been on the force's flight deck for six years. He was mid-forties, five years younger than Jacko; a university graduate with a public school accent, promoted on the fast track in his first force to miles beyond his capabilities, in Jacko's view.

He had fair, boyish looks, but the temper of a dyspeptic pensioner. The boys and girls in the Major Crime Squad reckoned he'd spoken to less than a dozen people. One of them was Jacko, but only to give him a blistering bollocking for bizarre behaviour while celebrating a successful outcome to an inquiry into a shot government minister's sister. One day, he'd solemnly vowed, he'd get even.

Knight was so uncommunicative that they had nicknamed him Silent, prematurely as it now turned out. Envious at the high TV profile attained by other assistant chiefs—rivals for the soon-to-be-vacant post of Deputy Chief—he had secretly booked himself on to a media training course. In his unexplained absence the rumour ran round the squad room that he was in hospital for a charisma bypass.

Before Christmas he stared to appear on TV almost nightly; bland studio interviews plugging campaigns against turkey rustlers and illegal fir tree lumberjacking.

The few conferences he'd presided over had been formal affairs, Perrier water alongside his nameplate on the top table, explaining boring community initiatives to even more bored local reporters who asked no questions to prolong their tedium, anxious for a quick getaway to stronger drink.

He'd never faced the national, indeed, the world media; hairy-arsed men and women who didn't give a shit for presidents and prime ministers, let alone assistant police chiefs, and who had been pissed about from pillar to post, warming themselves from hip-flasks throughout a raw January day.

'Oh Christ, guv,' said Jacko. It was a title he used to address only those chiefs he respected and admired, and would never be bestowed on Silent Knight.

Velma smiled quietly. 'You'd better take Hazel.' Hazel smiled dazzlingly. 'She's with divisional public relations.' Velma was only confirming what Jacko had already guessed. 'And afterwards chat up the media a bit. Find out what you can about Summers and his secret contained at Island Lodge. Keep an eye open for the missing McAllister.'

'I can't very well pull him in, can I?' said Jacko unenthusiastically.

'No,' said Velma, 'but you can offer him a trade.' She explained what she meant in some detail.

A good idea, thought Jacko, bucking up a bit.

'Will Hamb co-operate?' asked Velma.

'Bound to,' said Hazel. 'He's a publicity junkie.'

'If Mr Knight kicks up, well...' Velma shrugged, no need to add: I'll back you.

He knew that already.

'In fact...' She paused. 'Would Jackie mind if you stay the night?' His wife Jackie and Velma, divorced with a teenage son at college, had became once-a-week drinking pals after meeting a few months earlier. 'To book in and mingle.'

'It will stop us arguing about what side to have on TV,' said Jacko, who always liked a night out away from home.

'It will certainly save you driving back pissed,' said Velma.

'You should see the way they drink,' added Hazel, not at all disapprovingly.

He made up his mind about her then and there. It was more than her looks. It was the way she didn't pass judgements, accepted people the way they were.

'Both of us?' he said, brightly and rather eagerly. Velma frowned. 'Booking in, I mean?'

She and Hazel looked, then nodded at each other.

'Single rooms,' said Velma with mock sternness.

'Suits me.' Jacko shrugged, easygoing. 'I find it very tiring these days. Ruins my work rate next morning.'

'Really!' Hazel's dark eyebrows went up,

then down. 'You poor old sod. I find it rather invigorating.'

All three laughed.

They had plenty of time for a hot cup of tea and, for Jacko, a tasty corned beef sandwich at a mobile canteen, staffed by Salvation Army women, camp followers in all emergencies. In appreciative solidarity, Jacko always bought their *War Cry*.

Hazel chattered, soft-voiced but non-stop, about her job. 'The phone's never stopped ringing all day. You should hear their language. Fuck me O'Riley.'

This, Jacko knew, was not the name of an invigorating fella, but an all-purpose local phrase, rather nice, in his view, to express anything from astonishment to bewilderment.

Her mouth's wide, he began to suspect, from all the talking she does. He had no time to ask, 'What's been the problem?' She talked on.

'Mr Knight won't confirm Summers as the victim. He was so badly mutilated that he's ruled we can't make it official until cross-checks with teeth or DNA.'

Technically, Knight was right to be cautious, Jacko had to acknowledge.

A few years back they'd released the name of the owner of a car in a fireball road crash. It turned out the owner had loaned it to his twin brother while he was on holiday.

Sod's Law, the bane of all police officers, decreed that the surviving twin should be a Salvation Army bandmaster and *War Cry* prematurely recorded his death in its obits column headed: 'Promoted to Glory'.

With great glee at the police mistake, the tabloids had relegated him back to the land of the living.

Hazel, white raincoat dropped below her pencil-slim black skirt, had talked softly because journalists were standing around on the long grass.

Whisky fumes from two of them warmed an earlier-than-scheduled twilight, getting more misty and no warmer. They asked for black coffee—'and a blank bill.' Everyone who heard roared with laughter. A joke about an exes fiddle, Jacko speculated, smiling.

'I want to get back to real police work,' Hazel gabbled on. 'I'd love CID.'

'Can't you apply for a transfer, then?'

'Difficult domestically.' A sad shadow

crossed her lovely face. 'I'm dating...well, shacking up with the divisional detective chief inspector. 'So...'

A shrug and a bright smile now to confirm, he deduced, that there'd be no rumpy-tumpy, and he was pleased. A happy, uncomplicated working relationship and—let's be honest—sleep were far more important to him these days.

Jacko nodded: Message received. 'Lucky man.' He used a forlorn voice and wore a regretful face, so she wouldn't think he didn't fancy her.

Well, you don't like to disappoint them, do you? he told himself, showing off to himself, totally deluding himself up no end.

It was less like a conference venue, calm and orderly; more like the City on a frenetic day when the pound is going through the floor.

Seventy or so had squeezed themselves into the village hall, timbered, thatched and quaintly dilapidated.

Most weren't dressed for the City, though. Or for *Country Life*. More for a soccer match in duffel coats, waxed macs, some woolly hats. One was in black leather biker's gear and a crash helmet he hadn't taken off.

He was standing at a bar in a corner where a man and a woman had set out their stall—two small word processors and a pile of fat, green folders.

Behind them was a handwritten notice: 'Orange Squash—20p.' There were no takers.

The man was on a portable phone, as every other person in the hall seemed to be. One was shouting, 'You're breaking up.'

Jacko smiled to himself at a fond memory. When portable phones first came in, one was issued to a pal of his, a village bobby, as an experiment in high-speed community communications.

Instead of sitting at home all day, in the warmth of his office-cum-home, he was instructed to get out and about in the knowledge that any member of the community who needed him could reach him immediately. In addition, he was ordered to phone in to Control on the hour, every hour.

In his kitchen at home was a wall telephone with a loose wire which caused a high-pitched whine.

Every hour on the hour, he would sit

in his warm kitchen, sipping his coffee and nibbling his toast and phone Control. 'Checking in.'

'You're breaking up,' Control would reply. 'Where are you?'

'Just going under a motorway bridge.'

'Never moved from my kitchen for months,' he told Jacko rather proudly over a pint in his village pub.

Jacko loved cops like that, stories like that of bucking the system, taking the piss out of authority, memories that would warm his retirement years.

He mingled, Hazel at his side, heading for the bar.

Radio-pagers bleeped about them. From the hubbub came Continental accents, a few American, and lots of Scots. It always astonished him how many Scots worked on English nationals. Most had hard accents out of the Gorbals that could make 'Have a nice day' sound like a demand for money with menaces.

In the old days, his early days, Jacko reminisced, even big press conferences used to be attended by about a dozen, no more; all with notebooks and pens, just one tape recorder carried by the BBC man in a big green box.

Nowadays, said Hazel disdainfully, with a radio station, often two, in every sizeable town, TV in every region, four national channels plus satellite, freelance agencies spreading like weeds in a garden, they were more like gatherings of warring clans with zooms and booms and mobile phones and laptops as their weapons.

They reached the bar. The man with the pile of green files, balding, burly with a black moustache, used an Ulster accent down his phone. 'Is that sterling or dollars?'

The man in biker's gear seized his chance as the Ulsterman went silent, awaiting the reply. 'Dispatch from Beeb, Brum.'

The Ulsterman spoke to the woman at his side. 'Have Pebble Mill put it in writing?'

The woman, fortyish, bespectacled, keyed in numbers on a computer, no bigger than a lunchbox. 'Yes.'

He handed over a folder, got the dispatch rider to sign a form.

The woman keyed on. 'The *National Inquirer's* offer is in the mailbox.'

He typed one-handed into a twin machine. 'Yer,' he said into the phone. Then, 'Sorry, mate. You're outbid.' He thumbed the off-button.

He looked up at Jacko. 'Yer.'

'McAllister of Fine Focus about?'

'That's me. Where'ya from?'

Police Gazette,' said Jacko, unable to resist it. 'We want a word with you.'

'Can't you see I'm busy?'

'After the conference will do. Across the road at the Finch's Arms.' He jerked his head back in the direction of the village pub, then allowed a small smile to play on his lips. 'Don't leave town.'

For almost twenty-nine years he'd wanted to say that; thought he might not get the chance again.

The hubbub had not abated, so, until he turned round, Jacko hadn't noticed that Silent Knight had made his entrance.

Smooth, pressed uniform tailored to a tall lean frame, he was sitting, placing his nameplate in front of him on a trestle table on a stage with red and white canvas skirting at the other end of the hall. Behind him was a walnut piano with one castor missing so it stood less than upright.

A second nameplate on the table indicated that the uniformed officer at his side was the chief superintendent from division, who spoke, shouted, really, first. 'Thank you, ladies and gentlemen.'

Knight waited until phone conversations had ended and bleeps had been silenced. Then he stood, script in hand.

He read a long appeal for witnesses, boaters, bird-spotters and the like, to come forward. Everyone took notes, dutifully doing their public service bit.

He stopped as Lord Hamb strode in, cutting a swath through the crowd, retinue in his wake. There were murmurs of appreciation from the audience, none of whom had sat on benches and fold-up chairs by the wooden walls.

Not a wallflower among them, Jacko noted, but then theirs was not a job for shrinking violets.

'Sorry, sorry,' Hamb mumbled loudly as he took an empty chair at the table, beaming about him. 'Carry on. Carry on.'

Knight gave out a long list of the various agencies involved in the inquiry, then sat down abruptly.

There was the sort of stunned silence that comes from a soccer stadium's popular end when an unjust penalty has been awarded against the home side. Then the storm breaks, as it broke now with shouts of: 'You mean, you're still not officially naming him?... 'Is that all after six hours of being buggered about?'...and, in a Scots voice, 'Fucking polis chiefs. I've shat 'em.'

Knight looked disbelievingly from one shouter to another, having never even been spoken to in all his life like this. 'You must understand—'

'And what you must understand, sunshine...' From somewhere near the centre. '...is that this is a matter of grave public concern. Now give us the facts.'

'I've told you all—'

'You've told us nob all all day.' A woman's voice.

'Tell us, please.' The baying voice of a royal correspondent, his florid face known to Jacko from television which always made him look like the Widow Twanky. 'Did Prince Charles see or hear the explosion?'

The reply was No to the first part, Don't Know to the second, and Can't Say to a supplementary on what part he'd played in the aftermath. 'Not germane to the inquiry.'

A Press Association reporter, a sober heavyweight Jacko had spotted knocking on doors in the village, asked a clever, slow-burn question. 'Do you think Summers was the target, or someone else?'

'We're unable to confirm anything at this stage.' Knight permitted himself a little smile, intended to tell his questioner: I'm not falling for an old one like that.

'You see,' the PA man went on, 'villagers tell us that Mr Matthew Hamb also drives a white VW Golf...'

This was news to Jacko. His eyes found the tall, dark man he'd seen in Hamb's study an hour earlier who was now standing beside the stage, neck craned up. If he was the Hon Matthew, he looked distinctly uncomfortable.

'...so naturally, we're bound to ask—'

Unwisely, Knight didn't let him finish. 'Too early to speculate.' Then, foolishly, 'We're not ruling out anyone as the intended victim, absolutely no—'

'Anyone?' came a joyful chorus.

'Well...er...' Knight was all too aware that he'd just ruled in Prince Charles as the possible target, never mind Hamb Junior, and retreated. 'No further comment on that aspect.'

'Was it a land mine or a car bomb?' a local reporter asked very politely.

'Examination of the scene is not yet complete,' came the brusque reply.

'Any claims of responsibility yet?' asked a newspaperwoman.

'No, but that doesn't mean we're ruling out any illegal organization.'

'Any?' Another gleeful chorus greeted a direct link between royalty and terrorism. Knight spotted his mistake too late and added, very lamely, 'At this stage.'

'Look.' A Gorbals voice. 'We know from him...' He flicked his head in the direction of McAllister standing at the bar. '...that it's Verne Summers. The world knows now. Can yer no confirm it?'

Knight, face whiter than the balmed Willis, tried to regain control, again saying more than he'd intended. 'We can confirm it was his vehicle but we can't say for sure at this stage who was driving it until—'

'Hey. You.' A slurred voice. 'Why not...' Pause. 'What's your name again?'

The chief super lost his temper, another mistake, pointing to the nameplace. 'Can't you read?'

'He can't write either,' came an even more slurred response. The small group around them chuckled merrily. Among them were a couple Jacko had seen at

75

their hip-flasks when he first arrived. They were virtually holding each other up.

The man who had originated this line of questioning finally got round to completing it. 'Why not call in the big boys from the Yard? We might get some sense out of them.'

It was a cutting (cruel, in fact) remark to direct to any provincial police chief, but Knight was so on the defensive now that he replied by listing the Met agencies already involved and thanking them profusely.

'Creep,' came a call from the front and 'Plonker' from the back.

Knight had the dead look of a greenhorn who'd gone over the top in battle for the first time and could see the whites of the enemy's eyes.

He glanced helplessly, pleadingly about him. Jacko's eyes went down in case he was called up as reinforcements, a hopeless mission with the mob in this mood. Besides, he was rather enjoying it.

'Lads. Lads. Lads.' An oop north voice.

Come the hour, cometh the man, thought Jacko, looking up.

Lord Hamb was on his feet, conducting for silence.

He breathed in, pushing out his mighty chest.

'Assuming it was your colleague...' A broad wink. '...it's a terrible tragedy and a minute's silence is called for, don't you think?'

He lowered his head and clasped his hands together at his groin. The room went from fortissimo to pianissimo accompanied by just a few burps, quickly silenced bleeps and embarrassed foot-shuffling.

'Now, lads,' he resumed, still chauvinistically ignoring half his audience, prompting Hazel to press her lips tight together in disapproval.

He held them in his hands for a twenty-minute question and answer session. Yes, he confirmed, Prince Charles was a regular visitor and he detailed when and for what sporting purpose. So was his brother Andrew. 'To get away from the normal trials and tribulations of life.'

Code for crumbled marriages, he means, Jacko realized, and so did everyone else.

He patiently explained why he didn't consider Prince Charles was the target. 'He always flies in and out by chopper, never uses that road off the island.'

A girl reporter next to Hazel sighed,

'Shit. That's torn it.'

He praised the bravery of Willis, crediting him with more courage than the captain had claimed for himself. On medical advice, he couldn't sanction interviews or give out a home address, other than to state his proud parents lived at Uppingham.

Jacko held his breath, worried that his bargaining chip, the ace he was to play for McAllister, would be revealed.

'He's quite ill. Resting when I left.' He repeated most of what Willis had said in hospital.

When someone asked if Willis had recognized Summers as the bombed car's driver, he ignored the question. Instead, he moved on to fawn over Prince Charles's coolness at the controls of the helicopter on the airlift to hospital.

A collective dreamy drone went round the room, and Jacko knew the danger had passed.

'A terrific angle,' said the girl reporter, enthused again.

'No bad. No bad,' a Scotsman concurred, praise indeed.

Assuming the victim was Summers, Hamb continued with another broad wink, well, yes, paparazzi photographers could be a bit of a pest to royalty and nobles like himself—'but we live in a democracy.'

He endeared himself to the tabloids, alienated a few always-serious, self-important quality and broadcasting staff by favouring a voluntary code of conduct rather than privacy laws.

Yes, he said, his son Matthew—he looked down at him—did own a white Golf VW, but he regarded it as a coincidence. 'Lots of young trendies have them, especially in Fleet Street, I'd imagine.' Matthew smiled weakly.

Unabashed, he answered personal questions about the cost and size of his Lodge and threw in a bit of local history for the colour writers. 'Do you realize that on this very stage have stood Noël Coward and Sir Malcolm Sargent when they were guests at the old hall before it became a hotel?'

It was the cue for a tabloid man to stage whisper, 'And now we've got Bernard Manning of the Lords.'

Everyone, apart from Knight, laughed, Hamb louder than most.

It was a masterly performance, a virtuoso at his peak. 'That it then, lads? My London PR is on tap for any further inquiries.' He gave the number. 'Don't phone home, right?'

'Thanks, guv,' called a Cockney voice.

Knight climbed weakly back to his feet. 'Shall we call another conference at, say—'

'Piss off, yous useless bastard,' growled a Glaswegian amiably.

'And piss off, he will,' said Hazel, watching a shrunken Knight following Hamb out, like a uniformed footman, lost among the lickspittlers.

Never to be seen on the inquiry again, thought Jacko; terrific. Little Velma would be in sole charge now.

Half the room had emptied ahead of Hamb and his retinue. The rest were shouting into phones or had sat on the benches, fingers poised over laptops.

They strolled back to the bar.

'Not now,' McAllister protested.

'Now,' said Jacko, sternly. 'Across the road. In private.'

'I've got—'

'The media world and his wife are here. It will be on the wires by now,' said Hazel.

'I've got Sydney coming up to deadline.'

'And I can put you on to a picture that they'll hold their front pages for,' said

Jacko, tantalizingly.

'What?'

Jacko gave him a taster.

'Twenty minutes,' said McAllister, eyes ringing up currency signs from around the world.

'Ten,' said Jacko, 'and I'll spend them reading this.' He helped himself to a green folder from the diminishing pile, but didn't offer to pay.

6

Fifteen minutes, as it turned out; time enough for Jacko to down a pint of lager, smoke a cigarette and browse through the folder as he sat alone on a brown leather bench by an open fire in the Finch's Arms, a cosy pub with low, beamed ceiling and a cottagey feel.

It contained a portfolio of Summers' work that had won him awards as Young Cameraman of the Year in the early eighties, runner-up in Foreign Photo of the Year with the late eighties and a highly commended in the Royal Picture of the Year a couple of years earlier.

Startling shots of blazing riots in Brixton and Belfast and grim war pictures from the Middle East made his later royal stuff look tame by comparison. Several showed Charles hunting and shooting, a few of Andrew water skiing, all taken on Rutland Water.

An accompanying double-spaced script detailed his twelve-year career, anecdotes of derring-do leaving the impression that he was as addicted to danger as Lord Hamb was to publicity.

There was a string of laudatory quotes from McAllister which put him in the same league as Donald McCullin, the old *Sunday Times* man; in Jacko's view, the best of this strange breed. There was also a quote, just two paragraphs, from Marilyn Moore, which talked of her shock and her love for him.

'That package is priced at a grand.' An Ulster voice at his shoulder. 'A ton to the *Police Gazette.*' McAllister laughed as he sat down on a stool at the round, heavy table. 'Terrific, eh?'

'Flogged many?' asked Jacko.

'Eight here, a dozen abroad.'

Twenty thou in one shift, Jacko calculated,

plus what he'd earned from his first tip-offs round the nationals.

Presently Hazel joined them. 'Got it.' She opened a black leather shoulder bag. All she got out were Jacko's car keys which she handed back to him.

McAllister made no move to buy a round. Staffers, Jacko had noticed, were always generous with their employers' money; freelances not so, because they were self-employed, he supposed.

He went to the bar and returned with another pint for himself and scotches for McAllister and Hazel.

Before he had time to resume his seat, McAllister asked, 'What's the deal then?'

Jacko sat and took a long drink first. 'You give us the complete rundown on Summers, access to his files, contacts books, everything, and immediate access to his lady, and you get the picture.'

'What's it show?'

Hazel hugged her shoulder bag. 'Charlie, Hamb, a horse and Willis, the hero of the hour. It's worth a mint to you.'

'When?'

Jacko again. 'When we're satisfied we've got the lot.'

'Tonight?'

'Depends on you.'

'Tomorrow's no good.'

'It may have to be. It could take time.'
McAllister frowned, uncertain.

'Look.' Hazel palmed the portfolio on the table. 'Tomorrow's papers are going to be full of these.'

She patted her bag. 'This will keep. Releasing it now will mean you're competing for space with your own stuff, plus everything the staffers and other agencies have taken today. Bad business, surely? This job will run for weeks. It gives you a flying start for Wednesday morning's papers. Leave something for tomorrow, eh?'

A brilliant sales pitch, Jacko decided, approvingly, but McAllister was still not wholly convinced. 'How do I know I can trust you?'

'The alternative,' said Hazel darkly, 'is for us to give it to PA and they'll push it around everywhere, home and abroad, and you won't earn a bean.'

'I trust you,' said McAllister, hurriedly.

Jacko had cleared the trip with Velma and collected the bag (containing one shirt, one pair of underpants and socks, a clean hankie, toilet gear and the Good Pub Guide) he always carried in the boot of his car.

Hazel travelled light—just her shoulder bag. Sitting in the back, she said, 'I'll buy some new knickers in the morning.' A slow sexy chuckle. 'Unless I declare a no knickers day.'

'What?' said McAllister, chin over his shoulder, leering, as he waited to turn right from the peninsula road and drive along the north shore of Rutland Water.

Hazel told of an old school pal on the south coast who was sometimes in the doldrums because of an errant husband. She herself often got the blues over her married DCI. 'So we phone each other and declare a no knickers day, just to cheer ourselves up.'

Jacko, in the passenger seat, laughed but thought: Good lord. In his mid-teens, the girls at the downtown grammar school wore brown knickers with elastic at waist and legs. Harvest festivals, they were called, because all was safely gathered in. Times had changed.

McAllister drove steadily, as if nervous about the policeman at his side, towards Stamford. He added to the script in his package. 'Like a son to me, he was.'

Summers, he said, came to his agency as a twenty-year-old straight from a year-long news photography college course in Sheffield. He was hired to make the tea and do the head and shoulder shots which the agency's team of jet-setters regarded as beneath them after jobs like the Falklands War.

When the Brixton riots erupted, they'd been short-staffed and had to pitch him out of the office. He came back with amazing stuff that made him the Young Cameraman of the Year.

'Gave him itchy feet, though. Kept him happy for a while with trips to Belfast, but he wanted the big time.'

Three years on, McAllister accepted he couldn't keep him, so he came to a deal. 'I bankrolled his move to the Middle East in return for first rights marketing his work; my equipment as a retainer.'

'What was in it for you?' Hazel asked, brightly.

'The usual. Ten per cent home sales, twenty foreign.'

'Do well?'

'Yeah, right through to the Gulf War.'

Summers operated out of Nicosia where

he set up home with Marilyn Moore, an air hostess with some Mideast line. 'Two years older. Not much to look at. Seen bigger tits in a bird-bath. But a good girl.'

'Anybody before that?' asked Jacko.

'A fling with a Page Three girl in London. He was too busy to do too much chasing.'

'Name?'

'Sally Masters. She's on TV now. Some game show. Funny thing is...' He looked across, tilting his head slightly, seeking something. '...she popped up on one of his feature jobs a few months back. Some kiss-and-tell involving some politician. Can't remember his name.' He gave his head a shake. 'It'll be back at the office.'

'So they were still in touch?'

McAllister said he didn't really know.

A sex triangle, Jacko mused, with love, money or both the motive, and a hit man hired? It's been known. He'd check it.

'Did he visit you often when he was aboard?'

'Spoke every few days, but I only saw him when he was home to visit his widowed mum.' She lived in Mansfield, he continued; capital of the East Midlands coalfield, but Jacko didn't need to be told.

He knew it well. He'd been there, in the town's court, just over six hours earlier.

'She's been ill recently, real bad,' said McAllister.

They were on the A1 now, heading south. Immediately, he picked up his black BMW to eighty. Dipped headlights cut through pockets of mist, picking out the red rear lamps of slower cars and lorries in the inside lane he seldom used. It remained a smooth ride.

'What happened on the Gulf?'

'He wasn't picked for the photo pool.' That, McAllister explained, was a group of cameramen who got special facilities laid on by the military, briefings, guided tours, airlifts and so on, but they had to pool everything, share what they got with any media outlet who wanted it.

The same arrangement applied to official royal visits at home and overseas tours. The rota, they called it. Photographers were given privileged positions to work from, but they had to pool the shots they got.

'Is that good or bad?' asked Jacko.

McAllister shrugged. 'Outside the pool or the rota, you can miss the action, but you can go where your nose takes you.

You're a free spirit, not bound by their rules. And you don't have to share what you get. You can sell it where you like.'

'Where did his nose take him in the war?'

'Kuwait and up into southern Iraq. Got some good desolate shots, bodies in burned-out convoys, dying wildlife after that oil spill and the like. Sold well.'

Bypassing Peterborough, he continued. 'He came back all of a sudden; ahead of most of the troops, in fact. Said he was following up a biggie. Wouldn't say what till he'd checked it. Said he was going to spend a couple of days up north with his mum and he'd turn it over on the way.'

'Didn't he confide in you?' asked Hazel.

'Only in so far as it might turn out to be a words job when he had the necessary pictorial proof.'

A words job meant he'd have to team up with a reporter who'd make the inquiries and write the piece. 'They put words to the monkey's music,' said McAllister with a light laugh.

Wordsmiths called cameramen monkeys, he explained, because they spend a lot of time hanging out of trees, lunching on bananas and scratching their arses.

Hazel laughed delightedly from the back.

'Verne never worked with a wordsmith that I know,' McAllister went on, 'except Nick Dilks who does our captions. And Nick didn't go north with him.'

'So what happened to this big scoop?' asked Jacko.

'Must have petered out.' He hunched his shoulders over the wheel into a shrug. 'Didn't stand up. Often happens.'

Summers flew back to Cyprus but returned within a month. His lady and furniture followed. He told McAllister he wanted a change of scene and direction; fancied a shot at the royals.

'Had he ever expressed any interest in that sort of work before?' Hazel asked.

'No, and I told him it was an overcrowded market, heavily staffed; that he'd be better off in the Middle East, but I couldn't talk him out of it. So we came to another deal. He continued to use some of our equipment, plus a subsidized car. We got first rights to his stuff.'

Jacko again. 'Is it possible he just got sick of wars?'

'Lost his bottle, you mean?' McAllister's thick black eyebrows went up, then down. 'No chance. Brave as a lion. He got lost in an Iraqi minefield and took photos of the guides coming to get him out.'

He took his right hand off the wheel and flicked index finger against thumb. 'Shit. Should have used that in the script.'

Jacko went silent for a while, thinking: He'll sell it tomorrow; a good tale, in the circumstances of his death. Then: 'Did he do well back here?'

'Reasonable. Had to do some celeb snatching and sport as well.'

Jacko gave a frustrated sigh. Sure, it was decent background, but it wasn't getting him very far. 'All this royal stuff was taken at Rutland Water. What do you read into that?'

'That's where his contact was. Must be. He can't have had a, say, Sandringham or Highgrove source or he'd have gone there, too.'

'Who was his contact?'

'Come on. No journo will spill that, not even to his editor. It's the only real ethic we've got.'

He told a story to demonstrate how hard it was to identify a source. For years, his agency was being beaten on animal pictures, a lucrative line, by a one-man operator.

'He was first on the scene for rescues, raids, the lot. Know what was happening? The RSPCA inspector was giving his missus one and he was giving him tips to get him out of the way. In the end they ran off together. Know what hubby did? Flogged the story to a Sunday. That's the only reason it all came out.'

No worse than making twenty grand plus out of someone who was a son to you, thought Jacko, mind momentarily wandering. His mind came back immediately from its travels. 'Are you trying to tell me something? Was Verne giving somebody one for info?'

'Hell, no.' Positive, a touch shocked. 'Honestly no. He didn't play around. Nothing like that. I'm sure of it.'

Jacko wasn't; something else to check. 'Did he make good money out of his Rutland royals?'

Depended, said McAllister. Get a moody shot of Charles fishing, alone and looking pensive, during his marriage troubles and it would sell like hot cakes, including the States. Capture Andrew enjoying himself when there were complaints about the cost of the civil list, ditto.

Jacko could never understand the public

obsession with the royals. There were much more important things in his life—like would his beloved Lincoln City get promoted (forget glory, a division up will do) and would the new pills from the vet cure his dog's tummy bug?

Deep in his heart, he was a republican, approved of elections, even if he didn't always vote. He was opposed to inherited wealth and power. But he accepted the Queen ruled (if that's what you want to call it) by common consent. How long her gilded children would retain that loyalty was hard to judge. Basically, he didn't give a tinker's toss one way or the other.

They had only themselves to blame for the publicity they attracted. Any family who'd appeared on that appalling TV programme *It's a Knockout* were in on the tacky end of showbiz, as far as he was concerned, and had to take the consequences.

'So what did he earn in a year?'

'He wasn't home long enough to be front rank, hadn't built up the contracts yet. His royal stuff wasn't very, well, spicy, er, sexy, was it? No secret trysts, eh?'

Finally he got round to answering the question. 'Thirty, say. Thirty-five. But one royal biggie would have doubled it.'

'What are the national staffers, the sort on this job today...' Jacko flicked his head back and northwards towards Rutland, thirty or so miles behind them now. '...what will they be on?'

'About the same; a bit more perhaps.'

'I don't follow.' Jacko frowned. 'They get paid holidays, liberal exes, office cars. Lots of perks. Pensions, if they—'

McAllister saw the question. 'He couldn't come back and walk straight into a staff job. It's all short-term contracts these days, casual shifts. That's why these youngsters leap around all over the place, putting hours in, in the hope of eventually landing a staff job.'

Jacko was expecting a lament for the old days (the sort of nonsensical nostalgia he came out with, drunk in the Fairways, the HQ local, on a Friday night) but McAllister snorted out a hard laugh. 'The smaller the staff, the fatter the freelance fees, that's my sentiment. Besides, Verne could go where he liked, do what he liked.'

His phone rang, surprising Jacko, who was stubbing out the trip's second cigarette in the tray above the bracket that held the receiver. He unclipped it and handed it to McAllister who took it right-handed, so Jacko wouldn't hear if the news was bad. He said so little there was no way of telling. He passed the receiver back. 'Marilyn's on tap at eight.'

Jacko looked at the dashboard clock. More than two hours, he thought. Time for a drink in Fleet Street, perhaps. For some unaccountable reason he'd always wanted to drink in the Cheshire Cheese.

Hazel, quiet in the back seat for some miles, came up with a question which Jacko, to his secret shame, had missed. 'Did you know Verne was coming to Rutland Water this morning?'

Yes and No, McAllister said.

On Saturday, Summers got a day's work from a Sunday paper for a soccer game in Nottingham. He'd stayed the night at his mum's in Mansfield. On Sunday Marilyn relayed a message from Verne to him: 'There may be some royal stuff to market by mid-afternoon tomorrow.'

'That all?' She sounded disappointed. Not Jacko, though. Much of this media stuff, about rotas and fees, she must have already known in her PR post. Not once had she shown off and interrupted the

95

briefing. A smart operator, he decided contentedly; the perfect partner on this job.

'All she said,' McAllister replied. 'Maybe she knows more.'

Round about Sandy, Jacko gazed out of his window into the mist. Fifty miles were behind them now, fifty to go, and he'd do it in less than an hour even through the tail end of London's rush hour.

He looked at the clock again: six. He nodded at the radio. McAllister switched on the news. They heard edited highlights of Lord Hamb's solo performance on the stage at the village hall.

7

'Mum. Mum.' Her small always-complaining voice started up again as soon as he used the remote control to change channels.

He'd been flicking between them all day, imagining the TV set blowing up, giving himself a kind of charge, randy almost, that he'd never experienced before. This time her bellyaching stilled the sensation. 'Shut it,' he hissed.

'Mum. Mum. Mum. He turned off *Neighbours* and—'

'Shut it, I said.' Transfixed, he was having yet another bird's-eye view of the peninsula and the mangled wreckage. A still shot of Prince Charles on horseback quickly replaced it. Now Lord Hamb was talking to a reporter with a hand mike held to a frozen face.

'No *Neighbours* and now he won't let us watch *Home and Away*,' the young girl piped on, forced tears welling, sitting cross-legged on a shabby carpet in front of a gas fire on low.

A flabby woman in a stained lime green jumpsuit shouldered open the sticking door to a small kitchen. She held a cigarette in one hand; a tarnished fork in the other. The smell of fish fingers filled the thinly furnished lounge; not appetizing.

'What's this about?' Her puffy face was set in a severe scold.

'Crow won't let us—'

'Yer and who pays the frigging TV licence?' It was something his father always said automatically to his mother in mild programming disputes, usually *Dallas*

97

versus football. He realized too late that in this household it didn't apply. Nobody paid the licence fee.

'Not you,' the woman reminded him firmly. 'You pay for next to nothing. All you've done...'

He sank deeper into the lumpy sofa and thumbed an inner button to mute, blocking her out, to concentrate on the set. He was desperate to find out if the BBC had anything to add to the ITN coverage that had baffled and angered him with references to a bungled attempt and speculation about a mistake by terrorists.

'...is sit on your bloody arse all day watching telly. What's a matter with you? You badly or something?'

Two pictures of cars appeared side by side; one an aerial shot of the mangled Golf, one a photo of the same model, looking brand new. '...of the type Lord Hamb's son also drives,' the newscaster reported, and he went on to hint at a case of mistaken identity.

Crow felt sick, fevered.

Her brat of a son, usually an ally, shuffled round on his bottom on the carpet, turning on him, upping his temperature. 'And you promised to take me to the lake to try the boat.'

'Too windy,' he said quietly; then to himself: Ignore him. Don't cause a ruck by telling him he should have been at school. They seldom went, either of the little bastards; always feigning illness. Just concentrate.

'Shut up, you,' his mother snapped, 'and go and get the chips.'

Another old picture of Prince Charles at the controls of a helicopter came on to the screen.

'But Mum...' The boy again, whining still.

Then, making Crow pitch forward on the brown couch on which he had lounged since midday, an entirely new photo appeared.

He wore the white band of an officer cadet around his black cap and his face was a dozen or so years younger than Crow remembered it, but it was him all right.

'Shut it,' he rasped, not quite a shout. The woman and her two children went deathly quiet, always did when his pressure cooker temper began to steam free.

Just in time he caught an unseen woman's voice confirming his identification. '...to hospital where Mr Willis, a former army captain, is tonight reported to be in no danger.'

Now Lord Hamb re-filled the screen, praising Prince Charles's and Captain Willis's coolness in equal measure.

The auld shit, thought Crow. So that's where the queer wound up. Fifteen miles up the road. 'That shit,' he repeated out loud.

'Who?' asked the woman, quieter, still standing at the door.

'What?' He wasn't really aware that he had spoken.

She nodded at the TV. 'What's all that about?'

'That bombing...'

'I know that.' A sour face. 'Think I'm thick or something? It's been on all bloody day. Do you know him?'

'Who?'

'That officer.'

'No.' He spoke softly, shaken by his own stupidity.

'Was he with you in the Gulf?' asked the boy, his ally again.

'Never saw him. Heard of him. Same outfit, that's all.'

'In the TA?' asked the woman.

He did not reply.

Get out, he implored himself. Get clear. Think. Plan.

'Chips,' said the woman, looking down at the boy.

'Oh Mum...'

'I'll go,' said Crow, stirring.

'But you never—'

'I need some fresh air.'

'Should think so after sitting there all day.'

Listen who's talking, he said, talking to himself, as he heaved himself up. Over this thick green sweater, he put a black donkey jacket he'd been using as a pillow. She's the one who normally loafs all day. A couch cabbage, his disapproving mother called her. Couch potato, she really meant. But his mother was always slightly out with in-phrases and, with her fondness for green, it was an inadvertently appropriate name for her.

'I'll no be long,' he said, walking out.

He left the van where it was, parked outside the terrace house, fifties design, but looking pre-war with broken fencing and an overgrown front garden.

He'd walk. He wished he hadn't used the van this morning; risky, really.

There were so many things he would have done differently if only he had had more time to plan. He wouldn't have hired a vehicle, though; traceable. He'd have nicked one.

Still, he'd covered his tracks after that grey Merc from the hotel had overtaken him. Putting on this donkey jacket and dropping in at the newsagent in Stamford was a good idea, buying the *Mirror*, making a show of asking for directions to a stately home where he already had a tree-clearing job lined up.

If the polis came, he'd say he'd left home at gone eight and the woman would not say otherwise; couldn't. She slept till ten every morning.

She'd still been in bed when he got home. He told her he'd landed the tree-felling contract, because his expertise with dynamite was needed to shift some spreading, ancient roots.

He'd changed and dumped the fatigues in the bathroom next to an already overflowing laundry basket. He'd have liked them washed straight away, to get rid of any explosive traces, but knew it would be a week or more before she got round to it. He daren't alter routine and launder them himself. She'd rumble something.

If those forensic scientists who'd been filmed by TV at the scene examined it, they'd find traces, that's for sure, but then, he comforted himself, his job was a ready-made explanation.

The rest of the operation he'd have left as it was, even with more time to plan. The bomb was a belter, couldn't be bettered, and he'd certainly use the same technique again, no sweat.

A terrific job, perfectly executed, and the more he thought about it, the more the slipshod way it had been reported infuriated him.

You can't even trust the BBC, with all the licence fees we pay them, incompetent bastards; praising that poofter, ignoring me.

OK, I don't want them to know I did it, at least until I'm paid in full and well clear, but I'm entitled to the private satisfaction of credit where credit is due. A bungled attempt? The wrong target?

A white Golf, right? I got the white Golf. Didn't know who was in it. Now I do. Some cameraman called Summers, they think. Now I know I still don't care.

Nothing to do with me.

All that matters is that he was in a white Golf. Check? Check.

OK, Hamb's son has a white Golf. A coincidence, like that fat old fart said on TV. Must be. Otherwise it doesn't make sense. Willis was thirty yards away. In a Land Rover, according to the telly. Not a white Golf. Check? Check.

He'd killed the right man. He was sure of it. I'm a professional, for fuck's sake. A fucking professional.

Pangs of panic crept up slowly behind him as he walked through a rundown estate with several windows boarded up and covered with graffiti; an indefinable suspicion that he was being set up somehow; the beginnings of a plot to deny him the fourteen grand he had coming with a cock-and-bull story that he had botched it.

The bastard won't get away with it, he swore in a private oath. I'll kill him first and take the money. I've killed before, the perfect crime, and I'll kill again, if I have to.

Warn him to play it straight or else. How? Send a message, hinting at the truth coming out if he pulls a double-cross.

How? Can't phone. Everyone's line will be tapped and taped for miles around on a job like this. I'm not seeing him till Thursday, when I collect.

How then? Via the media, perhaps. Use them. They cocked it up. They can put it right. That's what bombers do, don't they? Phone a radio station or something and make a statement and claim responsibility.

He reached the fish shop. A long queue snaked outside. He recognized the man in front, nodded. 'Hi, Mac.'

'Bollocks to this,' said Mac. 'I'll come back when it's quieter. Fancy a bevy, Crow?'

'Broke.' Clever that, thought Crow. Let no one know you're flush with that grand in advance. That almost did for us in Cyprus.

Mac left the queue, grumbling. Crow stepped into his place. He knew no one ahead of him. Good, he declared. Time to think.

The public ought to be told, or at least pointed in the direction of the truth. If the message is clever enough, it would sound a warning, too.

But how? Can't nip into a phone box and ask Directory Inquiries for the number of the BBC or the *Evening Telegraph*. They'll trace it.

He reached the warm, stainless steel counter and stood before it. 'Chips, twice, please.'

A woman in white tossed two large scoops from the drainer next to the deep-fat fryer on to greaseproof paper with plain wrapping paper beneath it. 'Salt and vinegar?'

Crow nodded. 'Lots.' She never had any in at home.

Tart-smelling brown liquid sizzled as it sprayed the golden chips. 'Nice and hot,' she said, wrapping them up. 'One-twenty please.'

He gave her a newish twenty note, regretted it immediately as she held it up to the yellow strip-light. Must change 'em into something smaller, he vowed.

She seemed satisfied and turned to the till. While he waited for his change, he took the *Mirror* from his jacket pocket where it had been, folded and unread, since he bought it.

He slipped the wrapped-up chips inside it, beginning to double-wrap them, to keep them hot on the walk back, still wondering who to phone to make his statement to the world and how to get their number without it being traced back to here and him.

His eyes fell to the bottom of the back page, but he wasn't reading about football. He held out his hand for the change. There was a fifty pence piece among it.

8

A phone rang in the car, not the tinny sound from above the ashtray; muffled and from Jacko's pocket.

He lifted it out with his right hand, transferred it to his left, thinking: *Touché;* repaying McAllister for his secrecy.

'Carole Malloy.' She never gave him her rank. 'Where are you?'

The street with terraces of four-storey buff buildings that had seen better days was unrecognizable to Jacko who usually travelled to London by train. He relayed the question to McAllister and his answer to Velma. 'Ten minutes from the City.'

'Good,' she said, sounding happy. 'I've another little job for you.'

Oh, good, thought Jacko, anything but

happy, in dire need of a pee. Stick a hose on my nob and I'll wash this bloody car for you, too.

'The Yard have just had a man on from the *Daily Mirror.*' She gave his name, extension number, an address in Holborn and briefed him. 'Fix up to see him, will you? And keep in touch.'

Jacko pecked out the number with his forefinger and made an appointment for five minutes' time.

'Drop us off at the *Mirror* building first,' he said to McAllister.

'Why?' He was so startled he gripped the wheel which he'd steered lightly for most of the hundred miles, sometimes with just index fingers on the bottom, grandstanding.

'I have to see a potential witness.'

'About what?'

'Confidential.'

'You're not doing a deal with them, are you, over that photo you promised me?' His expression was very flustered, betrayed almost. 'Cutting me out?'

'Would we?' said Hazel, teasingly, from the back.

Within a couple of minutes he drew up on double yellow lines outside a tall square building, red, white and blue, an odd bit of patriotic flag-waving from a Labour-supporting paper, colourfully out of place on the edge of the sober City with the floodlit dome of St Paul's just in view as they'd approached.

Jacko got out. 'She's got your picture. You can hold her as hostage, if you like.' Stooping, he gave a little wave to Hazel in the back. 'Not that anyone would pay much of a ransom for you.'

'More than you can afford,' said a smiling Hazel, never at a loss for honest, hard-hitting words.

A short man with a chubby, friendly face waited behind revolving doors, got him through turnstile security, up a swift, silent lift to the third floor, chatting amiably. He pointed Jacko to the toilets opposite a block of empty red phone boxes, a bizarre sight in a humming hi-tech hive; museum pieces, he supposed.

Relieved, he stepped back on to the huge L-shaped editorial floor, glancing at steel desks with screens and keyboards, most empty. He guessed their occupants were all where he'd just travelled from.

He was led into a small narrow room

where a petite, dark woman was at a cluttered desk talking on a phone and into a much bigger, thickly carpeted room with a breathtaking view of the City lights through smoky mist.

Standing at a big desk was another short man, late forties, rather plump, in shirt-sleeves and a striped tie that looked old-schoolish. Around him were three men and two women, none of them particularly well dressed for the money McAllister had said they must be earning. They were in animated conversation, looking down at white lined tabloid pages on the desk. All had drinks in their hands.

Jacko was pointed to a long fawn wall couch. 'What do you want?' said his guide.

It came out rather bluntly after such a warm welcome, and Jacko was thrown. 'Well, er, as I tried to explain on the—'

'No. A drink. What will you have?'

'Beer, please,' replied Jacko, having just made room.

The man walked on to a well-stocked cabinet behind the desk, helped himself to two bottles of expensive lager from a small fridge, poured them into slender glasses and returned to the couch, sitting down. He took a packet of cigarettes from the pocket of a creased beige suit. 'Fire away.'

'I was hoping to speak to the reporter...' Jacko took a cigarette and light, impressed by all the hospitality. 'Thanks...who took that call.'

It wasn't a reporter, said the man, who had a northern accent. It was the deputy news editor. He prodded his chest. 'Me.'

'You fire away then,' said Jacko.

His phone on the news desk rang at 6.37, precisely, he said, looking down at a quarto-sized scratch pad resting on thick thighs. He could be that precise because he'd noted down the time. He turned the pad towards Jacko, jabbing his cigarette at figures which were circled and stood out clearly on a page filled with a mixture of long and shorthand.

A switchboard operator said, 'Got a geezer on with a statement for you about the mine incident at Rutland Water.'

Although he'd been on the desk since nine, phones ringing dementedly all day, the deputy news editor took it, anxious not to miss any scrap of information about the biggest story of the day, indeed of the year, so far.

A different man's voice came on. 'I have a statement for you about the mine incident at Rutland Water.'

'Who's calling?' The desk deputy thought it might be a PR from the police or the Palace or somewhere calling back with previously requested information.

'I speak on behalf of Animal Vigil.'

'What's that?' asked the deputy, suspecting a crackpot and losing a bit of interest.

'The statement reads: "We claim responsibility for the incident. Summers will not be the only one to go down if the terms aren't met." Got that?'

The deputy, all interest now, noted it down and, at the same time, asked, 'What's this mean?'

'That is all.'

He made another note which he slipped to an assistant to his right. 'Tell the police to get this call traced.'

As he did so, anxious to keep him talking, he said, 'Listen, mate, anyone can phone up a newspaper and claim a bombing—'

'It was a mine.'

'So you say, but how do I know this isn't a hoax?'

112

'Have the police told you the mine contained fifteen pounds and was detonated by remote control?'

'Not yet, but—'

'It did, and you'd better believe it, pally.'

'I don't want to be rude, mate, but I've never heard of your organization. What do you stand for? Is this some campaign against blood sports?'

'It's a campaign for fair play.'

'These terms you're talking about—what are they?'

'Payment in full or else.'

'Are you holding someone hostage, then?'

'That's all you get.'

The line went dead just as his assistant got through to Scotland Yard.

'Sorry, mate,' the desk deputy said, regretfully, 'he gave me no chance to keep him talking.'

'Good try.' Jacko nodded his thanks. 'Did he give a code?'

A solemn headshake.

'You made those notes at the time?'

'Those.' The deputy pointed to Animal Vigil and a line of squiggles that contained Summers' name in longhand. 'I jotted down the rest immediately afterwards when it was fresh.'

'What accent?'

'Obviously disguised. Slow, deliberate. A bad imitation of BBC.' He stopped in thought. 'But there was a hard edge about it. Celtic, certainly. Ulster, I think. A bit like Paisley.'

Can't be McAllister, trying to keep a lucrative story running, Jacko thought. He'd got two alibi witnesses.

The crowd around the big desk drained their drinks and wandered out with the pages now filled with pencil marks as thick as black crayons.

The plumpish man sat down behind a big desk. A silver-haired veteran with a pink face to match his shirt walked in and up to the mini-bar. Uninvited, he helped himself to a moderate measure of gin and tonic.

The man at the desk looked at Jacko. 'What do you make of it?'

'Dunno,' said Jacko truthfully, not wanting to say: More then my job's worth to discuss it here with you, so he added, 'Yet. Never heard of Animal Vigil, have you?'

Silver-Hair took a short sip from his

glass. 'Not a line about them in the library.'

'Is he right about the mine?' asked the man behind the desk. He had an Oxbridge accent, strange on the British working class's paper.

Jacko didn't know about that either, decided he needed help in this high-powered company. Playing for time, he asked instead to speak to the switchboard operator.

'Is it right?' asked the man at the desk, not letting go.

'I'll try to find out.' Jacko nodded to three phones on his desk. 'Can I use one of those?' He patted his pocket. 'Mine's running low.'

The man slid one forward. Jacko stood and walked to him. He was told what to dial for an outside line, then rang the command post and asked for his boss.

'Yes, Jacko.' He'd had to wait some time for Little Velma to come on.

He briefed her fully, then said, 'They want to know if the info about a mine is right.'

'Why?'

'I suppose they, like us, want to gauge its worth.'

'Who's the boss man there?'

Jacko lowered the phone and looked down at the man behind the desk. 'You the boss here?'

He put on a put-upon face. 'Not that you'd notice sometimes.'

The other two laughed briefly.

'Have a word, will you, with my chief?'

The man nodded at the door to tell the desk deputy to close it. He switched on a loudspeaker line, so everyone could hear. Jacko put the phone on the desk and returned to his seat as the man identified himself as the editor and Velma introduced herself.

No surprise was expressed by word or expression over the fact that the detective chief superintendent in charge of the year's biggest police inquiry was a woman.

Cleverly, she didn't patronize him with fulsome thanks or seek to mislead him. Instead she came completely clean. 'It will take a day or two for Forensics to confirm, but the statement has a ring of truth about it.'

'So you are taking it seriously?'

'Yes.'

'It was a mine, not a car bomb?'

'There's a good chance, yes.'

'Will it cock up your inquiries if we report this call?'

'No. But say we're treating it seriously. The public will expect us to. If it doesn't turn out to be a hoax, they'd regard it as unforgivable not to have had it checked.'

'We've never heard of Animal Vigil. Have you?'

'Not off the top of my head, but we'll obviously run the name through intelligence nationwide.'

'Can we say that?'

'You can say what you like and I wouldn't try to stop you, but I'd prefer you not to use the line about Summers not being the only one to go down unless these unspecified terms are met.'

'Why?'

'It reads a bit like a probable hostage situation, but we know of no kidnapping and have certainly received no demands for ransom. I'm just playing safe, that's all. Without that and the bit about demands, I can see no harm in it.'

'Can we say it was a land mine?'

'I couldn't argue it wasn't.'

'Do you want us to run an appeal for him to get in touch with us again?'

'That would be helpful. If you agree, we could monitor the line.'

'How long do you want us to hold off on this...' He stopped for a second, looking down at a print-out on his desk. '...this sentence about Summers not being the only one?'

'A couple of days. Just to give us time to poke it. Look, I can't tell you—'

'No.' The editor broke in, paused, then: 'OK, then.'

And that, apart from the goodnights, was all that was said.

The editor told the desk deputy to take out the lines Velma requested, run the rest and bill it 'world exclusive'. He added, 'Get a feature writer up there and do a profile on her.' He nodded down at the phone. 'She sounds sharp.'

True, thought Jacko, but Velma was so without self-regard that she was going to hate it.

A pale, bespectacled man was ushered in, the switchboard operator. The caller, he said in a Cockney voice, used a public coin box, not a private phone, because he heard a car beep in the background. Since it wasn't a transfer charge call, no number had been passed on.

He gave no code, just said he had a statement to make about the mine incident at Rutland Water, so the operator connected him with the news desk, where all such offers of information went.

'Accent?' asked Jacko.

'Difficult, that.' A moment's ponder. 'Sounded like...well...as if he was talking with his mouth full. Eating something, I mean. Or maybe it was the old hankie to the mouth trick.'

'Just testing,' said Jacko in his flat, uninteresting tone, 'but anything like me?'

'North Midlands, I'd say,' said the operator, smiling. Jacko shot him a beam of admiration. 'Nothing like.'

'Or him?' Jacko looked at the desk deputy.

'No.' The operator motioned towards the editor. 'Nor him.' The editor joined the laughter.

'If I had to stick one on him, I'd say, close to Scottish.'

'Not Northern Irish?' asked the desk deputy, looking and sounding surprised.

The operator gave this some thought, but stuck to his original view. 'No. This side of the sea, but west coast. Around Glasgow rather than Edinburgh.'

Jacko thanked him. 'Get many calls like that?'

'Used to get a few to the Belfast office, particularly, in the early days,' said the desk deputy. 'Not so many these days, genuine ones, anyway. Most seem to go to the Beeb or PA who've got the codes and can tell whether it's the real thing or a nutter.'

'Well, thanks,' said Jacko, standing. 'Can I buy you a quick drink?' Secretly he was hoping for another freebie.

The desk deputy shook his head. 'Still lots to do.' The editor didn't look up from yet more page proofs which a soft-footed messenger had brought in, but he said, quietly, 'We'll keep in touch.'

It was the nearest anyone had come to suggesting there might be anything extra, something exclusive in it for their co-operation.

'Nice bloke, your boss,' said Jacko as the deputy accompanied him into the lift.

'Not always,' said the deputy with a grim smile.

9

Twelve to twenty-four hours

Her hollow eyes were not red because, Jacko suspected, she had not been left alone yet to shed her private tears, but there was no doubting Marilyn Moore's grief.

The ghostly, absent look, the fidgeting, the blinking silences—all clues to a detective who'd conducted too many interviews like this; not enough, though, never enough, to escape a feeling of being an intruder.

Her rail-thin, boyish body seemed to be fading away within a blue knitted dress which hung from her in what looked like folds of fat.

She sat on a double bed in a room with creaking floorboards two floors below the separate singles Jacko and Hazel had taken.

In the old days, McAllister had said, pulling up in an elegant curved terrace that was the Aldwych, the Waldorf Hotel would be the last place to hide a buy-up, making Marilyn sound like another one of his commercial packages.

He'd have whisked her to a country hideout, far from Fleet Street. These days, after the newspaper's desertion along or over the river, it was as good a safe house as any.

'A tabloid's got her for a couple of days and then we'll try her on the women's magazines,' he'd said, just managing to stop himself rubbing his money-grubbing hands.

Even his nickle-plated tongue could find few words after the formal introductions. He soon departed for the bar, taking with him his deputy Nick Dilks, around forty, seedy, dandruff and cigarette ash on his deep blue suit, brown suede shoes curling up at the toes.

Jacko had ordered from room service—plain omelettes all round. Normally he would have added, or at least thought, here in the Waldorf: 'And nuts to your salad'—but not tonight, not in this sombre mood.

Marilyn managed only a few mouth-fuls as Hazel did what she was good at—talk—leading her through her early days with Verne Summers.

In a soft, warm voice from somewhere around Manchester, she told of taking a job with a Middle East airline after the Ringway-based charter firm she'd worked for collapsed in the eighties.

She met Verne in a hotel in Jordon. Dating was spasmodic with both of them often on trips. Eventually she moved into his large flat in Nicosia. She made the arrangement sound a matter of convenient economics, until she talked about her fears for his safety when he was away at wars, fears that police wives share and seldom talk about. Jacko knew then that she had cared for him deeply.

In their brief spells together, they didn't live the expat's life—beach barbecues, cold drinks round hotel pools, embassy parties. 'It was prime time we wanted to share, just the two of us.' To Jacko, the phrase sounded a touch trite, out of a woman's magazine.

His plate clean, Jacko asked his first question. 'Did you meet up with Lord Hamb over there?'

No, she said, but she knew that between more risky assignments Verne had taken some pictures of the family's place in the Troodos Mountains for a house and garden glossy. 'A nice easy job, well paid. He quite liked Hamb's wife. A batty old biddy, he called her, but they got on well.'

She shook her head when he asked if Verne had met or talked of Hamb's son Matthew or an army captain named Willis who'd been stationed there. A politician called Blewis rang a distant bell, but she couldn't think why.

'My mind's in such a whirl.' Her pale face was lined with the effort of keeping inner emotions intact. 'Questions all day. That awful phoney...' She nodded at the door through which Dilks had gone. '...wanted me to say I was pregnant, so he could write "love child of a hero" and all that crap.'

'He'd have been short of evidence within nine months, then,' said Hazel with a cautious little smile.

'Oh, he had that worked out. I could have a miscarriage because of my heart-ache. It would have given him a follow-up, you see. Can you believe it? I don't know why I let myself in for it.'

For the money, Jacko cynically supposed.

'Mercifully, the paper sent their own woman reporter with a bit of tact and decency.'

Hazel took her on to the Gulf War and rephrased a question Jacko had used on the way down. 'He came back straight after that. Was that because he wanted a quieter life?'

'Oh, no.' A look both startled and sad. 'For my sake. You see, I've...I picked up this tropical thing, a parasite, on my travels.' She placed a hand to her stomach, painfully thin beneath the flattened folds of her dress. 'Eats away the lining. Couldn't shake it. The doctor recommended a cooler climate. I got a transfer to ground staff at Heathrow.'

So, thought Jacko, Verne Summers had given up worthwhile work for the shallow, meaningless life of a paparazzo to bring her home. That had to be love.

But, being a detective, he wondered what the stomach bug had done to their sex life. He recognized he ought to ask her about Verne's old flame, Sally Masters, but couldn't bring himself to; not here, not now. He'd tackle it another way.

'Wasn't it difficult for him?' asked Jacko. She knitted her eyebrows, a shade darker than her mousy hair. 'I mean, starting again back here from scratch after building up all those contracts over there?'

'He said he'd got something which would give him a head start with a broadsheet paper.'

'What was that?'

'Something to do with arms smuggling.'

Normally such a reply, sensational really, would have shocked him into silence for a second or two. He surprised himself by coolly and immediately thinking of Midshires Munitions, Hamb's company in Corby which his son ran. He approached the clue with care. 'He never mentioned that to his agent.'

'You've met McAllister. Would you?' A faintly bitter smile faded. 'He never mentioned much about it to me, either. Just that it might give him a start.'

'And did it?'

'He said he couldn't firm it up.'

'Did he try?'

'On a trip to see his mother.' Christ, thought Jacko, controlling his excitement. Corby is just a slight detour on the way to Nottinghamshire. 'And?'

'It didn't work out.'

Lots of careful follow-up questions only

produced the replies that he'd never mentioned names or companies. 'He only talked about his work in general terms.'

Jacko couldn't suppress a frustrated sigh. 'So where did that disappointment leave him?'

A shrug. 'Shrugged it off, said he'd specialize in royals for a while.' An abstracted headshake. 'He didn't find it very challenging work after...well...still...' Another shrug that told Jacko beggars can't be choosers.

'Did that work?'

'Reasonably. It wasn't very fulfilling but...' Her voice trailed off.

'All his royal pictures were taken at Rutland Water.'

A brief nod.

'Which suggests he'd got a good contact there, tipping him off.'

'I know.'

'Do you know who it was?'

'Somebody he cultivated in the month he was here and I was still in Cyprus waiting for my transfer.'

'Who?'

'Never said. He was always evasive about informants. Never talked about them. Ever.

They're all like that.'

True of detectives, too, Jacko conceded. He shared almost everything with Jackie, his wife, except the names of his own informants. Still, he comforted himself, maybe Verne's contact books or records would tell them.

He moved her on to Saturday when she last saw him. Summers had got a day shift on a Sunday quality which took him to Nottingham. He'd used portable equipment to wire back his soccer photos. Then he went up to Mansfield to see his mother.

'Devoted to her, he was,' she said. 'Sent postcards from every place he visited, wrote a long letter every week when he was in Cyprus. He phoned me on Sunday to say he was staying an extra night at his mum's because he had a call to make on the way home on Monday.'

'Did he say where?'

She gave this deep thought. 'Not in so many words. He asked me to tell McAllister he might have some royal stuff for him on...' A puzzled pause as if she had lost track of time. '...today, so I just assumed Rutland Water. That's where he got all his royal pictures.'

'So sometime on Saturday or yesterday he was in touch with his informant?'

'Must have been.'

Terrific, thought Jacko. All we'll have to do is check the phone records.

'And he phoned you from his mother's?'

'From a coin box at the end of the street. She's not on the phone. That's why he always wrote.'

'Why not use his car phone?'

'It doesn't work up there. It's a dead spot on his network.'

'So he used his phone credit card?'

'Doesn't carry one; doesn't need one with a car phone.'

Stumped, thought Jacko, dejected for that moment it took to find another way in. 'What does his mother say about it? Have you spoken to her today?'

'Can't. Nobody can. She's in a nursing home, a stroke. That's why he was always nipping up to see her.'

Jacko's tongue was paralysed and the only part of his brain that still functioned was wondering if this was what a stroke felt like.

Hazel picked up the pieces. 'In that last phone call, did Verne mention anything else?'

'We talked about his mum, naturally, a bit about the game he'd covered, what I'd been doing and he said he fancied a pasta for supper tonight.' She bit her lower lip. 'And small talk like that.' Tears made their first glistening appearances at the corners of her eyes.

'Anything else?' Hazel prompted.

'Not to put supper on too early because, well, something about while he was in Fine Focus dropping off his film he'd have to spend a bit of time looking back through old work—marine stuff, he said—so he might be a bit late...'

The tears flowed now, for her man who would never be coming home, and Jacko felt more than an intruder; more like a violator.

Sometimes he wished hell had this God-awful job.

Jacko drank an incredibly expensive lager, sitting alone in Edwardian splendour in a soft burgundy chair (deep purple would have matched his mood) on a balcony terrace. He looked down on a marble ballroom decorated with white fairy lights, palm trees in terracotta pots dotted here and there.

It gave him the feeling of being a first-class passenger on a luxury liner in the great days of transatlantic travel. To add to the illusion, he felt sick. Over the pain he'd had to put Marilyn through. About the absence of phone records. Over the lousy, stinking job. About the shittiness of life in general.

McAllister had said he and Dilks would be waiting in a bar off the balcony, warming themselves by a fire. He decided not to join them. He was sick of him, too, and his commercial exploitation of a tragedy so close to home. He wanted to be alone for a while, nursing his blues in private, trying to dispel them, to crank himself up again.

Presently Hazel joined him, looking the way he felt, as if suddenly aware that there was as much counselling as detecting in CID life. 'She's settling down.' She dangled a bunch of keys. 'She agreed.'

He ordered another lager for himself and a scotch with lots of soda for her. She swished her drink and stared vacantly into it. 'A sickener about the phones, eh?'

Jacko gave her a grave nod.

'Makes it bloody difficult. Are we ever going to crack it?'

'Yes.' An immediate, firm reply, his inner resilience returning. He was never down for long.

'Don't see how,' she said glumly.

'By working hard.'

He had been brought up in CID to labour with life-shortening urgency in the first seventy-two hours of any major inquiry. He'd come to believe that, if a case isn't cracked in those vital hours, the days became weeks and then months, and they might never crack it at all.

'It's all...well...' Hazel gave small, helpless shrug. '...so high-powered and widely scattered.' She looked at him, appealing. 'How, Jacko?'

'Told you. By working hard.'

'Yes, but for how long? We can't keep up this pace. You can't anyway. Not at your great age.' Her smile was back, warming him.

Jacko liked affectionate abuse. He smiled back. 'Inside seventy-two hours.'

Her smile was replaced by a frown, sceptical and challenging. 'Impossible!'

His smile remained. 'A pint says so.'

'Done,' she said, and she was chatting merrily and non-stop again when Mc-Allister and Dilks came up behind them, hovering, telling them it was time to go.

Outside, Hazel flagged a black taxi to take her to a Tube station to journey south on the Northern Line. With her she took keys that Marilyn Moore had trustingly handed over to their flat close to Clapham Common.

For Jacko, a much shorter ride by car beyond the deserted law courts back up Fleet Street, McAllister at the wheel, Dilks beside him. They turned left into side streets heading back towards Holborn and the *Mirror*.

They stopped outside a 1930s four-storey building, squat alongside its neighbours, with a rounded corner and double doors of glass in black wrought iron.

Lights shone into the dark narrow street from all the windows on the second floor. To reach them they climbed a cold, echoing staircase, framed photos hanging each side.

The office was open-plan and ill-planned—grey steel desks and green cabinets in no clearly defined pattern, piles of dusty newspapers in no particular order, every shelf filled with boxes, big brown envelopes and camera bits and pieces.

Dilks sat down at one of three terminals and tapped twice on its keyboard. A long list of dates, captions and codes rolled in white letters on to a black screen.

The life's work of Verne Summers was not filed in one cuttings book, McAllister was explaining, but scattered through files under different names and subjects.

It took seven cigarettes, much, much longer than Jacko had expected, to examine negatives and transparencies through a small, square magnifying glass, bending over a frame topped by white glass with a bright light beneath it; the light box, they called it. What made it longer still was that their colours were reversed and it took time for his eyes to accept what they were viewing.

He found nothing that he hadn't seen already in the portfolio under any member of the royal family; no secret trysts, for example.

Dilks disappeared and returned with a big bundle of papers under his arm. 'The midnights,' he said, dropping them on Jacko's corner desk next to the light box. A clock above him on a grimy cream wall showed 11.15.

McAllister tore excitedly into the pile

like a dog digging for a bone, scanning several front pages at the same time, rapidly and noisily turning pages, joyful now: 'Terrific.' Then, angry: 'Tossers.'

Every one of next morning's first editions, even the pink *Financial Times,* was soon spread out and coming apart on three desks.

'How do you get all tomorrow's papers at this time?' Jacko asked, astonished.

Neither answered and he guessed there was a big black market in operation.

'Jesus.' McAllister jabbed at one. 'They look bad.'

Soon he picked up a ringing phone. After a few gruff 'Yers' he lost his temper. 'It's been on offer all fucking day... You want it now, it's still a grand... Send your own night car. Your editor won't be going home yet, not by the looks of this heap of shit.'

Jacko imagined every news desk doing just this, right now, comparing what they'd got with their rivals and, more important, discovering with horror close to panic what they'd missed, frantically trying to catch up for their last edition by commissioning photos they'd earlier rejected and stealing the words to go with them.

'Heads should roll tomorrow,' said McAllister with a satisfied smirk as he replaced the phone.

It rang several times more as Jacko, giving his eyes a break (a change, anyway), sat and glanced through the bundle. Everyone, even the staid broadsheets, had ignored Silent Knight's caution and named Vernon Summers as the victim, not qualifying the identification with 'thought to be' or 'believed to be'.

All the tabloids had Royal and Outrage in their banner headlines. Most overlooked Lord Hamb's dismissal of a royal target by simply dropping his quote that the Prince always went in and out by air. Instead, they played up Knight, ruling no one out.

The *Mirror* had splashed on their exclusive phone call, but mentioned nothing about demands.

McAllister's package of photos, not so many of Dilks' words, had made it here and there on inside pages.

The tabloid piece on Marilyn Moore included the phoney-sounding 'prime time' quote but was otherwise understated and sensitive, the sort of article a dignified police widow might put her name to.

Underneath her ghosted words was a

paragraph which said, 'By request of Miss Moore, payment for this article is being forwarded to the Newspaper Press Fund, a charity which runs retirement homes for journalists.'

Jacko felt a deep stab of shame and did what he always did when assailed by uncomfortable emotions—got back to work. He stood and bent over the light box.

He went through Hamb's sheets, only finding the Troodos house feature; nothing at all on his Honourable son. Nothing either under Willis.

On to Toby Blewis, whom he'd never seen in the flesh. Just one strip of him, rather tubby, fortyish, leaving a night-club with a curvy blonde with a painted-on smile.

So what? Jacko told himself.

Sally Masters Next. Lots of strips of her, some stripped to G-string.

Suddenly he was staring down, bespectacled eyes no longer tired, on the same shots he'd seen in Blewis's sheet. The very same. Blewis and Sally Masters. Together.

No wonder his name rang a distant bell for Marilyn Moore, he thought, thrilled.

He bided his time until the phones

stopped ringing. Then he summoned McAllister to the light box with an upward flick of his chin. 'Is this the job you mentioned on the way down here in the car?'

McAllister arrived, took the magnifier and squinted one-eyed through it. 'That's the one.'

'What's it about?'

He called across two desks to Dilks. 'Were you on this?'

Dilks sauntered up, took a peep himself. 'Nar. It was a GI stunt.'

Jacko frowned, baffled.

'Find the piece,' said McAllister sharply. Global Images was a showbiz PR outfit, McAllister explained while Dilks strolled away to rummage among the piles of newspapers.

He returned with a Sunday tabloid. Only one picture had been published above Summers' byline. It showed Sally Masters arm-in-arm with Toby Blewis. Her look was lovey-dovey; he was caught wide-eyed in the camera's flash.

The story beneath came almost entirely from Sally who talked of her love for mature, powerful men ('A real turn-on') and hinted at romance with Blewis. His one sentence was much less forthcoming. 'I never discuss my private affairs.'

A stupid thing for a politician to say, Jacko decided; a give-away. But then again what would you say if you emerged, Hazel on your arm, from a night-club as a gust of wind billowed up her skirt to reveal no knickers and, flash, a photographer recorded the happy scene for use under the headline: 'Caught with pants down'?

He asked for a print, deciding there'd be no night-clubbing tonight.

Well past midnight, and the phone rang again, this time for Jacko.

'Nothing,' said Hazel, light classy voice weary and weighed down. 'No name of his Rutland contact in his paperwork.'

'What about his accounts and cheques stubs?'

'Not there, either. Odd thing is that there are payments to night-club bouncers and the like, but not this source.'

'Maybe he paid cash?'

'Can't have been much then. He always used holes-in-walls—two hundred tops at any time and well spaced out.'

He got Dilks to order a mini-cab for her to take her back to the hotel and to bed.

Jacko put down the phone. Nothing, he thought slowly, but without disappointment. Sometimes it's what a detective doesn't find that amounts to something.

Maybe there was nothing to find. Was Summers rewarding his tipster a different way? By holding back, not publishing something spicy? Put the other way, maybe the contact was buying Summers' silence with exclusive info.

He was thinking faster now, just one word on his mind: Blackmail.

Not really interested, not now he'd got a possible lead, Jacko worked his way routinely through Hamb's separate companies.

He reached Midshires Munitions and Shipping. This time what came up at him through the looking-glass wasn't so much thrilling, more bewildering. Not a face or a place; not even taken by Summers.

By now he was used to the way negatives reversed the colours—reds for greens, for instance. This was black and white. He was looking at a dark wooden crate (which meant it was light) with white stencilled lettering, which meant it was black. 'Danger. Midshires Munitions.

140

Made in Corby, England.' Switching the shades in his mind, the crate looked to be standing on a muddy, frozen battlefield; not a sandy desert scene.

He summoned McAllister back to the light box. 'What's this all about?'

He squinted, studied it, pulled a baffled face and called across Dilks.

Another short saunter. 'Nothing to do with this job,' said Dilks after a glance that was no more than cursory. 'Why?'

McAllister replied for Jacko. 'Just answer the fucking question.'

An unconcerned shrug, used to his boss's bluntness. 'It's ten years ago; more. Verne had only just joined then.'

'Tell him anyway,' snapped McAllister, protecting his investment.

'It was taken by a staffer who covered the Falklands. He spotted the crate after the ceasefire behind the Argie lines. Thought, mistakenly as it turned out, he'd uncovered some great arms scandal, so he snapped it.'

Dilks got the job of checking. Yes, Midshires Munitions agreed, it did come from their factory at Corby, and, yes, it was part of a consignment shipped to Buenos Aires.

'But it was dispatched long before the Argies invaded or any arms embargo and the company had the EUC to prove it.' End-user certificates, he explained, had to be issued before any registered arms dealer could export an order. That was the way sales to warring countries were banned.

'It's a law that's easily bent, but not in this case. They showed me the papers. They were in order. It just didn't stand up, so I dropped it.'

Wouldn't trust you with a dog show, Jacko decided. He'd check it himself. 'What would it have been worth as a story if it had stood up?'

'It's a bit heavy, more quality than pop, I'd say,' McAllister pronounced, like an expert on BBC's *Antique Roadshow*. 'A few grand from a Sunday heavy. They're not great payers compared with the pops.'

'Would Verne know about this?'

'He was with us in '82. Just. Could have seen it in the files, I expect. Could have filed it himself.'

Jacko asked for a copy of it, too. Dilks disappeared for another ten minutes, the time it took to print one.

'Meantime,' Jacko said, 'can I see his animal stuff?'

'Ah, ah,' McAllister trumpeted. 'Thought you might ask for that.' He nodded at the *Mirror,* on top of the pile, with its story about the call from Animal Vigil. 'That why you dropped in there?'

Jacko shrugged, non-committal.

'Beat you to it.' His face shadowed with disappointment. 'Nothing on anything called Animal Vigil. In fact, only these...'

More negatives were placed on the light box and Jacko studied a very small collection that included camel-racing and black birds covered with white gunge, which Jacko's now expert eye transposed as black oil from a slick on white gulls.

'Animals were never his scene,' said McAllister.

No RSPCA inspector giving his lady one, thought Jacko, reminding himself of what Marilyn Moore had told him. 'What about his marine stuff?'

That took a long time to collect together from files under different headings and was every bit as disappointing—a Limassol launching, refugees from Beirut on a ferry, school-children on an education cruise and a six-man crew, all but one white-skinned, lining the stern rails of a battered black coaster called *Froura Zo.*

McAllister pointed to the last one. 'That's a collect.'

Jacko, back aching, legs very tried now, frowned.

'He picked it up for a paper in Manila who wanted it after the boat sank in the Med. It was Cyprus-registered but had a Filipino crew.'

Jacko shook his head, exhausted, lost.

'Verne didn't take it personally,' McAllister explained. 'Just copied and air-freighted it here. We sent it on to Manila.'

Jacko was still shaking his head.

'If the boat's gone down,' said McAllister, very patiently, 'obviously you can't personally take its photo, unless you're an underwater cameraman, of course.' He laughed, Jacko yawned. 'So he'd borrow a snapshot from an old shipmate or the family of one of the crew. It's a pick-up, a collect. Like you collected that photo from Hamb.'

He looked hungrily at him.

You've got to give it to him, thought Jacko. Gone two, and still hustling. Would that all police officers worked this hard.

Keeping to the bargain, he reached into the inside pocket of his jacket and handed over the photo Hazel had collected from the Island Lodge.

Dilks and his boss held it between them, fingers and thumbs lightly pinched to opposite top corners, admiring it, connoisseurs viewing a work of art, trying to value its worth.

Considerable, by the delighted looks on their faces, Jacko deduced.

He walked back alone down Fleet Street, almost empty apart from a dustcart manned by a team of half a dozen, black donkey jackets over yellow overalls, cheerfully making dins with their bins in an alley that led to the closed Cheshire Cheese.

Only the lights in the solid, stone building that housed Press Association and Reuters shone down on this great street where, just a few hours ago, in hot metal days, it would have been rush hour.

The black glass palace, no longer home to Express Newspapers, was boarded up. The *Telegraph*, too, had vacated the off-white stone building a few doors away for some distant dockland.

The dome of St Paul's behind him was almost lost in a thick, very cold mist from the river down side streets to his left.

His mind was quiet and clear. He didn't yet know who was putting the bite on whom, but he had a motive.

Blackmail, he repeated to himself.

10

Kip. You must kip. Remember the golden rules.

How many times had he told that wee bastard, his erstwhile ally, sleeping next door with his scarecrow sister, 'Nosh and kip wherever and whenever you can. You never know when you'll get the next chance.'

Not that the boy believed him any longer, wanted to listen any more to his war stories.

He didn't really know where these sayings, his golden rules, had come from. Not the army, not serving in that outfit under that queer officer. Not from the army cadets. He'd never joined; too like Boy Scouts, all toggles and sodding singsongs.

He made them up as he went along—a

line from this 'Nam video, a sentence from that survivalist magazine.

He'd broken the golden rule twice in the last twenty-four hours. He hadn't eaten, apart from a few chips in his fingers in the phone box, waiting for the *Mirror* switchboard to answer, waving at Max who had pipped as he drove by in his banger. Now, for the third night running, he couldn't sleep.

When he'd got back from the fish shop, he'd been slagged for letting the chips go cold. He'd told her where to shove 'em and he took the van to join Mac for three pints of heavy, but only paid for one round and then out of loose change.

The kids were still up when he got back. This time he did pick a ruck over their legging off school. He ordered the telly off and them to bed.

'You've eaten,' he'd told the boy. 'Now you must kip. Remember the gold—'

'Bullshit,' the boy had retorted. 'You talk crap and all my pals know it.'

'Outa order,' he'd snapped. 'If you knew what I've done today you'd be...' He stopped there, just short of saying something stupid.

147

'Buggar all, that's what,' said the boy's sister.

'Shut it.' His voice went up an octave between words, like his basic training instructor. 'Away upstairs.'

'You're not my dad,' the boy pouted in a parting shot from the peeling lounge door.

Too right, I'm not, and never would claim to be. He was so thick—can yer believe this?—that a month back he mistook the dynamite stockpiled in a holdall for pink plasticine and was moulding a model gun with it. No wonder his real dad took off.

The shouting match downstairs did him a favour, he recognized now. 'I'm cutting off your rations for that,' their mother had said. Thank Christ, he'd been excused her bedroom games.

She'd been asleep for a couple of hours now, back to back with him, his khaki boxer shorts against her green winceyette nightie, bulging at the backside.

No wonder her old man pissed off, he thought morosely. Cow. Cabbage.

Smashed, I was. Well pissed that night in the pub when I chatted her up, gave her the line about the army and the Gulf. 'Wear your uniform for me, will you?' she'd said, pissed, too.

He'd driven to his parents' place, collected all his clobber and changed into it in her bedroom. It was the first time he'd worn fatigues, black beret and green webbing belt since his discharge. Difficult to know that first night who was turned on the most. Gave her such a bayoneting that she woke the kids.

Six months (more, eight; it seemed a helluva long tour of duty) he'd lived here. Didn't notice at first—or didn't care—about beds, plates, underwear that were made, cleaned or washed at increasingly infrequent intervals; they were so busy in the sack, at it.

First time he'd lived with a woman; first regular screw since that forty-year-old in Limassol with the beginnings of a black moustache. What a dog. Not as bad as this one, though.

OK at first, she was, it was, away from the folks again. Here he could get away with things he couldn't at home, keep odd hours, no questions asked.

Once he bullshitted about the Gulf he

149

had to keep it up, live with it, so he told the tale to the kids and they had told the neighbours' kids, and one or two had come round and said, 'Show us your war wound, Crow.'

'Away,' he'd replied, not meaning it.

The first kid that had called him Crow got a good duffing in the schoolyard, but later he came to like the nickname so much he'd adopted it and taken it with him into the army at nineteen.

He recognized it as quite clever, a play on words, appropriate for a man who was six foot, powerfully built and very dark, and who could terrify the rest of the squad, especially those two card-sharp Cockney sparrows.

And lying there, close-shaven head on a pillow browned with grease, Crow permitted himself a mirthless smile.

'Oh, come on, Crow,' the kids used to chant in the summer days before the fickle fuckers tired of him. 'Come on. Show us your wound.'

And he'd rolled up his right cuff, wrist skywards, and they'd all looked down on a jagged, white scar eight inches long.

'Six hours in micro-surgery,' he'd said.

'In hospital for a week.' All true.
   'Hurt?'
'Like hell.' True again.
'A bayonet?'
'Yeah.' Not true.

Never told the truth about the wound, never to himself; too ashamed, but this night, having just proved himself, he finally faced up to it, lying there in that cold, bare bedroom.

Difficult to know who to blame.

Those Cockneys for reporting them to the squadron sergeant for not settling their gambling debts, making him and his mate look for a new poker school.

That wog skipper who cleaned them out of a month's pay and demanded dynamite in settlement.

That posh prick who had given them five hundred on top and told them they were helping to cut the enemy's supply lines. Bullshit. What enemy? What lines? Think I'm thick or something?

That poofter officer for sticking his nose in when the boat was reported sunk.

Arms smuggling, it was, or an insurance job, one or the other, had to be. Why else would the prick have popped up again and offered a grand to take out the one survivor?

Difficult (harder, almost impossible) to focus on what happened then. He rushed it through, like he used the zapper to reprise the best bits in Vietnam videos, only this was the worst bit.

Blades glinting in the dockside darkness...a seaman fighting like a cornered rat...the shock, the panic at the sight of blood flowing from a cut he hadn't felt...his knife clattering as it hit the quay...slumped in a corner watching his mate and the seaman in a cursing, shouting, bloody pile...cradling his mate's head in his good arm while he died slowly, his guts hanging out, screaming, agony in his bloodless face.

It was his first taste of death—double death, because the seaman died, too. All the films he'd seen and magazines he'd read had not prepared him for it; nothing like the quick, clean endings they portrayed, a softly spoke message to mum or the girl left behind before his eyes closed and his grip slackened. Nothing like it at all. Slow torture.

He got off lightly, scot-free really, telling those Special Investigations berks that it was the seaman who jumped them. Booted him out, of course; medically unfit. He just missed the Gulf War, but he wouldn't have enjoyed it. Being behind the lines, with the SAS, fair enough, but not sweeping up mines behind the front line. No medals in that.

For a fleeting second, he sees himself at Buckingham Palace being decorated by the Queen, a recurring fantasy that has stayed with him since schooldays.

For the investiture, he is in Corps uniform, as cover, and wears his solemn modest face, talking shyly of his exploits, reluctant hints about the numbers he'd had to kill. 'It was them or us,' he hears himself saying. Prince Philip nods understandingly: enough said.

There'll be no publicity, of course. Never is for the SAS. But they'd let him take a guest. Mum? They'd gone off each other since he'd moved in here. He dropped in for ten minutes to exchange inexpensive presents just before Christmas, feeling so unwelcome that he hadn't gone round first-footing a week later. No chance, no way, would he take this scrubber lying next to him. A classy bird, he'd take, but he didn't know any classy birds. The fantasy faded away.

From the day they turned him down for the SAS, he'd wanted out, would have bought himself out sooner, if he hadn't lost so much at cards, a bad streak, unlucky. So a medical discharge suited him.

Got paid that grand, too, for taking care of the seaman and kept it all because he couldn't send his mate's half to his family in the 'Pool without telling them it had been earned at the cost of their son's life. He passed it off to his parents as compensation for his injury. It tided him over, beer money, in the first few months in civvy street.

Back home that posh bastard had kept his word ('company policy to look after its recruits,' he'd explained with a clever dick smile) and found him bits and bobs of work where his army trade came in useful. Not much money in it, just enough to supplement her state benefits and head off her gripes.

For eight months, since he'd lived here, he'd squirrelled away a bit here and a bob there, like he and his mate in their army days. One day, he'd been sure of it, he'd be hired to do a safe-blowing job.

Easy enough to store the dynamite here, at the bottom of the built-in wardrobe, dry and cool. No houseproud mother to ask what it was, only that wee bastard poking around, mistaking it for plasticine.

'Show us your medals, Crow. Go on. Show us your medals,' the boy often chanted with the kid next door, the one with the suspicious young mother.

'Can't,' he'd said. 'There's no publicity in my mob.'

'Where are they, then?'

'In a military museum. I'll take you one day.'

'You still in the mob, then?'

'Reserve list. I'll be recalled when my hand's a hundred per cent.'

It would never be better than eighty per cent, the doctors had told him, despite squeezing a black rubber ball everywhere he went and walking up and down the path in the overgrown back garden with bucketfuls of soil.

He couldn't be sure if it was those exercises or the yarns he was telling the neighbourhood kids, but soon he was jogging, in PE kit at first and then in fatigues he got on mail order from one of his mags.

Calf-length combat boots, back-packs, bins and camping equipment were soon added to his growing stores in the built-in wardrobe. When she queried where the money came from, he'd said: 'TA issue; no charge.'

Once a month he spent weekends away camping outdoors by Rutland Water. 'Survival courses,' he'd called them.

'Who cooks?' she'd asked.

'Catering Corps, of course,' he'd reply, and he wouldn't mention that he survived long, lonely hikes by eating pub grub.

'Don't they pay you anyfuckingthing?' she'd demanded. 'You've not chipped in a brass farthing for weeks.'

'I get a big bounty at the end of it,' he replied, never wondering how he'd eventually explain away his continuing poverty.

These days he was fit, fitter than he'd been since Chatham, his RE depot days; fighting fit.

He'd been drinking heavies with Mac when he was motioned outside. Saturday night, it was. Christ, I don't think I've slept a wink since. What time is it?

He looked at his mail order black waterproof with a dial that illuminated the inside of his left wrist, his hundred per cent wrist: 03.17. Jeez. That's only, what? Fifty-something hours ago. So much has happened since.

He followed him to his parked car, thinking he was about to be offered a bit of urgent sub-contracting work. Instead, the silver-tongued bastard said, 'There's a must job. Call it a job for Queen and country, if you like.'

'What?'

'Someone is on to what happened with Animal Vigil in Cyprus. You know what that means, if it comes out.'

'Not me,' he'd replied, more stunned than stubborn. 'I didn't kill anyone.'

'Don't kid yourself. You were part of the conspiracy over that seaman. It amounts to the same thing.'

'What can we do about it?'

'See that he finishes up like that seaman.'

'How?'

He told him where he'd be and when. 'It's now or never.'

'How?'

'You're the expert. I'll leave that to you.'
He pushed an envelope at him. 'There's a
thou in there.'

Crow pushed it back. 'Take me for a
mug or something? Think I'm thick? You
must have made a mint out of it.'

'He's a security risk. He's got to go.'

'Not for a grand.'

'It's a down payment.'

'What's the balance?'

'Fourteen thou.'

'When's the pay-off?'

'Thursday. When the dust settles.' He
told him where to pick up the rest.

Fifteen grand in all. Jeez. A king's
ransom. Enough, more than enough, to
get away from here and her.

He had lain here, like this, just forty-
eight hours ago, planning. He knew the
layout, the geography, but what could he
use as detonation?

Then it came to him. The kid's
Christmas present from his dad; the
model boat's remote control.

He'd got out of bed, packed, sneaked
into the bedroom next door, took what he
needed. Nobody so much as stirred.

He was up early. This time she did stir.
'Where you going at this bloody time?'

'Told you. TA exercise.'

'Never did.'

'You never listen.'

'Bring us a cuppa before you go.'

She was asleep when he did.

He'd recced the peninsula, worked it all out. Ideally he'd have liked a full-dress rehearsal but there were always so many people about Rutland Water, even on a winter Sunday.

He'd made the mine, here in this bedroom, on Sunday night while the three of them watched TV downstairs.

And it had worked, mission accomplished. Perfect. Or had it?

He never told me Charlie Boy would be there, the bastard. I expected publicity, but not this much; never dreamt there'd be these hints about a different target, about mistakes.

There were battalions of cops on it, the Yard, too, and Home Office experts, they said on TV. These aren't dumb military or SIB berks. These are the tops, the cream and they're after me. Well, let 'em come. Let one get too close and... 'Once you've killed once...' he recalled reading in one of his mags. 'The more, the easier.'

The remembered words brought no

comfort, no sleep. Something was wrong, badly wrong. He felt a chill, much colder than on that dark Mediterranean night when his mate died, screaming in his good arm.

What would be the perfect result? The other fourteen grand in my tucker bag and no one left to talk about my part in the operation. Then away. On ma tod again.

Kip, you must kip.

But his mind worked remorselessly on towards the perfect ending and still sleep would not come.

11

Twenty-four to thirty-six hours

The freezing fog over London thinned to a mist by Luton and, come Kettering, a weak sun was beginning to show through.

There'd been just enough time, an hour, for a full British Rail breakfast, side by side with Hazel.

She hadn't been out to buy new knickers; so early when they left the hotel that no shops were open. Too early, Jacko told himself, too tired, too old, feeling nearer a hundred than fifty.

The police car Little Velma had promised when he briefed her from his bedside phone was waiting outside the station, which had angled glass roofs in grey-painted wrought iron; beautifully preserved, not looking big enough to cater for the combined hundred thousand-plus population of both Kettering and Corby which it served.

The peaked-capped driver made no mistakes at roundabouts, observing all road signs. They passed a sign to the hospital where, according to Velma, Cap'n Willis was still detained and reported to be 'comfortable'—an odd description for a burns victim, Jacko always thought.

Half a dozen miles north and the driver turned right off the A6006 on to a straight, rather featureless approach road to Corby, a new town (well, newish).

Wide grass verges, white with frost, had been invaded by unsightly molehills. Leafless trees failed to screen the grey boxiness of housing estates on either side.

Jacko expressed surprise at how many black London-style cabs were on the road.

That, their Pc driver knowledgeably explained in a Scots accent, was because the town was so working class that it had the fewest private cars per head of population in the country. 'Far cheaper fares, though, than London. Do a bomb round here.'

'Don't remind me,' Jacko was going to say, but it was still too early.

The sprawling estates were built to house the workers, thousands of them who came to man the steelworks, the constable chattered on.

Most were Scots; so many that children born here spoke without a trace of Englishness and supported either Rangers or Celtic. The parents bought almost as many *Glasgow Daily Records* as *Mirrors,* its London sister, and once a year families gathered with their clans at the biggest Highland Games south of the border.

'You local then?' asked Hazel.

'Born and bred,' he replied, rather proudly.

Like Geordie miners enticed to the East Midlands, the constable continued, many were thrown out of their jobs when the blast furnaces shut in the early eighties.

The works were pulled down and levelled

for a Disney-type fantasy-land, a dream of employment that hadn't yet come true. The firms that did materialize had managed to reduce the employment figure to around the national average, he went on.

And, God knows, that's bad enough, mused Jacko with the familiar shudder that always came with that subject.

'There's a terrific community spirit here,' the driver said.

Pioneers together, taking the knocks of a frontier town, supposed Jacko, catching a glimpse of its big concrete shopping centre with the obligatory McDonald's opposite civic buildings as colourful and as square as a Rubic's cube.

He tapped the constable's local knowledge to ask about Midshire Munitions and Shipping.

'Just announced more redundancies,' came the reply.

The dividend, Jacko guessed, of peace breaking out all over the world.

Midshires Munitions and Shipping stood behind double high wire, plastered with warning, danger and keep-out notices, on an industrial estate on the outskirts of town, surrounded by factories and warehouses that had more to do with the food trade than steel-making these days.

A uniformed commissionaire on a guard-room-type gate directed them to a two-storey admin block, a safe distance from the factory, clad in grey gun-metal.

A freckled-faced receptionist with a Scots burr led them to an upstairs suite of offices and a more glamorous secretary tapped on a pine door to announce them.

A surprise awaited behind the pine door.

At a polished conference table, legs outstretched, sat a man whom Jacko had only previously seen in Verne Summers' photos.

In the flesh, he was a bit tubbier, but there was no doubting that he was Toby Blewis, just about the last witness Jacko wanted to see right now.

At the far end of the light, long room, behind a teak desk, sat a man he had seen twice but not spoken to before—Hamb's only son, the Honourable Matthew.

Little Velma had ordered Jacko to confront them both, but not together. His stride faltered just inside the door.

Matthew broke off from a phone call, not cupping the mouthpiece. 'Yes.' He

164

sounded and looked harassed.

'Sorry to bother you.' Jacko gave his name and rank, not flashing his warrant card (seldom did) but, before he could introduce Hazel, Matthew went back to his call. 'Sorry. Yes...'

Blewis started to rise, rather languidly. He was dark-suited, short, jowly as well as portly for someone not yet forty. 'Make myself scarce.'

'We were rather hoping for a word with you, too,' said Jacko hastily. Then, pointedly: 'Afterwards.'

'Wait one, please, Dad,' said Matthew into the phone, then to Blewis, 'You, too, Toby.'

One of those nosy people who can listen to two conversations at once, Jacko decided, irked, but only because it was a knack he'd never been able to acquire.

He strolled further into the room, trying to catch what Matthew was saying to his father. Not much. A lot of yeses and noes, doing more listening than talking, not liking too much of what he was hearing, to judge by his worried face.

While Hazel engaged Blewis in small talk, Jacko stopped to glance at photos on the ivory-papered wall, the same collection

165

he had seen in Lord Hamb's study the afternoon before.

All apart from one showed barges, boats and that gleaming white ship in a shanty-town port, flag caught on the wind, Union Jack in the top left-hand corner, coat of arms in a white circle on a blue background. He couldn't put a country to it.

The exception was a cliff face coming away from a stone quarry a fraction of a second after dynamite had exploded behind it, by far the most dramatic, and it held his eyes the longest.

He heard Matthew say, 'Leave it to me.' He turned to see him replacing the phone.

Matthew pitched forward in a grey swivel chair with padded arms, comfortable and expensive enough for a chief constable. He put white-sleeved arms on the desk. 'What's this about?' His face and tone were unwelcoming. 'We spent most of yesterday with the police.'

He was his father's height, same dark, almost black, alert eyes, but was only two-thirds of his weight, with less than half of his commanding presence.

'So I gather,' said Jacko. Velma had

read their statements over to him on the phone.

'We've a meeting in half an hour,' said Matthew.

Jacko looked at Blewis. 'You, too?'

It was Matthew who answered, rather sarcastically. 'He is a director.'

Jacko was suspicious about politicians who moonlighted with directorships. Having a prospective MP on the board made commercial sense with all his contacts, but, to him, there was always a whiff of corruption about it.

He'd been planning to recap on parts of their statements before hitting them separately with his London leads.

Matthew had said in his interview that he was at the stables checking the horses when he heard the explosion and ran to the entrance just in time to see Captain Willis hot-footing it back to the Lodge from the burning Land Rover. Blewis had claimed he'd been indoors reading the papers.

Jacko began with Matthew. 'You told my colleagues yesterday that you knew of Summers by repute, not personally.'

He nodded sharply. Blewis frowned.

'Your parents knew him because of a

magazine feature on your family's place in Cyprus. Right?'

'That's right. Wasn't there myself at the time.'

'Ever been there?'

'Naturally, with my own family.'

'Once with me in tow,' Blewis interjected ingratiatingly.

Jacko let it pass. 'But in Cyprus you personally never came across Summers?'

'Told you that twice already.' Pause. 'Never.'

'Ever met him over in England?'

Matthew looked urgently at Blewis. 'No.'

Blewis looked nonplussed. Jacko turned to him. 'You?'

He paled. 'Er...' Deferentially, he gestured towards Matthew. 'He speaks for the company.'

The evasive bastard is lying, Jacko realized. They're both lying, but haven't got their act together. Right, try this for size.

He nodded at Hazel who took one of the photos he'd had copied at Fine Focus out of her shoulder bag. She handed it to him. He slipped it from a hard-backed brown envelope and placed it before Matthew.

'We found this at the agency which markets Summers' work.'

Matthew's mouth hung open slightly. 'What is it?'

'An exhibit.' A frightening, forensic word, Jacko congratulated himself.

'Of what?' asked Matthew, swallowing hard.

'Of a shipment from here found behind Argentine lines in the Falklands.'

'When was that?' asked Matthew of no one in particular.

'Early eighties, for goodness sake,' Blewis replied briskly.

' '82,' said Hazel, precisely.

'Thank goodness.' Relief flowed through Matthew's face. 'We didn't take over here until '84.'

Blast. Jacko's heart sank.

'Let me see that.' Blewis had reached the desk. He didn't study the photo long. 'Oh, that again.'

'Seen it before?'

'Some reporter from some London agency came here, oh, ten years ago now, and asked questions about it.'

'Long before we took over,' Matthew said, making sure Jacko had got the point.

'A reporter, not a photographer?' Jacko

169

asked. 'Not Summers?'

'Certainly not, no.' A positive answer. 'He, this reporter, wanted to know how the consignment got to the Falklands and we dug out all the papers for him. They were in perfect order. It was shipped months earlier to the Argentine, long before any embargo.'

Blewis couldn't recall the reporter's name, so Jacko asked for a description. He vaguely described Nick Dilks, McAllister's legman.

Shit, thought Jacko, knocked back. 'I see,' he said, trying to keep the dismay out of his voice. He played for time. 'Still, we'd like to see the paperwork, if you've still got it.'

'Inspector,' said Blewis, 'you can see all our paperwork. We run a very straight ship.'

Matthew broke in. 'I think that's a matter for the chairman. We'll clear it with him first, shall we?'

Blewis, put in his place, went silent.

A steady smile had appeared at the edge of Matthew's thin lips. 'That it?'

'Well.' Jacko had become uneasy, confused. 'The next bit involves Mr Blewis only, and it's not company business.'

'Out with it, Inspector,' said Blewis, heartily.

Jacko turned fully towards him. 'You've just confirmed to us that you'd never met Summers, either here or on holiday with him.' He flicked his head towards Matthew.

Blewis nodded mournfully, patently lying.

Jacko glanced at Hazel who produced another picture copied at the agency. She slipped it out of its envelope and gave it to Blewis, standing by the desk.

He looked at it with a frown, close to frightened.

'That,' she said slowly, 'was taken by Summers.'

'Grief.' There seemed to be genuine surprise in his round, smooth face.

Matthew had stood and walked round the desk, peering over Blewis's shoulder, letching a little at Sally Masters. 'She's caught up with you again, you old dog.'

Blewis was wearing a queasy smile. 'Ooooooh.' He stretched it out. 'Much ado about nothing, this, you know.'

'I know,' said Matthew, the smoothie again.

'Remember the occasion?' asked Jacko.

'Well,' said Blewis. He'd been having

171

a late supper at a nightclub with a party of friends, a Westminster MP among them. The girl—'don't recall her name' —had been deserted when her escort was summoned to the Commons for a division.

'I offered to see her home. That's all. All I remember is the blasted flash as I stepped out on to the pavement. Wouldn't recognize who was behind the camera; couldn't. I was blinded.' He nodded down at the photo. 'As you can see.'

'Ever met Miss Masters before or seen her since?' asked Hazel, smiling. 'She is rather—'

Blewis cut in, colouring slightly. 'Lord, no.'

Matthew let out a hollow laugh.

Jacko ploughed on, grimly. 'Why should she tell the paper of her feelings for you then?'

'Good lord, man. She's a popsy out for publicity, a TV hostess of some kind.'

'Did you sue or complain?'

A tight laugh. 'If we insisted on a correction for everything they write, politicians would be complaining every week.'

'What's the query here, Inspector?' asked

Matthew quite sternly.

'It's what's known as cross-checking. Mr Blewis has stated twice now that he didn't know Summers.'

'I didn't know who took it,' Blewis protested, more blustering than flustered.

'I don't see the problem anyway,' said Matthew, dismissively. He looked at Blewis, a sneaky look. 'It's not as if you had a wife waiting at home.'

Blewis blanched slightly. 'It was a stunt. To get her photo in the paper. Speaking personally, I can do without that sort of thing.'

'Oh, I don't know,' said Matthew easily. 'Can't have done you much harm. Even I'd vote for you if you can pull 'em like that.'

I wouldn't, thought Jacko angrily. Politicians shouldn't lie. They do, but they shouldn't. When I've got the evidence—and I know how to get it—I'm going to put this scheming shit through the wringer until the truth drips out of him.

And the answer, the truth, he suspected, was almost sure of it, was right here, somewhere in this room.

Heading north, looking east across the

frozen fields, Jacko remarked that the peninsula seemed to have risen out of the water since yesterday. 'Maybe there's been a mass evacuation of the media,' he said flippantly, just making conversation in the back of the police car.

'Could be.' Hazel had taken him seriously. 'News editors throw in body after body on the first day of a big story...' She was making them sound like First World War generals. '...and pull most of them out the next.'

A beautiful winter's day now; sun shining, very cold but windless. The vast expanse of water, three thousand acres of it, the largest man-made lake in Europe, was still and silvery.

Their car turned right as soon as it entered Oakham, a tranquil town of mellow buffs and russets, with an old castle and a public school; so civilized that even the stocks had a tiled roof over them to keep medieval miscreants dry.

Just a dozen miles from Corby, Jacko thought, but a world away.

Soon they turned right again on to the peninsula road. He could see why they had not drowned it with all the fields and farms around when the reservoir was built in the seventies. Its two thousand acres stood on high ground dotted here and there with copses that ran down to the water's edge, less than a mile at its widest, from either side of the road.

The trees looked to have been coated in icing sugar, brittle enough to be breakable under the slightest touch. Everywhere else had been painted in restful pastel shades.

The narrow road was quiet; so, too, the hamlet, though the spacious car-park to the pub was packed.

It was as if calmness had come with the overnight change in the weather, from a raw bare-knuckled fight for survival to winter's wonderland, good to be alive.

Or maybe it is the influence of this woman, thought Jacko, walking into an incident room established in his absence in the village hall to replace the temporary command post.

Trestle tables, benches and chapel chairs with boxes at the back for hymn books were in orderly lines.

Little Velma was talking quietly, patiently explaining something, over the shoulder of a young constable, one of a dozen or so, men and women, working at screens. Just as many were seated at the next table, their heads down over phones, making notes on forms.

The room was warmed by three portable oil fires, but too not warm, and well lit by six bulbs hanging in white shades from the high wooden ceiling.

There was coffee and tea in steel urns on the bar. Lunchtime sandwiches were being cut in a small kitchen off the far corner.

No First World War general was Little Velma, Jacko thought, gratefully. She cared for her troops, and, slowly, over the course of the previous year, Jacko had come to rate her professionalism and, very privately, to care for her.

There's a danger in that, of course, he recognized. Get too close to a CID chief who happens to be a woman and the rumour is bound to go round that you are bedding her.

He doubted if any man was. She was mid-forties, divorced, son at college. She lived alone in the next village to his. Her horse was the great love in her life. When she was away, Jacko's wife Jackie, her weekly drinking pal, got to groom and ride it, abandoning (callously, in his view) husband, son, dog, housework and gardening.

Velma waved a welcome towards them, turned and led them across the wooden dance floor to her desk beside the stage from which she could oversee the whole operation without lording over it.

All three sat down. She listened to his briefing on his talks with the Hon Matthew and Blewis, which he ended with, 'One or both are lying, but we're not ready to 'front 'em yet, are we?'

'Oh, no,' agreed Velma. 'We need more.' She looked away, in thought.

He sat back to await the interrogation that was bound to come. A standing joke in the squad room was that Velma only had five questions—when, where, why, what, how—and sometimes, Jacko believed, they were all any detective needed.

'Why should they lie, do you think?' she began.

'Because one or both hired someone to kill Summers,' Jacko ventured.

'Why?' she repeated.

'Let's say all this speculation in the media about the killer hitting the wrong target is wrong.' Jacko accepted he was speculating himself and might be just as wrong. 'Let's say the target wasn't Prince Charles...'

'I think I go along with that,' said Velma, very quietly.

'Let's say it wasn't Matthew, despite having the same sort of car.'

Velma worked her lips, less certain.

'Somebody in that Lodge tipped off Summers about the royal visit to get him on the island, for the sole purpose of having him killed.' Jacko anticipated her 'Why?' and went on. 'Because he was blackmailing them. Or to head off some scandal. It amounts to the same thing.'

'What scandal?' Velma beat him this time.

'Maybe arms smuggling.' Jacko shrugged, still speculating. 'Maybe a sex scandal.' In his experience, the motive for most murders boiled down to sex or money.

'And you say we can look at the paperwork?'

'Well,' Hazel replied, doubtfully. 'Blewis was game but Matthew passed the buck to his father.'

Velma sat back in her chapel chair, in deeper thought until a smile broke through. 'You stick to sex, Jacko.' Hazel gave a throaty laugh. Velma looked at her.

'He's better at it than paperwork.'

'How would you know?' asked Jacko, the macho man in him thinking: You should be so lucky. The Woody Allen within, always the more predominant, was neurotically wondering just how much his wife, her drinking chum, had confided in her.

Everyone switched off their smiles as Velma briefed them. Jacko knew she would have gone through it all before in the twice-a-day team talks she always called, meetings he kept missing on his travels. But she seemed happy enough to run through it again for them, and he guessed it was because talking it through helped her to marshal her thoughts.

Her opening sentence disappointed him at first. Forensics, she said, had ruled out Midshire Munitions by confirming the explosive was of the sort commercially used in quarries, mines and by civil engineers building roads.

'Fifteen pounds or thereabouts packed in a yard of drainpipe and buried just beneath the surface,' she continued. 'Professional, but home-made. No connection with anything produced for the military at Corby.'

'But then,' Jacko broke in, fighting for his theory, 'anyone connected with the company would be potty to use its own products. We'd trace 'em straight back. They'd be bound to call in an outsider.'

Which was why licensed shot-firers were being listed, she replied, already ahead of him, and stock-taking of ammo stores was being launched locally.

She nodded to the team on the phones. 'The public response has been fantastic.' Then at Hazel. 'Thanks.'

For handling the publicity over appeals for witnesses, she means, Jacko knew; a nice touch.

Nothing new, in fact, nothing at all, on Animal Vigil, she added.

Then she craned her neck back and up to the duck egg blue wall behind her. Pinned to it was a large map of the scene—blue for the water, green for the peninsula and Hamb Island, darker green for woods, deep yellow for recreation areas, red for nature reserves, black for roads.

Numbered pins in different colours seemed to have been stuck haphazardly, but only seemed to be, he knew.

Last year, in a case on which Jacko had not been involved, Velma used this system

180

on a girl's murder in broad daylight in a huge cemetery, which had been busy with visitors tending graves.

Every witness's position had been pinpointed; where they were, when, who else they'd seen. One by one they had independently confirmed each other's movements, ruling each other out, apart from one who'd come forward voluntarily.

He'd claimed to have been where other witnesses couldn't place him. She ordered a raid on his home, found evidence that he'd killed not once, but twice. Ghoulishly, he'd been visiting his first victim's grave when he struck again.

A brilliant piece of detection, even her detractors agreed (of which there were many, because she was, after all, a woman).

Velma stood, putting her right index finger on a pin, with a round head, coloured red and numbered one, which was stuck on a cross which symbolized a church. 'Red Spot interests me. Notice...' She drew with a finger round the southeast bank. '...the uninterrupted view of Hamb Island.'

Her finger went to a pair of yellow dots on a red-painted nature reserve. 'Two bird-watchers spotted him through their bins.' The finger moved to a blue pin on the water. 'So did this yachtsman.'

All three, she went on, reported seeing him on a stone-lined causeway which had been purpose-built to preserve the elegant old church Jacko had seen across the water.

They described him as tall, well-built, bare-headed, short-haired and wearing military-style dungarees. 'He seemed to be handling something. What? I ask myself. A control box perhaps, the sort they use with model boats? Hardly jolly model-boating weather yesterday, would you say?'

Far-fetched, thought Jacko.

'The yachtsman heard the explosion and saw the flames,' she went on. 'He's sure Red Spot must have done, too. Stuck out on the water in his boat, he couldn't raise any immediate alarm. Red Spot didn't, either. Half a dozen 999-ers were received, in addition to Captain Willis's call from Island Lodge. But no emergency calls ties up with Red Spot. Odd, eh?'

She fingered a white pin—a motorist, she explained, who'd been leaving a hotel on the south shore. He'd reported overtaking an old van streaked with yellow dust.

Velma looked at Hazel. 'Despite all our public appeals no driver of any van like that has come forward.'

'But,' said Hazel, not quite getting the picture, 'would the bomber hang around after he'd planted it?'

'He'd have to if he was detonating by remote control.'

'Like a model boat's controls?' asked Jacko, chancing a technical question, rare for him.

Velma nodded. 'There were bits and pieces of a battery and a receiver in the crater, but no wire.'

Not so far-fetched, Jacko conceded.

'So he'd have to stick around to detonate it,' said Hazel, not a question this time.

'Part of the fun anyway,' said Jacko casually.

'What fun?' Hazel again.

'Sometimes you get arsonists hanging around after they've started a fire.' He was grandstanding a bit, showing off his experience for Hazel. 'The flames and the engine bells are part of the turn-on.'

'And sometimes,' said Velma, looking directly at him, 'you get people who want to be the hero.'

Jacko knew that. There was a case, again

not one of his, awaiting trial, of an old folks' home attendant who doped patients so she could do the Florence Nightingale bit and save them. The tragedy was that she overdosed and killed two of them.

He knew, too, that she was thinking of Willis and that she would be checking deep into his background. 'How is our Cap'n?' he asked.

'Still detained. Being heavily doorstepped by the press.' Which explains why the hamlet was so quiet, thought Jacko. 'Not talking or posing, though, on Lord Hamb's orders.'

A self-satisfied smile played on Hazel's wide lips.

'Your doing?' asked Jacko.

Hazel pinked with pleasure. 'I just happened to mention to Old Man Hamb that it would help us if Willis didn't help the media.'

'McAllister will be pleased about that,' Jacko added.

'That's a terrible thing for a PR to admit,' said Velma.

They were laughing as the inquiry's collator, a veteran, Jacko's age, a close friend, ambled up and dropped a memo on the desk.

He didn't join the conversation; seldom did. A lugubrious man of few words, he was in charge of admin. He listened, read, thought much more than he ever talked.

'Ay-up, Happy,' said Jacko, chirpily, pleased to see him.

Happy replied with a sad sigh and trudged away.

Hazel's eyes had gone back to the map. 'What now, marm? Another media appeal for that missing witness?' She spoke with a reluctance that told Jacko she didn't really want the job, but, being in the force's public relations department, felt it her duty to volunteer.

'Not yet,' said Velma, looking undecided. 'If Red Spot is a suspect, why warn him?'

She paused, looking down at Happy's memo.

'No.' She'd made up her mind. 'Go with him.'

She handed Jacko the memo, which told him where and when Sally Masters would be available. 'It's PR of a sort, I suppose,' she added.

Jacko turned to Hazel. 'These studios are ten minutes from my home. You can stay the night. And don't worry. My missus has plenty of spares.'

'Oh, I don't know about that,' said Velma lowly, stifling a smile.

'What did she mean by that?' asked Hazel as they walked to collect his car parked by a red phone box outside the old post office.

'Don't know,' he said, huffily, to hide a lie.

He knew all right. Last year, women's pants kept disappearing from clothes-lines on the estate where they lived. Jackie had so many pairs she never noticed; at least, if she did, she never reported it.

Others had, and the village bobby kept watch. He'd actually caught the knicker nicker in the very act of peeping through the Jackson bedroom window as they were undressing.

The first this clueless detective, with a dozen murder arrests to his credit, knew about it was when the bobby knocked on his door holding the washing-line bandit in one hand and a pair of Jackie's briefs in the other.

He dreaded the boys and girls in the squad finding out he had missed a pinch on his own doorstep.

Now his own wife had shopped him to his boss.

What else had she mentioned on their girlie nights out? The Woody Allen within was anxiously wondering.

12

Ten years ago I could have fancied Sally Masters; five even, Jacko was telling himself.

Oh, for christsake, if you can't be honest talking to yourself, when can you be? OK. OK. Now. Right now. I fancy her here and now. OK?

Gorgeous. She was gorgeous; like one of those J Arthur Rank starlets he used to queue at the cinema to ogle in the fifties when nowt but a boy. He could see why Toby Blewis whisked her off into the night, lucky sod.

Those painted lips, painted eyes of china blue, high cheek bones beneath pancake make-up, long, blonde shining hair swept back above one ear from which a glittering ring dangled.

Her body, hardly changed from her Page Three days on display in Fine Focus files, had just about been squeezed into an off-the-shoulder black plastic dress that ended four inches above the knees.

She was sitting in a hard-backed chair in a bright, tiny dressing-room to which a twee production assistant had guided them after long rigmaroles at the security gate and the reception desk.

A radiant smile reflected from a dressing-table mirror as the assistant passed on some last-minute instructions with lots of dears and loveys.

She crossed her slender legs and Jacko closed his eyes. When he opened them the assistant had gone and she was wearing silver shoes, high-heeled and backless. Don't, Jacko, still standing, privately pleaded. Slingbacks had always been a turn-on. Don't do this to me. I'm too old and I'm spoken for.

Then studying the photo Hazel had handed her, she spoke for the first time. 'Wot's this abaht?'

Don't do that to me either, Jacko inwardly groaned, his lust evaporating, and feeling all the better for it.

She had an accent straight out of D

H Lawrence country a few miles north; ay-up me duck diction that always evoked tin baths in front of coal fires and mother complexes. His own accent would never win speech and drama prizes but anything, apart from Brum, had to be better than that.

(Nor, come to think of it, did he like Lawrence's style of spelling out dialogue phonetically. Working out what each word meant held him up and sometimes he gave up. 'You need a bloody glossary to read this,' he'd told his wife, tossing one of his books to one side.

He vowed that when he came to write up his life of crime, a bestseller, much bigger than any Lawrence, bound to be, he'd just drop in a couple of words here and there to give a flavour of the sound and then press on unimpeded.

He said more or less the same thing when he later reported the interview about to take place back to Little Velma.

'Oh, get on with it, you garrulous git,' she ordered.)

After she'd been told what their inquiries were about, Sally Masters said she and Verne Summers had gone drinking together with the same under-age disco crowd. 'Even before he went to college, he practised glam 'tography on me'—by which, Jacko knew, she meant pin-up pictures.

'We palled up in London; nothing serious. With the gang. Just good mates. He was luvly.' A deeply affectionate smile, not at all lustful.

'Sometimes we wouldn't see each other for months. We lost touch when he went abroad. Hadn't seen him for years till this.' Her glossy hair billowed over the photo.

'So he didn't arrange it?' said Hazel.

'Me publicist did that. He just hired Verne.'

She explained she'd signed up with Global Images when *Sun* readers 'grew tired of seeing 'em' and she glanced down to her shapely bosom. He fixed her up with promotional work—one-off jobs decorating trade shows or parading round boxing rings with the number of the next round.

'One day last year he asked me to do this club job. Why not, for a couple of 'undred and a free night out?'

'What did you have to do?' asked Hazel.

'Just be pictured coming out the club all over 'im.' She looked down on Blewis.

'Real method acting, that.' A streetwise little laugh.

'So it was all pre-arranged?'

'Course.'

'Was Blewis annoyed?'

A puzzled frown. 'Should he be?'

Hazel flicked her head towards the photo. 'He looks annoyed, that's all.'

'Part of the act.' She stopped, something to explain. 'He's a client, too. Or was. Same agent.'

Jacko lowered himself on to the edge of the dressing-table, shaking his head, not following.

Toby Blewis, she repeated, had consulted the same publicity agent.

'Why?' asked Hazel.

'Worried about his own image.' She looked at Jacko, grinning maliciously. 'That's the word on the street.'

Jacko laughed. It was a line from a zany American police comedy where the hero got every scrap of his info from a shoeshine boy called Leftie.

'What's the word on the street, Leftie?' he asked.

Her childlike laughter delighted him. 'That he's...' Still spluttering. '...dear me, must I spell it out...yer know...gay.' Her laughter had stopped, but she was still smiling. 'A problem for him. Gerrit?'

Jacko had got it all right, smiling through the shock. 'What sort of problem? Blackmail?'

'No. No. No. An image problem. He's a politician. Right?' Jacko nodded. 'And he was in line for some safe Conservative seat and was worried he might not gerrit if...you know.'

'If...'

Sally's face told him she had remembered something else and was determined to impart it. 'And he was having problems with his boss. You know how some people can be about it.'

Jacko had a fair inkling now what she was driving at but had to get it from her. 'About what?'

Knees together, she swivelled on her seat towards Hazel. 'Is he of this world?' Then back to Jacko. 'About employing gays. Can't understand meself.' She just refrained from saying, 'Some of my best friends etc,' and Jacko would have believed her. The lust had gone, but he had already come to like her a lot.

'So your agent fixed you up with a date with Blewis. To do what?'

'Have a meal and get snapped coming out.'

'Did you recognize Summers as the snapper?'

'Course, but I couldn't go up to him and give him a big hug, could I? I didn't know he'd been booked...' She made it sound like a showbiz engagement which, Jacko acknowledged, it was, in a sense. '...until I saw him.'

Genuine sadness filled her face. It was clearly her last sight of her luvly old drinking pal and Jacko feared that tears were about to ruin her thickly applied make-up.

He began to talk very fast. 'Let me get this right, Leftie.' She forced a smile. 'Toby Blewis went to your publicity agent and said: "Get me some space in the papers to save my political ambitions and my job which are being threatened by these unfounded rumours—" '

'I'm not saying they're unfounded,' Sally interjected, face very serious.

'Hmm.' Jacko let it sink in. Then: 'The agent arranges for you, who's on his books anyway, to have supper with Blewis at this club and Verne to be waiting outside to snatch your picture when you come out together.'

'At last,' she said, brightening.

At last, I'm getting it right, she means, Jacko realized. 'How much would Blewis pay the agent?'

'Don't know for sure.' A thoughtful pause. 'Work it out for yourself. I was on two. Verne, I'd imagine, would get, well, say, one, because he'd get money from the Sunday paper, too.'

A three hundred pound outlay. Bearing in mind McAllister's usual cut at Fine Focus, Blewis paid the agent three grand.

Jesus, he thought, but then: Well worth it for a safe Tory seat in the Commons after the next general election and a continued directorship at Midshires Munitions in the meantime.

'So what happened after the photo was taken?'

'Blewis took me home.'

'And?'

'Didn't invite the creep in for coffee, if that's wot yer mean. Not that he asked. If you ask me, the rumours are true.'

'And that was that.'

Not quite, Sally replied. Next day, the Sunday tabloid phoned. They had this exclusive Verne Summers picture of her and Blewis looking coy, as their reporter put it, and would she care to comment?

'The agent had it all written down, like, wot I was to say.'

'So the whole thing...the picture...the publicity that followed...was stage-managed?'

'Happens all the time. These wild men of pop who smash cameras pay for 'em next morning, part of the deal. These kiss and tell are often stunts, too. Marriage break-ups are cooked up. Haven't you noticed? Only hard-up has-beens do it.'

Have, now you come to mention it, Jacko concurred.

'They get desperate without their names in the paper,' Sally went on. 'They need the plug, see.'

Jacko thought he saw. 'And it's all a con on the papers?'

'Some papers are in on it; know and don't care, as long as it's exclusive and they're not going to be sued.'

The real con was on the public, Jacko finally realized.

'Still...' A bare-shouldered shrug, not sexy to Jacko now. '...can't complain, can I? Didn't do me any harm, did it? Got me spotted in the paper and landed me this contract.'

True, Jacko thought. Life could be hard

on a Page Three girl past her lust-by date. Acting was out for Sally. Not many parts would be offered with that accent. She was a bit young to play one of D H Lawrence's whinging women, even though the diction was spot on.

Still, she was back in the limelight, with her face on TV and her photo in the papers which was all that she craved.

OK, it wasn't much of a job, mincing up to a smarmy game show host and saying, 'Our next contestant is Ivan from Ilkeston and he's an imbecile,' but then everyone on games shows, especially the easy-to-please audiences, was an imbecile. She made some people happy (me, too, for a while), so good luck to the girl.

She and Hazel chatted on. She was still clearly very upset about Verne. 'A straight bloke but...' A trouper's shrug that said: The show must go on.

Presently the twee production assistant popped his head round the door. 'Overture and old crows,' he cooed.

Sally Masters giggled, unoffended. 'Stop and see the show recorded, if yer want.'

'Busy,' said Jacko.

On balance, he'd rather watch a re-run of *It's a Knockout.*

Walking on blue tiles down a grey-walled, low-ceilinged corridor to the studio canteen, Hazel said, 'Nice girl beneath the warpaint.'

'Mmm,' said Jacko, giving nothing away. 'Pity about the accent.'

'Really?' Her classy tone, slightly querulous. 'I thought she spoke rather like you.'

Women! There's summat abaht 'em as can piss a bloke off some days, he chuntered to himself.

Hazel bought two teas, with a sausage roll for her ever-peckish partner, but she wasn't buying his latest theory.

'I can't believe that Blewis killed Summers just to stop him exposing him as a gay. Good God, this is the nineties. You don't murder to cover up your sexuality any more. You don't even have to pay out blackmail; not for that anyway.'

Once she'd started talking, Jacko had noticed, it was difficult to get her to stop. He decided to hear her out as they sat across a table in green fabric chairs in the studio canteen beneath an angled roof with wooden slates, much smarter than any police canteen.

'Being a director of Midshires Munitions doesn't make Blewis the bomber any more than Hamb or his son,' she continued, over the rim of her cup, her drink going cold. 'Look at him. He's the company's salesman, a negotiator. I doubt if he knows one end of a fuse from the other.'

Me, neither, Jacko concurred, glancing out of a huge triangled wall window. The sun had gone. Mid-afternoon and it was already getting dark.

Finally she took a small sip of tea.

Jacko fingered crumbs from a corner of his mouth to stop himself giving her a sour look. 'No one is suggesting Blewis killed Summers. He can't have done. He was in Island Lodge with a royal alibi witness. He hired someone to do it.'

'But—'

'Listen for a change.' He waited for her silence and attention.

'You might not be bothered by his sexuality, but Lord Hamb could be. He's high Tory—'

'And high church, according to his news cuttings file,' Hazel butted in, 'despite all his blokey effing and blinding.'

'There you are then.' Jacko beamed, justified. 'Old attitudes die hard. He's not

198

a modern thinker like you.'

'But—'

'Let me finish. The Labour and Liberal parties might not give a shit, but backwoodsmen in some Tory shires still do. I'm telling you it's a valid theory.'

Hazel sipped again for a thoughtful moment. 'So Lord Hamb is the family's homophobic, not Matthew?'

'Matthew likes Blewis. That was obvious when we spoke to them both this morning, surely?'

Hazel nodded agreement. 'What did Summers have on Blewis?' She wore an uncertain look. 'If you're right.'

'Hard to say. But he was often lurking around the island, camera at the ready. Maybe, while waiting to snatch a royal, he snapped Blewis up to something in the woods.'

'Who with? It takes two.' Pause. 'Matthew?'

'Married with two kids, according to the statements.' Another pause. 'Doubtful.' Jacko looked doubtful.

'Proves nothing,' said Hazel, bluntly.

Jacko gave this some silent consideration, then: 'No. Matthew's more like you. Nearer to your age and your views. He probably knows...he must know...his old chum Toby is truly a bachelor gay, but, like you, he doesn't care.'

More thought. 'Or maybe with all Toby's foreign contacts bringing in orders when the arms business is so slack, he can't afford to care.'

'But—' Hazel blurted it, barely able to hold back a further contribution.

Jacko pursed his lips into a shush. He liked frank exchanges, but didn't want to be overheard. Regional newsroom staff were bound to be mingling with make-up and continuity girls and best boys and grips, whatever they are.

'Sally...' She resumed, softer. '...implied that if it came out he was gay it would cost Toby Blewis his directorship with Midshire Munitions.'

'Mmm,' purred Jacko quietly, 'but while the Hon Matthew runs it day to day, his old man is the chairman. And a hands-on chairman, judging from this morning's long call to his son and his grasp of the balance sheets.'

A moment's meditation. 'No, if it came out, his Lordship would tell his son: "Get rid of Blewis." And Matthew would. Everyone is so terrified of that fat old bastard they jump automatically, do what he tells them.' Me, too, he confessed privately and guiltily.

'If Blewis's lover isn't Matthew, who is it?' Hazel demanded.

'Who knows?' A speculative shrug. 'Cap'n Willis?' A suspicion was dawning. 'When I saw him at the hospital yesterday he struck me as, well, a bit...' He was going to say 'effeminate' but changed to '...of an oddball.'

'What do we know about his background?'

'Don't worry. Velma will be finding out.'

'Does it matter at this stage?' Hazel looked away, unsure. 'I mean, it could be a stablehand, a domestic at the Island Lodge, anybody.'

'Agreed. Verne might not have got the dirt on Blewis at Rutland Water. If the publicity agent briefed him as fully as Sally Masters, he could have kept watch on him after that night-club stunt and dug up the dirt in London.'

'Don't believe that. Verne strikes me as a decent sort.'

Jacko knew then that Hazel had detected posthumously something special in Summers, that ability to care which

201

Marilyn and Sally experienced live; the way women do.

He let her down lightly. 'Through no fault of his own he'd hit hard times. A man can do odd things when the love of his life his ill and he needs money.'

She smiled at him, right chord struck. 'Assuming, just assuming, you're right, what did he have on Blewis that made him so dangerous he had to be killed?'

'Pictorial evidence,' Jacko had in mind photos of two bodies entwined in some Grecian pose but failed to stretch his imagination as far as the portly Blewis in the buff.

'But where would he keep them?'

Where indeed? Jacko was asking himself. He could understand Summers not handing incriminating photos on to McAllister at Fine Focus for his sidekick Dilks to put grubby words to, but Hazel hadn't found anything interesting at his Clapham flat either. He stayed silent.

'I know where.' Hazel was answering her own question, a clever smile on her wide mouth.

'Where?'

'That's the trouble with men. They're

not as close to their mothers as girls. But Verne was.'

Jacko gave Hazel the portable phone before she slipped gracefully into the passenger seat. 'Better use that now.'

When he was turned on by a case and working well, and he judged he was doing that today, he had total recall, a phenomenal memory for detail, and he'd remembered Marilyn Moore had talked of a dead spot for some phone systems that had cost a possible clue.

From her room at the Waldorf Hotel, Marilyn gave Hazel directions and the name of the neighbour who held the key.

The pylons of Field Mill, getting ever closer, prompted a soccer story out of Hazel as they drove thirty minutes later into Mansfield.

Before her chief inspector, she'd been chatted up in the force's press office and dated by a journo from the *Chron and Echo* in Northampton. 'A fund of stories, he was.'

They nicknamed the local football club the Cobblers because Northampton is a shoe-making town. One Saturday, the team travelled here to Field Mill, home of Mansfield Town who were called the Stags because the pit town was so close to the deer parks of Sherwood Forest.

The game ended in a high-scoring draw and the local paper carried the headline: RAMPANT STAGS HELD BY COBBLERS.

Jacko laughed long and loud. He loved stories like that, liked working with people who made him laugh.

Within sight of the Field Mill pylons was the terraced street where Verne Summers' mother, a widow, lived for years before she went to hospital with her paralysing stroke.

The small house, two up, three down, was so cold, like entering a fridge, that Jacko longed for his long johns for the first time that day.

No phone, he confirmed in a quick look round the three neat but dusty ground-floor rooms. He went upstairs and noted without much interest that Verne had dutifully tidied his small bedroom after his weekend stay. There was nothing else of note.

He'd left Hazel downstairs, rummaging through a sideboard, apparently knowing what she was looking for and where she'd find it.

He came downstairs, not too disappointed, thinking he'd have time now to drop in at the Old Railway Inn near the court-house for the drink he'd missed out on yesterday.

She had a huge thick book open on a round table. Mrs Summers had proudly kept her son's cuttings, from his first mug shot of a schoolboy runner, sold on space to the local *Chronicle and Advertiser,* to his war work the qualities had used and the royals the tabloids had run.

Near the middle of the book was a loose coloured photo, not a cutting.

There was not much colour in it, shades of white, pale wood on darker sand; nothing like the sexy picture he'd expected to find.

Bang goes that drink at the Railway again, he knew.

13

Thirty-six to forty-eight hours

'Listen, kids,' said Crow, quietly, sitting, unusually for him, in an upright position on the splitting sofa.

'Ah, Mum,' groaned the scarecrow girl, on her stomach on the threadbare carpet as close as possible to the gas fire, not looking away from the TV. 'It's only just gone eight.'

'We want to watch this,' said the boy cross-legged beside her. 'What's the idea of having the movie channel if—'

'Then shut up and listen,' their mother said, raising her voice, then herself up out of a slouch in an armchair with stained, shiny blue fabric. She screwed out another tip in an already full black ashtray between wide-apart feet, and flopped back again.

Makes a change for her to tell the bastards to do what they've been told, thought Crow.

His surprise vanished when she looked

at him and said, 'Turn it up a bit.'

Listen to the telly, not to me, the cow means, he realized. He kept his anger under control, but didn't reach for the remote control on the sofa's arm next to him. 'No one's saying anything about anybody going to their pit.'

The room went quiet, apart from Bruce Willis on the movie channel.

Crow lifted a buttock and reached into the back pocket of his brown cords. He took out some twenty-pound notes, folded, previously counted, so he knew he was holding a hundred and eighty pounds.

With the half grand spent on a second-hand Land Rover that lunchtime, fifty pounds for a quarter's insurance, forty on two new receivers and transmitters and twenty he'd broken into at the chip shop the night before, that left two hundred and ten upstairs in a pocket of his fawn denims. His Gulf gear, he called it. He'd already decided to wear them on his next mission.

'Will ya no look then,' he said.

No one looked from the screen.

He peeled off two notes, nipping the rest between his knees, and held up one in each hand.

The girl heard the crackle and glanced

over her slender shoulder. 'W-o-oooooooo.' She pushed herself up to her knees.

'For you.' He offered it to her.

She snatched it, examined it briefly, pushed herself up further, like a runner on a starting block, and dived on to his lap, kissing his unshaven face noisily and wetly.

'What about me?' the boy pouted, not interested in Bruce Willis any more.

The girl was kissing Crow's lips now, his right hand in the middle of her back to stop her falling. He couldn't reply. He held out the other note for the boy to take. He grabbed it and, shrieking, jumped into the scrum on the settee.

Crow pulled his head back and looked towards their bewildered mother. 'The rest is yours.'

In the scrum, head down again, he felt, but did not see, a hand removing the notes from between his knees and then his testicles being playfully tweaked.

'Give me room to breathe.' Gasping, laughing, he roughly pushed both children away and pulled himself upright again. The girl dropped on to the carpet and sat, back to the TV. The boy ducked under his arm and snuggled closer.

The woman had returned to her armchair

208

and was counting out the notes, all beams. She stopped. 'Where did you get it?'

He tickled the boy's stomach hard. 'Well...'

'Turn it down,' said the mother.

He killed the sound. 'Army pay.'

She started counting again, from the beginning, savouring the moment, making it last.

He'd already worked out what he was going to say. He'd worked everything out, thought of nothing else all day.

He'd taken the van mid-morning to the nearest newsagent to buy the *Mirror*. It had run his message, but only part of it. Should have phoned the sodding *Sun*, his usual paper, he thought bitterly.

He drove on into the countryside, recceing with his bins the spot where he was due to collect the rest of the money, fourteen grand, in thirty-six hours' time.

He remembered that other golden rule: Decide priorities. What are they? One, to get paid in full. Two, to cover his tracks.

How best to cover his tracks? To have no witnesses.

He couldn't complain, could he, that posh prick? It was him who had ordered the elimination of the seaman from the sunken ship in Cyprus. A security risk, he insisted he was. What's he to me? The same. It's unsafe, bad tactics, to leave him around, to talk. Check? Check.

Dark thoughts, thoughts of betrayal, had blocked out the sun that shone a broad, bright path across the still water.

Maybe he's ahead of me already. Maybe his plan is to get me out here in the country, miles from anywhere. Maybe his idea is that I should finish up like that seaman. Dead.

You or me, prick.

So—slowly—not me. You.

The decision was that quick, that simple. 'Work out your tactics,' he ordered himself.

His seven by fifty bins scanned the rugged man-made landscape for a long time. The more he looked, the more certain became his conviction that he was being set up for an ambush.

He was pleased now the *Mirror* hadn't used his message in full, with its implied threat. Why tip him off to what lay in wait for him? He decided the place to plant his second mine. He knew from experience how to make it, how to detonate it.

He doubled back to Kettering, not his own doorstep. Smart, that, covering his tracks.

He ate a trucker's meal at a transport café, working out his shopping list.

He bought two new transmitters and receivers for model boats, one to replace the accessories he'd taken from the boy's present. Good thinking, too, covering his tracks again.

He helped himself to another yard of piping from an unattended building site in the side street where he had parked the van.

He had twenty pounds of plasticine left in his wardrobe. He'd build it tonight.

Three-quarters would go on the mine. To cover contingencies—like a cop getting too close—he'd use some of the rest inside the casing of the white grenade he'd brought home as a souvenir. He'd also arm and prime that other little black beauty he hadn't thrown on a night exercise.

One or the other would be used against his sub-contractor. He was bound to have hired one. He'd never carry it out himself, wouldn't dirty his hands, wouldn't know how.

He'd toured second-hand car lots and

put down five hundred on a Land Rover, signed an HP agreement he'd never keep, taken out temporary insurance, got a green slip for travel in Europe.

'There's a sailing at two on Thursday, sir,' said the girl at the travel agency. 'No need to book this time of year. Just be there half an hour at least before departure.'

In forty-eight hours' time, less, I'll be on the Continent deep into France. Where from there doesn't matter. Bosnia. Africa. Anywhere they wanted a proven saboteur with two scores to his credit.

He felt wonderfully free, alive.

She had counted out the money twice.

'Collected it today,' said Crow, casually. 'Have to pick up a truck tomorrow.'

'Can I have a ride?' asked the boy, cuddling him.

'If I've time. We'll try out that boat in the park.' He looked at the mother. 'It means a month away.' He nodded at the notes she was holding. 'There'll be plenty more where that came from, four times.'

'Where are you going?'

'Scotland, on exercise.'

'When?'

'Thursday, earlier than a sparrow's fart.'

'You been recalled then?'

'If the hand stands up.' He held up his right hand, turning it, examining the scar.

'SAS?' asked the boy, eyes wider than Crow had ever seen them.

'Shush.'

'Really? Honest?'

'Say nothing,' said Crow softly but urgently. 'Promise me. Nothing to nobody. None of your mates. Nobody. Just say I'm away on some temp job. Remember the golden rule: "Careless talk costs lives." Want me dead?'

The boy shook his head solemnly and was rewarded with a hug.

His mother tucked the notes in the breast pocket of a grey jumpsuit, but left her hand there, fingering it, squeezing it. She worked her dry lips and looked up at the ceiling, towards the bedroom.

He unwound himself from the boy, beginning to stand. 'I'm off up to the wooden hill. A bit of packing.'

'I'll help,' said the mother eagerly. She nodded to the remote control. 'Stick the sound back on.'

The boy picked it up and gunned it at the screen.

'You got wax in your ears or something?' said the mother from the door. 'Louder.'

Crow was climbing the bare wooden stairs ahead of her. I'd rather be packing the pipe, he was thinking. Still, plenty of time tomorrow. She was certain to get up early, early for her, and out, shopping for daft things; for herself, seldom the kids.

He ran the day back through his mind. The plan was in place. Check? Check.

He'd obeyed all the golden rules. He'd eaten. He'd recced. He'd worked out his tactics, allowed for contingencies and plotted his withdrawal. Check? Check.

Reaching the cold bedroom he made up another rule. 'Screw when you can because you don't know when you'll get the chance again.'

14

Eight-thirty, Little Velma had told him when he'd reported what they'd found on his phone from home (more secure than a mobile, as certain members of the royal family were finding out to their cost). 'Be here at half eight.'

He'd dropped in at home and made more of a fuss of his dog than his wife. He'd picked up his passport. 'Might be a trip to Cyprus in this,' he'd told her; he loved his little trips.

He'd cancelled a planned dinner for three she had prepared and Hazel's bed. He didn't remember until he was the other side of Melton Mowbray that he'd forgotten to bin his dirty washing and top up his overnight bag with fresh things, but he didn't turn back.

They were in the village hall for eight thirty. Velma wasn't.

'Oakham,' said Happy, the incident room collator, grim-faced. 'You're to join her there at the local nick.'

For a very private chat, Jacko deduced. 'Trouble?'

He nodded to the phone. 'The sound of Silent.'

Oh, Christ, thought Jacko, ACC Knight's back.

He was sitting erect, his I'm-in-charge posture, behind a green metal desk at the sub-divisional HQ, brown-bricked with sharply angled roofs in a back street, as modern and urban as the incident room was rustic and rural.

He was wearing smart grey civvies. Jacko guessed it was plainclothes disguise to avoid being recognized in public.

Marauding media gangs still roamed the streets, bar to bar in hotels booked up for miles around.

Complaints of bizarre late-night conduct had flooded into the station, Hazel's colleagues in the PR department had told her when she'd checked in.

One waitress, accused of slow service, had been ordered, 'Bring me the manager—on toast.' Having them spot Silent after his indifferent performance at yesterday's press conference might provoke a serious public order situation, Jacko acknowledged.

To one side of the desk sat Velma in a low armchair, body pitched slightly forwards, legs entwined, showing a smooth right kneecap, shining up at him when they entered. She nodded them to two straight chairs opposite.

Jacko was half expecting a bollocking for leaking the group photo Hazel had borrowed from Island Lodge to McAllister at Fine Focus. He was unprepared for what followed.

'Mr Knight,' Velma began, quietly, 'has had a complaint from the Home Office...'

'The Home Secretary's No 2, actually,' Knight interjected, rather self-importantly.

'...about the inquiries we have been making at Midshires Munitions.'

Jacko liked the 'we'. She wasn't passing the buck. 'What about, specifically?'

Knight answered that one. 'About your request to examine arms export certificates.'

Jacko disliked the 'your'. Silent was passing the buck. He made no reply.

'Why?' Knight raised his tone slightly. 'That's Customs and Excise ground, surely?'

Jacko didn't know that. He explained the discovery in the Fine Focus file of the photo of Midshires ammo in the Falklands and the questions they had asked about it.

'So what?' asked Knight. 'A simple check would have told you that Lord Hamb wasn't running it then.'

Velma smiled quietly. 'But Toby Blewis was on the board then.'

'Still don't see the point,' Knight persisted.

'Wait till you see what they've come up with now.' Velma widened her eyes and shone them on Hazel.

The photo Hazel had found in Mrs Summers' scrapbook of her son's cuttings was placed on the desk. Knight frowned down on a picture showing a neat stack of wooden crates piled high on sand. Most had 'Midshires Munitions' and 'Made in Corby' and a series of letters and numbers stencilled on them in black paint.

'Look on the back,' said Velma, invitingly.

Knight turned it over, frowned deeper, as he read a date and place written in pencil which Jacko had already dictated over the phone to her.

'That's well inside Iraq territory on the road to Basra a week after they withdrew in a shambles from Kuwait,' said Velma.

Done her research, thought Jacko, admiringly.

'So?' Knight's frown was more than worried now; alarmed over what he might hear.

'The Hambs had taken over then.'

'I still don't...' Knight's voice trailed.

Velma nodded at Jacko who had fine-tuned this theory with Velma, at length over the phone from home, and with Hazel, all the way back in the car, and he began to speak fluently, rare for him.

'A promising line of inquiry...' He was careful to emphasize the singular. '...has to be that Summers saw that photo as evidence of illegal arms running.'

Knight answered immediately. 'They could claim that it was authorized and shipped there months earlier to help Iraq in their war with Iran.'

Velma shook her head. 'An arms embargo was in place on both sides in that conflict from the mid-eighties on.'

Knight came back, in command of his facts. 'They could say it was captured from Kuwait, the spoils of war, which Saddam's troops had been taking home when they were overrun. They were perfectly entitled to export to Kuwait, surely?'

Jacko knew then he'd been well briefed on the arms trade by the Home Secretary's No 2.

'They can say what they like,' said Velma, very easily. 'It's what Verne Summers thought that counts.' She nodded to Jacko to continue.

'Let's say Summers comes home from the Middle East with that photo, travels to Midshire Munitions and confronts them with it.'

'Who?' Knight demanded.

'Toby Blewis, sales director, the Hon Matthew, managing director.' Jacko paused. 'Or Lord Hamb, chairman.'

Knight's confidence seemed to evaporate at the Lord Lieutentant-elect being named as a suspect.

Jacko pushed on. 'One, two or all three of them realize that publicity like that has got to be stopped at all costs. Imagine it. Making the bullets that were fired at our own boys.'

'So...' Hazel broke in, smooth-tongued. '...they offer Summers a deal. Keep the lid on that and we'll feed you tips on royal visits here, so you can get lots of lovely exclusive pictures to sell.'

Knight recovered, shook his head determinedly. 'That's a bit outlandish, isn't it?'

'Why?' Velma used her demanding tone now.

Knight had no answer.

'Look at it from Summers' point of view,' Jacko went on. 'He needs money. He's had to come home to England leaving a good business behind him in Cyprus because his lady's ill. He's no job to come back to. Times are hard on Fleet Street, no staff jobs.'

'That story...' Hazel nodded at the photo. '...would earn him a few grand, at best, from a quality paper. A constant flow of royal exclusives would net him a mint.'

'So,' Velma added, slowly, 'Verne trades his silence for info.'

Hazel again: 'We've found no evidence that he ever paid for his Rutland tip-offs. Someone on the island was feeding him. No one else knew about Prince Charles's travel plans. And Summers was getting the info free.'

'Makes sense,' Jacko summed up.

It didn't to Knight, who sat head hanging over the photo for several seconds, not really looking at it. 'Are you seriously suggesting that a peer, his son or a future MP would tip off the tabloids about private royal visits?'

'In their position, I would,' said Velma. 'Think of the scandal it was avoiding. It's got everything. Evasion, money-grubbing hypocrisy and corruption. They'd see it as the lesser of two evils.'

'Besides,' said Hazel, enjoying herself, 'Hamb loves his publicity. Having the world know his family and business friends rub shoulders socially with the royals would be meat and drink for his enormous ego.'

Daringly, she overdid it. 'Half the royal households seem to be leaking these days.'

A bit hard that, thought Jacko, so he toned it down. 'It was pretty innocuous stuff he was getting anyway. Annoying to the Palace, but tame compared with some shots the paparazzi have been snatching.'

Media-wise Hazel stronged it up again. 'Princes doing sporty things still sell. OK, they may not earn as much as princesses at play, but there's more money in them than Nottingham Forest versus Norwich City.'

Knight's face was full of doubt. 'If pictures of private visits keep on appearing, surely the royals would stop coming here?'

'Oh,' said Hazel, mischievously, 'they're just playing the media game. Their wives are getting so much publicity that if the princes don't get their photos in the papers now and then the nation will forget all about them.'

Maybe they should hire Global Images, thought Jacko, equally mischievously, but he refused himself a smile. 'We know from Captain Willis that inquiries were in hand to plug the leak.'

Finally Knight swallowed the theory

with a little gulp. 'What might have gone wrong?'

'Well,' Jacko shrugged, uncertain. 'Summers becomes a problem. Maybe he's greedy for more tips than they're prepared to provide. Maybe he was taking all he could get from them, but still poking around on the sanctions busting.'

'And they killed him?' Knight laced his voice with incredulity.

'Oh no,' said Velma. 'They're all alibied. Hamb was out of the country. His son was at the stables. Blewis was indoors. No.' She firmed up her voice. 'One, two or all of them paid someone else to do that?'

'Who?'

'Captain Willis can't be ruled out,' said Jacko.

'What? He almost got himself killed going to the rescue.'

'But,' said Velma, 'He was Royal Engineers. He'd know just what was required. He could make it look good, a close shave.'

The room went silent. Jacko felt a shaft of disappointment. She'd had plenty of time to dig into Willis's background. He anticipated far more from her.

Velma put a question that Jacko would

never have dared to ask. 'What did the Home Office say, sir?'

For a second or so, Knight's mind seemed miles away. On his diminishing chances of landing the soon-to-be vacant Deputy Chief's post, Jacko guessed. 'They said that they were acting on behalf of the Department of Trade, who'd had Hamb on.

'They pointed out in no uncertain terms that arms exports are politically sensitive right now. There've been one or two prosecutions over breaching embargoes that didn't look too good for the government. They're hinting to Customs and us that they're not falling over themselves to find another.'

'And what did you tell them?'

'Neither are we. We're looking for a killer.'

'Good,' Velma declared, primly.

'Yes...' A vaguely lost look. '...but I'm under vague instructions to tell you to refer all queries about export certificates to Customs.'

'And so you have, sir. Haven't you?' asked Velma.

A long silence. She broke in. 'We're

making tremendous progress. I've a good feeling about this one.'

Me, too, thought Jacko, but he said nothing. Neither did Knight.

Shrewdly Hazel found the key to his co-operation. 'It will be tremendous for the force's reputation and morale when a press conference is called and you announce that we've solved it.'

Knight brightened at the prospects of public rehabilitation. He cleared his throat. 'I could always say, I suppose, that I summoned you to HQ tomorrow to brief you and you were busy or the message didn't get through or something. That way I could buy you a bit of time.'

Maybe I've misread him, thought Jacko, warming to Knight ever so slightly for the first time.

'Give us forty-eighty,' said Velma, a line Jacko thought he'd heard before in every other crime film.

'I can't promise you that long,' Knight answered.

Jacko went cold on him again. That, he thought, is not what police chiefs are supposed to reply.

Trailing a cloud of grey smoke, Lord

Hamb was crossing the hall as a white-coated Filipino opened the front door at Island Lodge, its white stucco and black shutters giving it a Spanish feeling, out of place on a dark, cold winter's night.

He looked across his shoulder in their direction, but did not stop or smile. He was carrying a large glass of port in one hand. His other held a huge Havana to his mouth. He vanished into the room where he'd held court the day before.

The servant took their raincoats and nodded to them to follow. Hamb was already behind his desk, phone in hand, when Jacko shut the study door behind them.

The cloud had caught Hamb up and hung overhead, dancing as he waved a hand to instruct them to sit down.

He pressed a button with a podgy finger, flicked on the loudspeaker switch on the squawk box and placed the phone beside it on the desk.

Jacko could hear a number ringing. These conference lines were new to him; trendy toys for men of power, he guessed, designed to let them show it off. He could hear it still ringing out as he sat on a hard antique chair alongside Hazel.

'45—'

'Matt.' Hamb gave his son no time to complete his number.

'You've read them?' The Hon Matthew sounded anxious.

'Over dinner.'

They exchanged a lot of technical information about tonnages. Jacko, pretending not to listen, couldn't make out at first if they were talking about yields from their stone and sand quarries or their boats and barges.

Both, he decided, when Matthew reported that something sounding Greek had broken down in the Aegean Sea. He suggested immediate repairs in dry dock at a place that began with a 'Pye' and therefore sounded very Greek.

Hamb's face shadowed. 'That's two in two days. Is the entire fleet dropping to bits?'

Matthew laughed tightly. He used another Greek-sounding word that began with 'zoo' and ended with 'ko', followed by something sounding almost like 'Velma'. '...most certainly was. Corrosion.'

My beloved CID chief has had a ship named after her, Jacko thought, smiling to himself.

'The funnel was coming away from the superstructure,' Matthew continued. 'No alternative, Dad.'

Hamb cheered suddenly. 'Still a snip at half a million.' They laughed conspiratorially, Hamb's eyes on Jacko, enjoying himself. 'Got your friend here, by the way. Inspector...' He looked at Jacko. '...name again?'

'Jackson.'

'Oh.' Matthew sounded guarded. He explained that only a couple of days' delay was anticipated on repairs at somewhere beginning with 'Zamb' and Jacko amused himself by wondering idly if there was an African branch to the family.

'Pity,' Hamb said. 'That funnel looked rather rakish.' He gave Jacko a sly smile, irking him, taunting him almost.

'Can't be helped,' Matthew replied rather flatly.

Trying not to look as if he was listening—God knows why, because that was clearly the intention—Jacko let his eyes range the room, settling on the collection of boats he'd also seen on the wall at Midshires Munitions, but they were too far away to make much of a study.

Hamb had returned to the discussion

about the first ship and ordered that the Athens branch of their insurers should be contacted before any repairs were carried out.

He changed topics, enthusing about returns from the No 5 pit, the one Jacko had driven past on the Kettering-Oakham road the day before, feeling hijacked, a hostage. 'Give the manager a bonus.'

His son said fine. 'I'm there tomorrow for a couple of days if you need me.'

They went into a long discussion about something called alluvial deposits. During the course of it, Hamb raised his right buttock from his soft seat and farted extremely noisily, a real ripsnorter.

Jacko tried to blank his face, a facial feature he often sought, but never found. Beside him Hazel shook slightly as she tried to control a titter. Without embarrassment Hamb looked at her absently as he complained about output from No 3 quarry.

Jacko detected the odour of pheasant and port above the smell of cigar smoke, hardly listening as Matthew blamed the result on 'not shifting enough of the face'.

'Second time round.' Hamb lowered

his head towards the speaker. 'Show that manager what firing's all about.'

'You mean...'

'Yes.'

Another one for the dole queue, mused Jacko sadly.

Matthew changed the subject this time. 'Toby's Brussels-bound this time tomorrow. He hopes to—'

'Thank you all the same,' said Hamb, formally, 'but later...'

'You mean...'

'Yes.' He flicked off the switch without a goodnight.

He means your old man's been showing off his grip on his empire, his absolute power, to outsiders like me over his squawk box, but he doesn't want me earwigging on Blewis's travels and contacts, Jacko deduced.

'What do you two want then?' Hamb asked.

Jacko was used to his bluntness now, and, oddly, didn't regard it as rudeness, just showmanship.

'To thank you for that picture.' Hazel nodded to the wall where it had hung.

'Thought we ought to forewarn you that

it might be in most papers tomorrow morning,' Jacko added.

They had worked out this opening line, with Silent Knight and Little Velma, to flatter him. 'Don't push him about arms exports,' they'd decreed. 'Let him make the pace.'

Instead he looked displeased. 'Worth the trade, was it?'

Jacko said nothing, thinking: The old fart saw right through it.

'Find anything interesting in London?' A smile, not at all friendly. 'Apart from his war snaps?'

'Which war do you mean?' Smart that, Jacko congratulated himself.

'Any.'

Hamb studied the lengthening white ash on the cigar. 'It doesn't pay to pry. As you will soon be finding out.'

Jacko decided not to tell him he'd already got the message. 'How do you mean?'

Hamb puffed gently. 'If wogs want to kill each other, they might as well do it with made-in-Britain weaponry. Keeps our labour force gainfully employed.'

And your profits up, thought Jacko cynically.

231

Astonishingly Hamb seemed to read this thought. 'Business is bad enough as it is. If we don't supply 'em, someone else will.'

Jacko risked a rapped knuckle. 'Are you talking about the Middle East?'

'Anywhere.'

'Iraq, in particular?'

'Ah. Ah.' A delighted exclamation through a drifting balloon of smoke. 'Found that, too, have you?'

Jacko nodded slowly.

'Guessed you would.'

In for a penny, Jacko decided. 'Have you seen that Gulf War photo Summers brought back?'

Hamb nodded at the loudspeaker that had just relayed Matthew's voice to the room. 'He has, and Toby Blewis.'

Jacko stiffened, shocked. 'They told us they had never spoken to Summers. They made no mention of seeing it.'

'My instructions.'

'To lie to the police on a major inquiry like this?' Jacko was still shocked, but far from speechless. 'Why?'

Hazel shot him an anxious sideways glance, to remind him, he suspected, of their orders to go easy.

Hamb held his cigar sideways in further

examination. Jacko noticed the tip was hardly wet. When he smoked his annual Castella at Christmas, the end soon became so chewed and soggy that bits got in between his teeth.

Hamb took another short pull, relaxing. 'It's a very dirty business; cut-throat competition. Few scruples, I'm afraid. And very secretive. Has to be. Talk of police investigation can cost you customers. Word leaks out in the wrong quarter and you can lose a ship to sabotage. It's happened to us, Mossad, I'm sure of it.'

He chomped, for the first time. 'We try to be above board.'

'Many overseas orders?' asked Jacko, backing off, keen for background, to use later as ammo against him.

'We use Cyprus as a forwarding base for convenience...'

And tax reasons, I'll bet, thought Jacko.

'...and, let's be honest, there are certain tax benefits.'

He's a bloody mind reader, thought Jacko, unnerved. 'Why didn't Matthew and Mr Blewis tell us of this this morning?'

'We knew you'd find the photo. Eventually. I needed time to double-check. You'll find the paperwork in order. You'll find it in A1 order. That's all I'm saying.'

'That's not good enough, and you know it.'

He looked at him sharply, then sighed heavily. 'The end-user certification... Know what that is?'

Jacko nodded.

'...will tell you the destination was Nigeria, which is on nobody's banned list. Now. If the consignment is broken up in Lagos and parts of it shipped on...' A heavy shrug. '...that's their problem.'

Washing his hands of it, Jacko decided. 'How does the system work?'

Hamb drained his port glass, working his tongue in his mouth, not quite smacking it. 'Most governments have, on the face of it at least, tight laws governing the sale of arms. All dealers have to be registered. And we must obtain an end-user certificate to export.'

'In other words,' said Jacko, showing off (for Hazel, really) minimal knowledge gleaned at Fine Focus twenty-four hours earlier, 'proof of where your goods will end up?'

Hamb nodded, impressed. 'In this case Blewis set up a perfectly legal deal to sell to Nigeria. All we had to do was to provide a letter from their embassy.'

'London?' asked Jacko.

'Anywhere will do.' He flicked a switch and barked. 'Coffee.'

'So how can the system fail?' asked Hazel.

He sat back, happy to talk in a deep melodious accent that had lost all the eee-by-gumminess he'd used on the press. 'There's a vast demand from governments and organizations—terrorists, freedom fighters, call them what you will—who are on the banned list.

'Let's suppose a registered dealer—not us, never us...' For emphasis he jabbed his cigar towards them over the desk, spilling ash on it. '...hears on the grapevine that rebels in say, Rwanda are in the market for weapons. He knows he will not get an EUC to sell them. But his men in the field, the Blewises of the business, will know Third World countries with corrupt officials who will certify that the consignment is going to them.'

'For a price,' Jacko butted in.

The white-coated servant came in, almost on tiptoe, with a big cup of black coffee. Just one.

Hamb didn't say thank you or stop

talking in his presence. 'The deal may be worth millions so what's a hundred thou to that official in a Swiss account and, hey presto, an EUC. He ships the weapons to an African port, backhands Customs there, if necessary, and the crates make their way overland to Rwanda.'

His dark, almost black, mischievous eyes moved from one to the other, resting on Jacko, who thought he ought to say something. 'Much of it going on?'

'All the time. Governments, too. There's two I could name in Asia and two more in South America. They might sell direct to countries and organizations, drugs barons even, on the international stoplist. If they really want to cover their arses they use a foreign arms dealer.'

'The Middle East, too?'

'On my life.' A deep-throated laugh at a bad Yiddish impression. 'Exporting arms is a very important part of the Israeli economy. Wouldn't surprise me if we didn't lose our load at sea because of them.'

'When was this?' asked Jacko, frowning.

'Two years back. Lost in the eastern Med.'

'Sabotage?'

A shrug, saying: Who knows? 'Lloyd's settled. You'll find out all you need to know from them.'

He'd got his money back, all that mattered and sod the crew, thought Jacko.

Hamb resumed where he'd left off. 'The Israelis captured huge amounts of Soviet-made weaponry over the years, remember, and they sell them on, often under the counter, because most countries are loath to purchase them openly.'

He treated them to a story. The Israelis sold some captured Soviet Silk missiles to China, see, and, as part of the deal, sent Tel Aviv technologists to Peking to teach them how they worked, how to make them more efficient and, eventually, how to copy them.

'They were mightily pissed off when they discovered their little yellow friends had started on-selling these same missiles, upgraded, to Saudi Arabia who, of course, might one day use them against Israel. Hilarious, eh?'

Jacko smiled weakly to hide his disgust. And side-splitting, he thought, for the British Tommy being shot at in the Gulf by your Made-in-Corby ammo.

'Some of our rivals don't even bother sending them to the destination shown on the end-user certificate,' Hamb went on.

'How do they get away with that?' Hazel asked.

'They just send the ship's master fresh instructions *en route*. Plenty of shipping companies prepared to do it. Not ours, though. Got that?'

Jacko nodded. 'How does that work?'

'You have an EUC for Indonesia, say. You contact a shipbroker in Marseilles. A load bound for Jakarta, you tell him, but you add quickly and quietly that the destination might change. A deal is struck. The weapons are loaded. The skipper is told his final destination will be advised *en passage*. As they pass through the Suez Canal, he's told to set sail for Somalia, for instance.'

'Who checks?'

'Who indeed?' He ran the red glowing end around a black pot ashtray. 'No one, unless they're forced to. Politically, it's not good to have any sort of arms scandal so a government, even if it suspects something's wrong, turns a blind eye. There's millions in foreign exchange and jobs at home involved too. In any case, every country

238

has skeletons on the armoury.'

'But not you?' asked Hazel, sweetly.

'Never. Our hands are clean.' Beaming, he held them up in front of his face, for inspection. The he lowered them and his voice. 'But I wouldn't necessarily want the families of British troops to know that some of our ammo turned up on the wrong side of the Iraqi border. Bad PR.'

Having got the background, Jacko got down to business, but softly, softly, in accordance with Silent Knight's instructions. 'What arrangement did you come to with Verne Summers when he produced his picture of your arms pile to you?'

A surprised look. 'Not me. I never saw it, still haven't.'

'Your son and Mr Blewis then.'

Hamb had a point to underscore. 'I never met him over here. Our dealings—my wife's really—with him were in Cyprus.'

'But you knew he was being a pest to royal guests here?'

A cautious nod.

'What arrangements did your son and Mr Blewis make with him?'

'They told him the truth, I assume. We have nothing to hide.'

'And that was all?'

'What else could there be?'

Without hard evidence, Jacko didn't have the nerve to suggest that either his son or his sales director had been tipping Summers off about royal visits in return for his silence, which was now permanent. He said nothing.

'Nothing appeared in print, did it?' Hamb continued. 'Be honest, I always say, and people will be honest with you.'

His face filled with regret. 'Sometimes I think we're too honest. Look around and you'll find shady rivals who aren't laying off workers like we're having to.' He shook his head. 'Bad business.'

Crocodile tears, Jacko decided. He's just sacked a quarry manager without a thought for his family. He decided to push him. 'Tell me, if your hands are clean and your paperwork all in order and you believe honesty is the best policy, why did you instruct your son and Mr Blewis to lie to me this morning?'

'Economical with the truth might be a better in-phrase.' He laughed, uncomfortable this time. 'You know, I quite respect you, Mr Johnson.'

Jacko suspected now that Hamb had his name clearly fixed in his mind, but was pretending to forget it to belittle him.

'You've got what I call fighting spirit,' Hamb went on. 'When your thirty years are up, come and see me. We can always find room in the organization for someone with spirit.'

Now the cunning bastard is offering me a bribe, he thought angrily. 'You still haven't answered the question.'

'Really? Thought I had.'

'No.'

'Then let me.' He lent forward, threateningly, arms on the desk, a statement to make. 'I do not want the police prying into our affairs. Customs, we have to tolerate, but not the police, leaking to their media friends like you leaked that photo.' He looked to a gap in his wall collection where it had hung and then sharply at Hazel.

'According to you,' said Jacko, evenly, 'there's nothing to leak.'

Hamb smiled icily. 'I think that if you check with your superiors you will find everything is being answered at the highest level.' He switched subjects abruptly. 'Now, what else have you two troublemakers been up to?'

He's treating me like a bloody employee

already, thought Jacko. I'll show him how deep we're going. 'Saw your sales director's pin-up lady this afternoon.'

'Bimbo, you mean.'

Ungallantly, Jacko decided not to rush to Sally Masters' defence.

'Believe it?' asked Hamb.

'Believe what?'

'About her and him?'

Jacko shrugged, playing for time.

'Wouldn't if I were you.'

'Why not?'

Hamb raised his right buttock again. Jacko drew in breath, preparing to hold on to it in anticipation of another ripsnorter. Instead Hamb patted it, winking.

Jacko knew he was telling him Blewis was gay. 'Doesn't seem to bother your son.'

His face purpled. 'You're not—'

'Absolutely not,' Jacko replied, hurriedly. 'Their working relationship, I mean.'

The dark cloud lifted just as fast. 'He used to bring in a lot of business. Not these days, though. I'll be pleased to get shot of him to the Commons, for all the good it will do the rest of the country.'

'Maybe he's too straight.' Jacko smiled thinly. 'Business-wise, I mean.'

'Sod 'em.' Little Velma strode into a small, very basic country pub, Hazel's local, in the village where she lived outside of Oakham. 'Sod 'em all.'

Jacko turned to the bar, just a serving hatch, room for one only, to order her usual—white wine and soda.

'Make it a scotch,' Velma urged.

A real drink, a real paddy, thought Jacko. He wondered if Silent Knight had reneged on his agreement. 'Trouble?'

'Please,' she said with a mischievous smile.

All three laughed.

Jacko nodded at the barman. Velma asked for water to match her double. They took their drinks to a quiet corner in the flagstoned snug.

'I just can't understand it,' she said, serious again, as they sat down. 'I've had hassle from them all day.'

'Who?'

'The Ministry of Defence. Normally they're very helpful with military personnel background. This time they're clamming right up on Willis. All they'll do is confirm that he resigned his commission and departed with an exemplary character.'

'Are they covering up something?' asked Jacko. To him, the whole of Whitehall seemed to be conspiring against them.

'I asked point-blank if they got rid of him because they suspected he was homosexual. They wouldn't confirm or deny. Usually they'll give you a good steer in the right direction, at the very least. This time, zero.'

'You don't think he was SAS or something secret like that?' asked Hazel.

Doubtful, thought Jacko. The highest Willis would ever have made, in his experienced view, was a major, and then not a very good one with his lack of social graces in mixed company. But times had changed in the thirty years since he'd worn khaki and he couldn't be sure, so he didn't answer.

Velma wanted to know how they had got on.

'I was conned this morning by Matthew and Blewis,' he said, shame-faced, and he told her how. 'Everyone does what old Hamb tells them to do. He terrifies everybody.'

'Knight included,' said Velma, undiplomatically.

And me, thought Jacko, still feeling

244

guilty, so he added a partial confession. 'Everyone seems to toe his line.'

'Where's that all leave us?' she asked.

'We can't dismiss a cover-up on an arms scandal, just because Hamb has pat answers,' said Jacko. 'At least, not until we have turned over Matthew and Blewis again tomorrow.'

Velma sipped her drink. 'Let's up the pace a bit. Hit them with the hard word. They've asked for it. And Willis, too. He's being released from hospital to the care of his folks.'

Jacko nodded. 'We can't dismiss queer-bashing in reverse either.'

'I do,' said Hazel, positively. 'I just can't see Verne Summers dirtying his hands with blackmail.'

'Why not?' asked Jacko sharply. 'He was dirtying his hands with paparazzo stuff.'

'The royals and the showbiz crowd are in the public domain. The public pays their wages.'

'So are politicians. Haven't his prospective voters in his safe southern shire a right to know about Blewis?'

'Only if it affects his job or his judgement,' Hazel replied, firmly.

Jacko ended the debate, a more important

thought occurring. 'Maybe I'm looking at this the wrong way round. Old Hamb clearly hates Blewis. Quite apart from any sexual predilections he thinks his political work gets in the way of his job at Midshires Munitions.'

Velma, silent for some time, chipped in. 'I would have thought his international connections would be a boon to business, but go on.'

'Well, why doesn't Hamb fire him? He fires everyone else at the drop of a quarry stone. Maybe Blewis is the blackmailer. Maybe he's got something on Hamb or his son and Summers stumbled across it.'

All three of them left it there, too tired to think it through any further.

Velma enthused about the cosy bedroom a local inspector had turned over to her exclusive use—'for the duration,' she added, making it sound like she anticipated a long stay.

Jacko looked at his watch, a metal, wind-up cheapo: 11 p.m. He accepted he was unlikely to win his pint bet with Hazel now.

The tubby landlord, who knew Hazel was a police officer, loudly called, 'Time,' surprising and annoying the locals in the bar, clearly used to going home when they were full or falling over, and not before, the way it is in drinking rural England.

Jacko decided to recoup on his expected losses. He yawned. 'I'm awar te ma bed.' An appalling imitation of a Scots accent.

'Where you sleeping?' asked Velma.

He nodded at Hazel. 'Her little artisan's cottage. Her fella's away. On a course.' He held back from adding that everyone above the rank of inspector always seemed to be away on cushy courses because Velma had been on a few herself, and why upset the boss?

'In the spare room,' Hazel added, quickly and accurately, as it turned out, 'but my chap has left a few spare pairs of underpants behind, so he'll be cleanly attired in the morning.'

A brief laugh died. He eyed Hazel. 'I'll polish off the crossword before zizzville. I'm stuck for one. "Shipwrecked on a desert island." Begins with an M. Eight letters. Two Os together, but buggered if I can work it out.'

It was Velma who fell for it. 'Marooned,' she declared triumphantly.

'Mine's a double scotch, please.'

She looked at him as if he were the village's new idiot.

He put on his Glasgow accent. 'Ma rooned, you said, which translates hereabouts as "My round" and mine's a double scotch.'

Velma bought her round and Hazel, too, and all three again and the locals were still sipping steadily when they left at well past midnight.

15

Forty-eight to sixty hours

'Walking on the moon,' sang Sting on the car radio, an oldie these days. Jacko felt as if he was driving on it.

Ahead of him was enough white sand for the Sahara, mountains of it, piled high around a double-storey building and asbestos outhouses, but it was too cold for that illusion. More like the yard of a salt mine, crusted with frost.

He'd turned off the main road through an opened 'In' gap in a grass bank with the

248

notice: 'Hamb Aggregates'. He'd almost caught up with an empty articulated lorry rattling over a rutted single-line track which encircled a large lagoon.

On a road on the other side, heading slowly for the 'Out' gate, was a similar lorry piled high with sand, dribbling yellow water from it's tailgate.

It was a bitter morning, white all over. Ice edged the still water over which grey gulls and black crows swooped low, just above the tiny brown heads of paddling moorhens.

The lake had been landscaped with trees, leafless and silver, and sculptured with banks, tall, wild grasses dying back to a straw colour. It was a drop in the ocean compared with Rutland Water, but it was big all the same. A notice on a pole said: 'Private Fishing'.

Ahead of him the empty lorry seemd to be rising. His right foot rode the brake gently, almost stopped, until he'd worked out why.

The vehicle had forked right at a Y-bend and was climbing a blue-railed ramp; a weighbridge, Jacko realized. The track beyond it ran on behind the buildings.

There, another six-wheeled lorry had

backed beneath massive, twin tanks standing fifty feet high in the air on green metal pillars.

Its balaclava-ed driver was standing beside the cab and waving at a woolly-hatted man in overalls and donkey jacket who sat at controls behind a long window on the top floor of the double-storey, brick-built building.

Hazel got her bearings first, gesturing left, to a track that hugged the still lagoon. He followed it for another forty or so yards to a piece of ground roughly levelled into what passed for a car-park for the offices.

On it were a dozen vehicles, including a yellow bulldozer and a loader. The cars were all modest, mostly old, apart from an almost new White Golf VW steaked with yellow; confirmation that the Hon Matthew was where he'd promised his father over the squawk box last night he would be.

Jacko pulled up alongside it, switched off the radio and got out. Damp sand on the sharp air made the place smell like Skegness. A wind blowing across the ice-edged lake straight up his trouser legs made it feel like Siberia. He longed for his long johns.

As they walked towards the only ground-floor door in the two-storey brick offices, he saw a loaded lorry, leaking dirty water, rise into view on another weighbridge on the road to the exit gate, the balaclava-ed driver at the wheel.

Didn't take long, he thought, impressed.

Waiting for a word with the Hon Matthew was to take much, much longer, time spent in a bleak multi-purpose room, stamping his feet on a concrete floor that stuck cold up beyond his kneecaps.

With no one about to ask, he'd knocked on one of two black doors inside. Warm air fanned his face when a burly middle-aged man pulled it open.

Jacko told him who they were and who they wanted to see.

'Wait five,' called an unseen man, Matthew's voice.

Jacko looked about him—at the plaster-board walls, bare apart from coloured pin-ups, barer still, at a filthy sink in a corner next to a leaning table with chipped mugs, kettle, a half-empty bottle of milk and a packet of sugar standing on a check plastic cloth, even filthier; at greatcoats and yellow capes, hanging on pegs to dry, and blue hard hats all in a row.

He walked to a window, coated with ice on the inside. It didn't take long to work out that the lake had been landscaped and turned over to fishing for cosmetic purposes; to be seen and admired from the main road.

The real business was being done here, out of sight.

Towering draglines were creating a hill of sand, as high as the twin tanks, so fresh and wet that the top of it foamed white. Pipes sucked at the sand from the bottom, leaving a huge hole, and Jacko was reminded of drinking a banana shake through a straw in his milk-bar days.

The pipes ran up on railed gantries into the first building, the same size but a different shape to the one next door where the lorry had stopped.

He hadn't a clue how it all worked, what was going on, a familiar feeling on this job. He smoked a cigarette to create a fug, to try to give some semblance of warmth.

From above came the sound of footsteps on a verandah which ran round the building at first-floor level. Then they echoed on metal stairs and crunched the loose pea gravel which formed a path at the base of the outside walls, brick-skinned, roughly cemented, not built to last.

The other black door opened and what little body heat Jacko and Hazel had stoked up between them went out as the woolly-hatted man came in.

'Brr.' He looked surprised, but pleased, to see them. They told him who they were waiting to see, but not who they were.

'Cuppa?' He nodded to the sink. Normally Jacko would have refused the offer, the chipped mugs too off-putting. 'Please,' he said, eagerly. 'No sugar.' Hazel declined.

As the man made it, Jacko noticed his hat was maroon and white. He guessed, correctly, that he was a Northampton Town fan and they chatted about the Cobblers and Lincoln City for a while. Hazel managed a frozen smile for her only football story.

'Worked here long?' asked Jacko as he sipped from his cracked mug, letting the steam play on his face.

Two years, came the reply, after transfer from another pit which had become exhausted and where he'd also been the loading and weighbridge supervisor. 'This place is the best yet. Very advanced.

Electronic controls. Great production.'

'You don't waste much time filling 'em up,' said Jacko.

'Twenty-two tons in two minutes,' he answered with pride.

'How's it work?' asked Jacko.

The controller led him back to the window for a quick tutorial. He pointed to the ever-moving mountain. 'The surge pile,' he explained. 'From there's it's piped into the processing plant.' His finger had followed the gantry to the square construction on their left. 'There it's washed and graded.' On the high roof Jacko could see a rotating barrel and vibrating sieves.

His tutor pointed to more pipes running away and down to two more hills of sand. 'The sand is separated into builder's for cement and so on and sharp for horticulture.'

His finger went to the second square building, made out of wooden planks in green steel framing and linked to the processing plant by a conveyor belt. 'The stones get graded into hoppers there.'

Each hopper, six in all, had a steel bottom shaped like a petrol funnel, burnished bright by constant use. Below each funnel was space for the lorry to back, as one was reversing now.

A bare-headed driver climbed out and stood next to a notice which said: 'Safety helmets must be worn.'

'Six mil natural,' said the controller, mysteriously, but he had no time to explain. He took his drink with him.

Within a couple of minutes Jacko watched the lorry being loaded. Out of the funnel gushed a long, fast spurt of thick, brown water before small, glistening pebbles rapidly started to fill the back.

Before it was loaded, he heard the other door open and turned to see the burly man coming out. He was flushed and beaming; the manager, Jacko guessed, his bonus in his pocket.

'Come in now,' called Matthew.

Jacko went in, deliberately looking at his watch. They had waited twenty minutes.

'What is it this time?' asked the Hon Matthew, po-faced, sitting behind an old desk piled with paper that, Jacko suspected with unaccustomed bitterness, wasn't his own work.

Lacking his father's rumbustiousness, his bluntness did come out as rudeness, and

Jacko felt his temper and temperature rising; not altogether Matthew's fault.

Whisky always deadened his bones next morning, making him feel slow when he knew he ought to be quick. Just lately and with increasing frequency, he'd experienced inexplicable feelings of time running out on him; not to win that small drinks bet with Hazel, but on his police service, on life itself. Wasting precious time in a tip of an office in a gravel pit had brought him close to boiling point.

He strode up to the desk, pulling Summers' Gulf photo from an inside pocket as he did so. He placed it on the desk with a bullish flourish; none of this rehearsed, just short of snapping. 'About this.' He glowered down.

Matthew looked down, then up, unperturbed. 'I thought my father explained last night.'

'It's your turn now.' Sharp.

'I've nothing to add.' Just as sharp.

'I have.' Jacko dragged a ragged canvas chair to the desk and sat down, leaning forward, menacingly. 'Let me picture the scene. Verne Summers marched in here...'

'Down there, actually.' Matthew nodded

south towards Corby and Midshires Munitions.

'...slapped that on your desk...'

'Even he wasn't as obvious as that.' A disdainful look.

'...you looked at it, and what did you say to each other?'

'I gather from my father that he has already told you.'

So they've talked again—about me this time, Jacko realized. Worried about me, are they? Let's add to that worry. 'He wasn't present, was he?'

A hesitant headshake.

'So his evidence is hearsay, as we say. I need it from you. What was said?'

Matthew looked away to motion Hazel to a folded-down wooden chair by a grimy window. From beyond it, every so often, came the roar of water and pebbles rushing down silver chutes into waiting lorries.

His face, same strong structure as his father's, much leaner, was sallow and pinched. There were black bags under matching eyes. He *is* worried, Jacko sensed.

The sparse office was carpeted in fawn, not cleaned very often judging by grains of sand which had spilt from a red fire bucket near the door. The walls were plasterboard again. On them charts and lists were pinned.

The room was being comfortably warmed by a fan heater beneath a steel table stacked with trade directories and equipment brochures; so warm his light brown jacket hung over the back of a swivel chair. He was wearing a thick cream high-necked sweater and green cords.

'Well,' Matthew began, 'Summers only got in to see me in the first place by flannelling his way through reception claiming friendship with my mother in Cyprus. Normally, I'd never entertain the media. Leave 'em to father.' He smiled to himself.

'Did you meet him out there?'

'Told you that already.' A brusque reply.

'Originally, you also told us you never met him here either. Now.' A deliberate pause, often used in interrogations. 'Did you ever meet him in Cyprus?'

'No.' Emphatic. 'I'd heard mention of him from Mother, saw the magazine with the house and garden feature, but I never met him before either there or here.' Pause. 'Until then.' A troubled look. 'I can't prove that. You'll just have to take my word for it.' Jacko sensed he'd struggled to refrain from adding 'as a gentleman.'

'Let me get this right,' said Jacko slowly. 'Did you, as well as Mr Blewis, see that Falklands photo?'

'No. Never saw that personally until you showed it to me yesterday.'

'Just that?' Jacko nodded at the desert photo.

'Yes.'

'In what circumstances?'

'Well, when Summers and I were alone, well, just Toby was there—'

'All the time?'

'I'm coming to that.' Irritated. 'Summers produced this.' He fingered the Iraq arms dump photo. 'He told us he was just back from the Gulf and where and when it was taken. Frankly, I was thunderstruck.'

'Why?'

'He made it plain he had the *Sunday Times* in mind for a photo article. They're keen on this sort of thing.' Sanction-busting stories, he means, Jacko realized. 'It would have caused a bit of a flap.'

'What did you do?'

'Toby went off to track down the paperwork—the order, the export authorization and so on. That's his department.

259

Happily, he came back with approved documentation for Nigeria.'

'And Summers accepted that?'

'His face fell, but, yes, eventually he seemed satisfied. We parted on quite reasonable terms. Reasonable chap, actually, in any other line of business.'

Jacko lit up a cigarette, something he would not have dreamt of doing in Hamb's study the night before. 'Why didn't you tell me this yesterday?'

'Sorry.' A regretful face. 'After Summers left I phoned Dad.' It was the first time he'd called Hamb that. 'I tell him everything.' A tiny shrug, embarrassed. 'Best that way. He finds out anyhow. A workaholic. Tentacles everywhere.

'He approved my action, but told me that if the matter was raised again by anyone to do nothing till I heard from him; a favourite phrase of his.

'Yesterday morning, when I was informed you were in reception, I called him. We were sure you'd got your hands on this.' One hand covered the photo. 'He repeated that I should say nothing until he cleared it with Whitehall.' He was smiling when he finished.

Jacko wasn't. 'But you had the perfect

answer. The documents were in order, you claim.'

'Very true, but you miss the point. You don't go against his wishes. Not for you, Customs, the Board of Trade, anyone. Not if you want to stay, that is.' Another shrug.

'Why did Lord Hamb complain to Whitehall that we were asking questions about export orders?' asked Hazel, quite sternly.

'Best ask him.' A small wave, offhand.

Jacko glared at him. 'We're asking you. Help us. That's your duty. We're investigating a murder on his land within the sound, if not the sight, of a royal guest...'

'Summers was trespassing,' Matthew replied without apparent thought.

Jacko let shock fill his face. 'You're not going to give me the "Englishman's home is his castle" line, are you?'

'Sorry. No.' A long silence. 'I think that's what really concerned Dad. Charles being there, I mean. The old man has this paranoia about the press. He could see them drawing a line straight from royalty to arms smuggling.' He corrected himself. 'Alleged arms smuggling.'

Matthew emptied a tin of its contents—pins and clips—and slid it towards Jacko. 'He wanted to recheck the papers personally. Doesn't altogether trust Toby. He wanted time to consult the Board of Trade. He's a stickler for that sort of detail. Even now he's terrified it will come out.'

'Why?'

'Well, the end line is, isn't it, that our stuff turned up in Iraqi hands and the most authentic documentation in the world won't change that in the public's perception, will it?'

True, Jacko acknowledged privately. So what would the scheming old fart do? He approached the question in stages. 'So did you or your father come up with an offer to Summers to soften the financial blow?'

His dark eyes were on alert. 'What do you mean?'

'Well, another house and garden spread.'

A relieved look. 'That was my mother's doing.'

'Photographic PR work for all your companies to compensate for the story—well, half a story—he was passing up?' Jacko was thinking of those well-taken photos hanging in the boardroom at Midshires Munitions and Hamb's study.

Alert again. 'No.'

Go for it, Jacko, he told himself. 'Tipping him off about royal visitors to Island Lodge?'

A thunderstruck look. 'Why should we do that?' Barely above a mumble.

'So Summers would earn good money from the tabloid end of Fleet Street and forget all about arms-to-Iraq for the *Sunday Times.*' A numbed face now. 'Like your dad always says, that would be bad PR.'

A longer silence. His head dropped. His shoulders rounded.

'Tell us the truth, Matthew,' said Jacko, softly, screwing out his butt in the tin.

'Oh, Christ.' A defeated sigh. 'It's Dad's doing.' He shook his head. 'He's got this thing about having his name, better still his picture, in the paper. No matter in what connection. Provided it reflects well, of course. If it doesn't, he sues. It's a bloody obsession. Deeply embarrassing for the rest of us.'

'So what arrangement did you come to?' Hazel asked.

'He liked this Summers fellow, or at least liked what he'd heard about him from Mother. He takes a shine to people, strangers even, gives them jobs, hand-outs. Willis is another example.

'He asked me to ring Summers afterwards, just to say thank you for being so understanding, honourable, and offer a helping hand. Summers told me when we were alone about having to come back here and the difficulties of finding work. You know that?'

Jacko nodded.

'It wasn't a bribe, believe me. Dad's like that. Impetuous gestures. I have to clean up behind him.'

'And what was Summers' reaction?'

'Thanks very much, naturally. Really, Dad was using Summers. Every time a royal picture appeared from Rutland Water he got a mention. It tickled him pink. He saw no harm in it.'

'So no money changed hands on either side?' Hazel said.

'No, gracious, no.' Matthew looked disgusted at the very thought. 'Absolutely not.'

'How,' asked Jacko slowly, 'does your father's publicity seeking square with the media paranoia you mentioned?'

'Oh, he delights in what he views as

good publicity. But he has to control it. You saw him charm them on Monday.'

Jacko nodded. 'If he saw no harm in tipping off Summers, did you?'

'Most certainly. It's a breach of hospitality.'

'Why do it then?'

'Haven't I already told you? You do as you're told. Anyway, didn't last long. The royal detectives started to ask questions. About Summers' sources and so forth. It was so obvious, wasn't it? Far too close to home. You saw through it, too, didn't you? That's why you're here.'

Jacko repeated the nod and rephrased the question. 'What did you do about it?'

'Told him. Dad, I mean. Warned him. I told him his job as the next Lord Lieutenant was on the line.'

'Did he agree to stop?'

'He saw the force of the argument, yes. He told me to inform Summers about Monday's hunting engagement, but to tell him it would be the last.'

'How did you make contact with him?'

'He called.'

'Where?'

A nod in the direction of Corby.

'When?'

'Saturday.'

Jacko sighed deeply. 'And you withheld that from me, too?'

Matthew shrugged apologetically.

Jacko continued. 'A personal call or on the phone?'

'Both. He dropped into the office on Saturday. He knew I'd be there. I'm always there.' Grumbling again. 'He was on his way to some football match in Nottingham.'

'Did he often drop in?'

'Only two or three times. On his way to see his mother or on a job.'

'Wasn't that risky? Showing his face at your place of work?'

'Not really. No one would recognize him there, apart from Toby.'

Hazel butted in with a series of sharp questions. 'Was Mr Blewis there on Saturday morning?'

A headshake.

'What did you say to each other?'

'I told him there might be a hunting engagement on Monday, but it hadn't been confirmed. He said he'd ring later. Which he did, from a call box that night.'

'What did you tell him?'

'Just that it was definitely on, usual time.'

'How did you know that?'

'Willis informed me that Sandringham had been on and confirmed.'

Jacko frowned, thinking, lighting up another cigarette. 'You had Summers in the office and then on the phone. Why didn't you tell him to stay away, the source had been turned off and he was no longer welcome?'

'Father's idea again. He wanted Willis to catch him and chase him off. A bit of a security show to impress the Palace. Sometimes he thinks that simplistically. He's just a big exhibitionist. You must have realized that.'

Not half, Jacko agreed privately. 'Did Captain Willis know what was going on?'

'About?' A puzzled look.

'About you, on your father's instructions, tipping Summers off where and when to be for his royal photos?'

A horrified look. 'Good God, no. Absolutely not. All he knew was that Summers was becoming a pest. He only had to read the papers to see that. I told him on Monday first thing to keep a sharp eye open for him and send him packing.

267

That was supposed to be his job, anyway.'
Pause. 'Met him?'

Jacko nodded.

'Not the world's brightest spark, would you say, the army's best and bravest?' A sneer in his voice, he was feeling for a broadsheet newspaper in the pocket of the jacket hanging from his chair, pulled its masthead into view, pushed it back again. The *Daily Telegraph*, Jacko had just time to note.

Jacko, who hadn't had time to read it, or any of them yet, said nothing. First, his father smears Blewis, he was thinking, and now he's smearing Willis. Why?

'Did Toby Blewis know of this arrangement?' asked Hazel.

A long slow headshake. 'Only father and me and now you two. Toby knew about Summers staking out the island, of course. Every hunt member did. But that's all.'

Jacko decided to open up the alternative line of inquiry. 'You and Mr Blewis are very close, aren't you?'

His relieved look again, happy at the change of topic. 'He's good at his job and a good sport, yes.'

'Is he homosexual?'

His mouth fell open. 'Now look here—'

'Yes or no.'

'I refuse—'

'You look here,' said Jacko flatly. 'We're investigating a murder that's making the front pages all over the world. We suspected at first that covering up some arms scandal might be the motive. Subject to what my chief says, what you and your father have told us eliminates that.

'We also have to consider the possibility of hushing up a sex scandal. Your father has implied to us...' He flicked his head towards Hazel. '...that he is homosexual. So has another witness.' He was thinking of Sally Masters. 'Now.' Pause. 'Yes or no.'

He looked away, pain on his face. 'Yes.'

'Is Captain Willis a homosexual?'

The answer was immediate this time. 'Don't know. Wouldn't surprise me, not that I care, but I don't know.'

'Are Mr Blewis and Captain Willis close?'

'Ah, I see.' Enlightened eyes. 'No. No. Nothing like that between them. No.'

269

'Sure?'

'Positive. Toby has a long-term relationship; very stable.'

'You?' Jacko looked with a kindly expression over the rim of his bifocals, like a priest at confessional. 'Are you having a relationship with him?'

'What?'

'Are you homosexual?'

Matthew fell back in his chair in laughter, shocked and forced. 'Lord, no. Heavens, no. You must be very short of leads, Inspector.'

Jacko smiled grimly. 'We'll need to see them both.'

'Surely, not to—'

'Is Mr Blewis here?'

'His only association with our family business is at Midshires. That's all he has time for with his political duties. Lucky old him.' A martyr's features. 'Me? Here and six others, quarries and shipping, too.'

That's inherited wealth and power for you, sonny, Jacko wanted to say. Instead: 'Is he at Midshires today?'

'London.' A defiant look, then a short silence. 'Don't ask me where. I want nothing to do with this.'

'We'll find him,' said Jacko with absolute confidence.

'You do, then,' He was shaking his head angrily. 'You want him, you find him, without my help. I've said enough. I'm washing my hands of it.'

'We don't intend to tell him of this discussion, or your father that you've helped us clear up the riddle over Summers' source,' said Jacko, soothingly.

'Bloody well hope not.' He almost gasped it; then quieter: 'More than my life's worth.'

'Tipping off the press is not a criminal matter anyway. But it's useful to know.'

'I wish I'd never told you. Or about Toby.'

'You've been a tremendous—'

'I should never have—'

'Come now, Matthew.' Jacko put on an encouraging expression. 'You were only doing what you were brought up by your father to do. Be honest. Isn't that another of his favourite sayings?'

'I think I've been over-honest,' he said with a look of sheer misery.

'Pity you weren't yesterday,' said Jacko, very brusquely. 'You could have saved us twenty-four hours.'

16

'It's difficult sometimes...' Jacko was musing aloud for Hazel, doing his mentor bit. '...for a detective to decide just how to construct an interview.'

A bit like writing detective novels, he supposed. That problem was for the future when he retired. What preoccupied him now was how to approach Captain Simon Willis.

In the incident room they'd found time to scan the papers. McAllister of Fine Focus, had made his second killing in two days.

CAPTAIN COURAGEOUS, said several headlines over the collected photo, alongside Charles, his bay horse and Hamb. He was a national hero, an ex-military lion. A modest one, too. Not a word had he said to the media from hospital.

In the absence of what Hazel called 'I-was-there quotes', the press had dug deep into his background, quoting mainly neighbours and a few old schoolmates, but no girlfriends and nothing from his parents.

Nothing surprising in that, Jacko had decided, but what did make him think was his rather humble upbringing.

From Lord Hamb's press conference he'd learned that Willis's roots were in Uppingham, a genteel little market town with a fine array of stone buildings, nearer to Oakham than Corby in every way.

It was famous in Jacko's memory because of a cantankerous resident who refused to move his old banger from outside his house when police festooned his street with yellow no-parking cones to make way for Princess Di on a private visit (not an official engagement) to a friend's wedding. He refused to pay his court fine, too, and went off to jail—a happy martyr to his brand of republicanism. Jacko had rather admired him.

In normal people's minds the town is more famous for its public school. Automatically, he'd assumed the Cap'n's family would be upper middle class and that he would have gone there.

He had no strong feelings about fee-paying education but, in drink on wild nights out in the HQ's local, anyone

(Silent Knight, for instance) who was known to have attended one was loudly branded, not always behind their backs, as a public school poofter.

It was very wrong of him, he'd accept, apologetically, next morning. This mildly hungover lunchtime, he was conceding, he'd been wrong about Willis.

His father's National Service as a Service Corps clerk was in Cyprus during the EOKA troubles, Jacko had read. He still worked in admin with a local authority. His mother was formerly a district nurse.

They lived in a two-bedroom semi, bought from the council, and had sacrificed holidays to take their son out of the local comp at sixteen and send him to a sixth-form college that specialized in turning out officer cadets.

But he was sure (well, almost) that he was a poofter (albeit not public school). Not because Matthew had hinted at as much, but because of the way he'd acted so awkwardly, recoiling almost, when faced with that delightful Irish nurse at the hospital on Monday.

'How are you going to tackle it?' asked Hazel over home-made beef soup and crispy hot bread rolls in the Vaults on the tiny market square with cricketing photos and trophies on the walls.

'There are two basic ways—hard in, straight to the heart of it, or softly-softly, leading the interviewee gently through the story from A to Z.' His face was decidedly undecided. 'It's one of those choices you have to make and you know whichever you pick will turn out to be the wrong one.'

'You can't tackle him in front of his folks,' she said, unhappily. He shook his head. 'So how are we going to play it then?'

Willis sat in a pale green armchair, part of a three-piece suite. His back was to the bay window, the postage-stamp sized front garden and the press cars which blocked the cul-de-sac.

His balm-free face and arms, bare from the elbows in his white T-shirt, were lobster pink. His face coloured red when Hazel followed Jacko into a small, warm front room.

He got up immediately, ran up the carpeted stairs and returned in a thickish check shirt which looked uncomfortable at the neck.

'Good write-up this morning,' Hazel

complimented him.

'Embarrassing,' he replied in Jacko's direction.

Every question, all chatty, casual stuff, she asked he answered towards Jacko. For half an hour, they played it very badly indeed, getting nowhere.

Mrs Summers, a small slim woman, greying attractively, began to complain about being up and down all the time answering knocks on the door from journalists. 'We've had to take the phone off the hook.' Both parents had flat local accents, nothing like their son's which had been smoothed by Sandhurst and in officers' messes.

'I know,' said Hazel. 'That's why we couldn't ring to make a date.' She smiled at Willis, not at all simpering, but he immediately looked away to the gas fire in a cream-tiled hearth.

Mr Summers, quite tall, with a creased face, hooked nose and pot belly, grumbled morosely about not even being able to go down to his local for a lunchtime drink.

Jacko smiled through the sparkling spiel Hazel had prepared over coffee in the Vaults. 'Best to give them something in return for a promise to be left in peace.'

Willis listened with dismay on his face, too polite (or was it shy?) to protest.

She predicted all the questions the journalists would ask, the replies they were looking for. 'Why,' she said, as if a thought had just occurred, turning to Mr Summers, 'we'll tell 'em all to see us at your local.' He brightened considerably.

Pride in her eyes, Mrs Summers began to sort through a lacquered box of snapshots, Hazel helping to make selections that would have made pound signs revolve, like stars on a fruit machine, in McAllister's eyes at Fine Focus.

They went into the hall to put on their coats. Mrs Summers popped her head back round the lounge door. 'They're bound to ask why you left the army. What shall I tell them?'

'Just say I was head-hunted,' said Willis, coldly, not even looking at Jacko now.

'We're convinced that Verne Summers was killed by a professional.' Sitting on the sofa, Jacko went hard in, to the heart of it, as soon as the door had shut.

'We believe this hitman was hired to stop him exposing either an arms or a sex scandal. Let's deal with them in that

277

order. What, if anything, do you know about arms smuggling?'

'Only a little. Too little, as it turned out.' Willis's face was extremely sad. 'It cost me my commission.'

His reply was a riddle to Jacko. 'Let's go through that from A to Z,' he said, flexibly switching tactics.

Willis had been in Cyprus in charge of the same squadron that served under him in England. A cushy posting compared to his father's days there. Maintaining the peace line between Greeks and Turks, replacing the sandbags, extending runways for the RAF down south, building a firing range. Too cushy for him after spells in Ulster; boring in fact.

He'd taken up sailing, made lots of new friends at a boat club, a couple of local businessmen's sons among them. 'Picked up the lingo, too. Useful.'

One day the three of them were coming into Limassol. 'I noticed something I didn't regard as odd at the time.'

He went back even further. There were a couple of bloody-minded sappers in his sixty-strong squadron, troublemakers. One Scot. One Scouse. Willis claimed not to be too hot on discipline, but they wouldn't salute when top brass was about, bullied their mates, refused to settle card school debts.

'Both wanted to join the Special Air Services. They'd never touch them with a ten-foot pole. Certainly, they were strong enough, but they just hadn't got it psychologically.'

'In what way?'

'In the SAS you have to work as a team. They were Rambos. They'd have been...' Don't say it, Jacko privately pleaded. Willis did. '...loose cannons. They regarded themselves as great explosive experts. They were useless.'

'Overcooked it, you mean?'

'Undercooked it. They seldom used enough poundage. Once they failed to dislodge a tree stump, the simplest of tasks.'

He resumed his story. Sailing into Limassol that day, he saw the two sappers boarding a local-registered boat, an old rust bucket. A week later, helicopters were scrambled after an SOS from that same vessel that it was sinking in the Med and the crew was abandoning ship. The island's media speculated about sabotage because it was loaded with arms bound, according to the documentation, for the Royal Oman Police.

Willis asked his two sappers what they'd been doing on board. 'Playing poker with the crew,' they claimed. He'd been told by his sergeant that they were flush with money, unheard of with their duff bluffs. 'A winning streak,' they explained.

'I got to thinking that they may have been sort of syphoning off some of the explosives they should have been using—it would have explained their underestimating the required charge—and they could have sold it on to the crew.'

'Why?'

An unsure shrug. 'An insurance fraud or to facilitate an arms transfer. Both, possibly. It's not unknown in that part of the world.'

'What did you do?'

'Reported my suspicions to the Special Investigations Branch. They came back later and said the sole survivor from the crew had been picked up off the Lebanese coast. He blamed it on a boiler burst. No wreckage was found and no one could prove otherwise.'

Weeks later, at a diplomatic party in

Nicosia, he was introduced to Lord Hamb and his wife. 'We got talking about mutual connections with Rutland. Then I mentioned that boat business to him.'

Jacko asked 'Why?' again.

'It was one of his.'

The one Hamb himself had talked about last night, Jacko realized. 'He half suspects sabotage by Mossad.'

'He didn't mention that to me, just said it was a mystery.'

'What did you suspect?'

'You must be aware that I'm not entirely *au fait* with intelligence.' A self-deprecating smile.

He may have a lot more than they—or I—gave him credit for, Jacko was slowly beginning to appreciate. 'Then what happened?'

Within a fortnight, he continued, another SIB officer came to see him, of higher rank, and produced two statements alleging unofficer-like conduct. The complaints had been made by his two supposed sailing friends.

Jacko guessed what had been alleged, decided against asking him to confirm, not yet, anyway, and said nothing.

'Slanderous.' Willis shook his head, as

if he still couldn't believe anyone could behave in such an unsporting fashion. 'Incredibly vile. I denied it, obviously. I went to seek them out at the club—and I sorted them out, I'm afraid.'

'What do you mean?'

'Fisticuffs.' A guilty look. 'I was called in again. Colonels, the lot. It was made perfectly plain to me that I was to resign within twenty-eight days or I'd be court-martialled with all that would entail. Didn't see much option, do you?'

Jacko shook his head.

Willis went quiet for a little while. Then: 'You haven't asked me.'

A smiling pause, then Jacko asked, 'So did Hamb head-hunt you or is that just for media consumption?'

'Oh, yes. Phoned me up here on my return. Asked me round to Island Lodge. Said he was sorry to hear of my enforced departure. Offered me a job. I thought it would be in civil engineering, surveying roads to his pits, supervising dynamiting at his quarries—'

'Who does that, by the way?' This was not Jacko's end of the inquiry, but he thought it might be useful to know.

'Not sure. Never go there. Sub-contractors, I believe... Instead I got, well, this sinecure post, I suppose you'd call it, but I have my own quarters and, at least I get plenty of time on the water. It hasn't put me off sailing, you see.'

'What happened to the two squaddies?'

'According to a chum in the mess, the only one who still keeps in contact, they got themselves into a knife fight on the docks. Over gambling debts. A local seaman and the Scouse were fatally stabbed.'

'What happened to the Jock?'

'Almost had his hand cut off.'

'What was his name?'

'Starling.'

'Was he charged?'

A headshake, unsure. 'Shipped home, I hear.' A pause. 'Aren't you going to ask me?'

Jacko ignored it completely, covering some old ground. No, he'd never met the Hon Matthew or Toby Blewis in his time in Cyprus. Yes, he'd met them for the first time here in Rutland.

'Are you a particular chum of either?'

'Hardly see much of Toby. He's friendly enough. I get on reasonably well with

283

Matthew. A decent chap, I think you'll find.'

Yes, Willis confirmed, he'd spotted Summers lurking close to the island on previous royal visits. He'd never got close enough to speak to him ('Always scarpered') but he'd worked out how he got to the right hunt meet by following the right horse-box.

'First thing Monday,' he went on, 'Matthew told me to see him off—not literally, I hope you understand.' A friendly smile.

'What were his instructions to you?'

'To let him get on our land so he'd be trespassing and we'd have the law on our side; then to stop him, question him and read him the riot act to let him know that this was the way it was going to be in the future and not to come back.'

His face tensed. He straightened his back. 'I'm going to tell you. No, I am not. I know some people think so. Do you?'

'No,' said Jacko sincerely.

Should have known better, Jacko was chastising himself in the reflective few seconds that followed. You, above all people.

His recollection had taken him back to his own mentor, well into his sixties now, a judge's clerk in the years since he'd retired from the force. A bachelor, he'd lived with his mother and, after she'd died, his sister.

Jacko saw him still, occasionally; not often enough, never often enough for a man who'd taught him the basis of all he knew.

Not only had he never married, he'd never been known to date a woman. He had young cadets under his command. Never a whiff of misconduct, the slightest rumour.

He got on fine with other officers' wives and girls, buying them drinks, sharing stories, but if an unescorted, eligible lady walked into the room he'd go quiet, then excuse himself. He was like a gawky schoolboy in their company, terrified; yet he was a first-class detective, tough as police boots, when he had to be.

Jacko had never fathomed the reason for his shyness. Fear of rejection? Panic about sex, not sure he was any good at it? At heart still yearning for a young, lost love? Jacko had suffered all three symptoms after his first wife walked out. Celibate for a couple of years, he'd been, and not too bothered either.

What coaxed him back, made him seek them out, was not a need for sex, but for their civilized company, their conversation, the different, often better, way they looked at life, the things to be learned from them, and, in a couple of cases, their deep and abiding friendships; warm, trusting relationships that Willis might never discover.

'Thank you,' said Willis.

Jacko smiled to hide the sorrow he'd felt in that quiet little moment for someone who might never experience and value the true worth of a woman.

'Plan A or Plan B?' asked Hazel, eager to learn.

'A bit of both.'

'Did it work?'

'Hard to say.' For others to judge, Jacko judged.

They were backing out of the cul-de-sac to which around half of the press pack had returned, following Mr and Mrs Willis and Hazel from the pub, breaking promises to leave.

'They won't pester them, knock on the

door unless anyone else does,' Hazel explained. 'That way they can't be scooped. Insurance, they call it. News editors have to cover their backs. They won't let them leave until everyone else has left.'

The answer to that seemed simple to Jacko. 'Can't they come to a pact to piss off home and tell their desks that everyone's left?'

'Sometimes they do, but just as often, one of them will double back looking for Brownie points and, if he gets anything fresh, the rest are in trouble.'

What a fucking job, thought Jacko.

They hit the A6003. Hazel feigned rejection. 'You're not holding back on me, are you, after all we've come to mean to each other?'

Jacko laughed briefly. 'Would I—after you let me have the hot water bottle last night?'

'Come on then. Give.'

The only thing he held back was his mentor memory, and he gave another in its place.

Years ago, as a young detective constable at the height of the cold war, he'd been assigned to go with a senior SIB man to the offices of a small-town weekly paper.

Its one reporter had a statement from a local who'd been scavenging on a rubbish tip and found a load of secret papers from a nearby RAF station. Being fair-minded, the old journo phoned the base for a comment. 'Call you back,' they said.

Instead he got a personal call from the SIB man who had no civilian powers, so Jacko was holding a watching brief. At first the SIB officer tried to patronize the veteran reporter ('national security and all of that, old man')—but was being given short shrift.

He changed tactics. He produced criminal and medical records which showed the local totter to be a pathological liar and thief, and samples of the documents he'd claimed to have found; all low-grade restricted stuff. The newspaper decided it couldn't trust his evidence and dropped the story, which all of Fleet Street would have eventually picked up and developed.

In the car afterwards, the SIB man admitted the records had been concocted, the papers had been top-secret, useful to any enemy, and should have been incinerated, not dumped. He'd prevented a major security scandal.

'No one fights dirtier than government departments when their back's to the wall,' said Jacko bitterly. 'Willis acted by the book. He reported his suspicions. The SIB dropped it. Fair enough, perhaps on the evidence of the rescued crewman. Willis doesn't drop it. He goes on about it to Hamb. What happens? They stitched him up completely, smeared him.'

'Who?'

'Hamb and the MoD. Willis had got the scent of a scandal, so they got rid of him. Those homo allegations were fabricated. Probably this two so-called boating mates had been up to something shitty—drugs, say—and they co-operated to stay out of jail. That's why Whitehall were leaning on Silent Knight and were so chary with Velma.'

'And that,' Hazel suggested, 'is why Hamb hired Willis. Not out of the goodness of his heart, but to make him beholden to him.'

Jacko nodded. Like he fancies making a lapdog out of me, he thought.

'How far up does it go, do you think?' she asked.

'Up to, but not including, the Palace.'

'Bastards,' Hazel hissed. 'This time we'll

289

not let them get away with it. Right, Jacko.'

'Right,' said Jacko, but secretly he was fearing that most of them would. Not all of the bastards, though, he vowed.

17

Sixty to seventy-two hours

Mine, grenades, luggage, all packed. Check? One more time Crow felt inside the khaki handgrip on the unmade bed. Check. He zipped it up.

Passport, what's left of the cash, vehicle insurance, in the breast pockets of desert fatigues. Check? Bearded chin down, he unbuttoned both pockets and fingered through them again. Check. He refastened the buttons.

He sat down on the bed. Most of the day, he had been up here alone.

She'd risen miraculously early for her, and had dragged the kids to school for the first time that week, but it took a bribe to end their sobbing protests.

On the way back she bought food. She had fried a brunch, but had not washed up the pots and the pan.

At noon, she'd gone out to mix more shopping with drinking. The kids had been told to meet her outside Woollies in the shopping arcade.

The plan had been to take a cab to Peterborough, a twenty-five quid trip, to go round a classier shopping centre, then out to a multi-screen cinema and, afterwards, have anything but Big Macs with double fries. 'A nice change,' she'd told them.

He knew she would have run through the money like no tomorrow, would be almost spent up. He felt in the left breast pocket for the five notes he'd set aside.

The house that had been so quiet all day burst into noisy, squabbling life downstairs. He stood and picked up the grip from the bed.

'Crow.' The girl craned her neck up and he stooped, so she could kiss him on his cheek's black growth, more than stubble after four no-shaving days. She grimaced as it prickled her lips. 'They should call you Blackbeard.'

'Or Blackbird.' He forced a short laugh

as he put the grip on the untidy table. 'Good time?'

'Smashing.'

Crow looked down at the boy who had already clambered over his luggage, turned on the television and was sitting cross-legged on the carpet in front of the screen. 'Good time?'

'Yeah.' The boy didn't look up.

Their mother had followed, carelessly placing colourful plastic shopping bags on to a heap the children had already started just inside the door. With his two big back-packs, the rolled and strapped-up tent and sleeping bag wrapped in his buff-coloured cape-cum-groundsheet, there was little leg room left.

'More parcels than Christmas,' she purred, pleased. Her tone changed. 'Brr. It's freezing in here.' She glanced at the unlit gas fire, then him. 'Aren't you freezing?'

'Been upstairs packing and changing,' he said.

She picked her way, not at all nimbly, through the piles of luggage and shopping to the fire. 'What a sodding shambles.' She pressed down the ignition button and held it in place for the ten seconds it took to fire.

She stared at him. 'Why you dressed like that already? Aren't we going for a few drinks first?' Her face was flushed, not just from the cold, he suspected. Her voice was thick, and he was certain she had already had more than a few at lunchtime; a real lagging for the effects to last this long.

'Change of travel orders.'

'Bloody hell,' she sighed exasperated. 'What now?'

'The major was round while you lot were gone.' He nodded down at the packs and tent. 'That's why I stowed everything.'

'Thought you said dawn,' she said. Drinking heightened, never impaired, her memory. Coming down from a long session, she could be questioning and quarrelsome.

'Changed to twenty-one hours.' He looked at his waterproof watch. 'Less than an hour to spare.'

'Where?'

He told her.

'Why?'

The answer to this had bothered him. He'd thought of saying: 'The OC wants to break the back of the trip north overnight while the traffic's light on the A1.' But he needed this place as a bolt-hole, if the mission had to be aborted. Sound contingency planning, he'd convinced himself.

'Night exercise to bed us in,' he replied.

She shot him a silencing look. She panted for him to talk about night exercises in the bedroom, encouraged all his manoeuvres, like being taken prisoner and manhandled, but regarded it all as Top Secret, not to be mentioned in front of the kids. 'It's fucking freezing out there. Feels like snow.'

Crow had made contingencies for that, too. He was wearing his arctic gear between top fatigues and long johns. They served a dual purpose. For a quick change of camouflage, if it was white over in the morning. And because of a new golden rule he'd taken from a magazine: 'Several thin layers of clothing are preferable to one thick layer to insulate against cold.'

He nodded to the strapped tent. 'I'll be under that.'

'Rather you than me.'

'I've got to go through it, if I want to get back in the outfit. You'd like that, wouldn't you—steady pay?'

She did not respond.

'Married quarters?'

'Got to be better than here, I suppose,'

she replied without enthusiasm.

'A posting to somewhere warm like HK border patrol?'

She nodded, even less enthusiastically. She didn't want to leave her drinking pals or her mum, and never would. He already knew that. But he had to leave; to test himself over and over again and earn big money as a mercenary and perhaps win a foreign equivalent of the Victoria Cross.

Still standing, she held a cigarette to the bars of the gas fire until it glowed and smelt of scorched paper. He hated cigarettes and their smell, the way they damaged people's lungs and slowed them down. She was a chain-smoker when she had the money. He loathed the habit. Once, when he said so, she had poured a pan of cold baked beans over his shaved head.

'What time you setting off?' she asked.

He'd planned for this question and didn't want to pitch the reply too early, in case he had to return to change clothes and transport in an emergency.

The collection had been fixed for eleven thirty. He'd be there fourteen hours before that. A long time, true, but he had things to do.

He'd kip, if he could, in the tent by the water. He'd eat before and after sleep from rations he'd packed in greaseproof and double-wrapped, in the *Sun* this time.

Long before dawn he'd use the flash to plant the mine in the road at the spot he'd pinpointed yesterday.

It would be a long sentry-go, no two hours on and four off like his square-bashing days. There'd be no bunking or dozing off. He'd do what a guard should do—keep vigil. Clever that, he'd thought. A play on words. He wondered if it had been too clever.

He'd maintain observation, watch him arrive and make sure no one else, another hitman, arrived earlier and was lying in wait. If so, he'd grenade him first, collect the fourteen grand and let that prick escape down that road until... Transmitter to hand? Check? He patted a pocket at his thigh. Check.

Straight out of the textbook; as good as anything he'd read in his magazines.

He accepted from painful personal experience that there was no such thing as a perfect plan. No one could foresee all possible circumstances—lovers screwing too long in a car, an unexpected visit from a postman or milkman or newsboy; all potential witnesses.

Anyone can have the sort of unlucky break we got in Limassol when that poofter officer just happened to be sailing by and saw us boarding that ship.

So this place was his fall-back position. If he had to return he could claim that one of the vehicles in the convoy had broken down and he had to pick up the van.

All of this he had thought through so his answer was immediate.

'Noonish,' he said.

'Tomorrow?' she asked.

He nodded.

'Bloody hell. Why go now?'

'Told you. Night exercise and then a kip before hitting the road.'

'Will you be able to nip back here for something to eat?'

For sex, she really means, he thought, and that means she's too fagged to fancy it now; good.

'If there's a breakdown,' he ad-libbed, making it sound a possibility.

'How yer going to get there?' she asked.

'It's miles from anywhere.'

'Being picked up in a jeep outside the *Evening Telegraph* office.'

'Taking the van?'

He shook his head, then flicked through the uncurtained window to the street where the van was parked by the kerb. 'Leaving it here.'

In reserve, he'd decided. In case of unforeseen circumstances, if he had to retreat back here by foot, it would serve as standby getaway.

'Want me to run you up there?'

In your state, he thought, with no licence or insurance? The cops will pull us in before the mission gets under way. He kept this to himself, not wanting a row. 'What—and have all my mates taking the piss?' He was smiling. She wasn't. 'Shank's pony. Break in my boots.'

He hadn't far to walk, just a few hundred yards to a free council car-park where the Land Rover had been all day.

No smile from her still, trouble brewing, he cautioned himself. 'Use the van as a runabout while I'm away, if you want.'

Her face clouded. For some time he'd sensed that she had never really accepted his stories, except in the bedroom. Now he knew she'd never believed what he'd been telling her about being recalled one day. He was leaving, actually going. She hated being on her own with the kids, needed a man about the house. At her age, and with her looks and habits, she'd have difficulty finding another.

'Listen.' Still smiling, he undid a breast pocket. 'The OC gave me an advance. Subsistence allowance. For travel.' He took out five folded twenty-pound notes. 'Have it.'

He handed it over, thinking: I'll have it back tomorrow, if I have to. She can't spend it by noon. She's not normally up that early, not two days in a row.

'What about us?' said the girl from the split sofa.

'Ask your ma.'

'Mum?'

'Shut up,' she replied, disturbed as she counted it.

'I'll be off then.' He lifted his gear on to the table and wriggled his shoulders into the harness. He'd not strap the tent and wrapped-up sleeping bag to the top pack, as per regulation. He'd carry them under his arm to his transport. No one that mattered would see him.

It took some time—and some trouble—to kit up and he got no help. The children watched TV and their mother lit a new cigarette from the butt of the old.

He picked up the grip last and turned, forcing himself to smile. 'How do I look?'

'Like that English parachutist in that Eighth Army film,' said the girl.

'British, if you don't mind.' He smiled. She half stood on the sofa and kissed him again, on the lips this time.

'So long, son,' he said to the boy.

'I'm not your sodding son,' said the boy, not looking from the screen.

'Shut it, you ungrateful little bastard,' shouted his mother.

'What's a matter now?' asked Crow, much softer.

'Don't suppose you fixed the boat.'

'You've been out all bloody day. I wanted you to be—'

'You promised.'

'We'll sail it when I come back.'

The woman followed him to the door. So laden was he that he had to twist one shoulder to manoeuvre himself through the frame.

Pitched forward under the weight on his

back, he turned to her. 'I'll send you a postcard.'

'Just you bloody well behave yourself with all those Scottish slags.' Her puffy, flushed features set severely; no joke there, a deadly warning.

This, he hoped, would be the last word he'd hear from her, the last sight he'd see of her. A feeling of freedom flooded through him, a fabulous feeling.

She did not take the cigarette out of her clamped mouth and he made no attempt to kiss her goodbye.

He turned away into the cold night. Even before he reached the always open back garden gate he heard the kitchen door slam shut.

18

For almost an hour they had been hanging around the airport desk where, after a few calls back at the incident room, they'd established that the elusive Toby Blewis would have to check in for the flight he'd booked to Brussels.

'Another five minutes and we'll have to close,' said the red-suited hostess.

'Are you absolutely sure he hasn't cancelled?' asked Jacko. He'd asked it twice already. This time she couldn't be bothered to answer.

Hazel had finally spotted a spare place in a block of green seats in front of the large square check-in desk, but moved too slowly to claim it, beaten by a back-packer who'd been squatting on the fawn-tiled floor.

The departure hall was crowded and noisy. Jacko had a headache from the almost constant tannoy announcements, the droning of the air conditioning and the squeaking of the wheels on the luggage trolleys. He felt as if he was in a busy supermarket. He hated supermarkets. At least he could smoke here. He lit another, dragging on it deeply, adding to his headache.

On the M25, they had hit rush-hour traffic and it had taken well over two hours door-to-door to get to Heathrow.

It was hot, and Jacko was glad he hadn't collected his thermals when he'd picked up his passport on his flying visit home more than twenty-four hours ago now.

Making him hotter, beginning to sweat, was a nagging suspicion, without any foundation but real all the same, that Blewis had conned everyone about his travelling plans, had made alternative arrangements and, with all his foreign contacts, was at this very moment disappearing off the face of the earth.

Why the hell can't he turn up in good time like everyone else; me, for instance? he inwardly fumed. He was an anxious traveller, arriving so early at airports that he often spent more time in the departure lounge than in the air.

Then he saw Blewis appearing out of the open-plan W H Smith shop, *Evening Standard* tucked under an arm. One hand held a small case, the other his passport and ticket. A heavy blue coat was slung carelessly over a black pin-striped shoulder.

Unhurried, the seasoned jet-setter, he strolled past the Body Shop. Only then did he see Jacko, whose anxiety did not lessen with the knowledge that, unless he talked Blewis into postponing his trip, he wouldn't get to talk to him much at all.

'Half expected to see you,' said Blewis, not unfriendly, as he placed his ticket and passport on the cream plastic counter.

'We've been looking for you most of the day,' Jacko said; moaned, really.

'I've had a meeting in town.'

'We have a few more questions.'

'Have to wait, I'm afraid.'

'There's seats on the six fifty-five tomorrow, same airline. I've checked. You can have a room on us at—'

'Got a supper engagement.' Blewis didn't look at him as he opted for a non-smoking seat and for his case to go as hand luggage.

'It is important. It's a murder after...' Jacko stopped in front of the hostess.

Blewis didn't. 'Are you detaining me?'

'Of course not.'

'Then I've every right to go about my lawful business.' He swept up his passport and boarding card.

'Yes, but...' Jacko was left with his mouth hanging open as Blewis, without looking across his shoulder, started to walk, still unhurried, beyond a line of more shops towards the departure gates.

Decision time again and whatever you decide will be wrong, Jacko thought pessimistically. 'Got any seats left?'

'Yes,' said the hostess. 'But you need...'

He slipped his passport and credit card

wallet from an inside pocket. 'What's the earliest you can get me back?'

She keyed into a screen. 'First flight tomorrow at seven twenty their time.'

'Book me on that, too.' Jacko felt in another pocket and handed his car keys to a tired-looking Hazel. 'Go home. Get a car to pick me up at...' He looked at the hostess.

'Seven twenty-five our time.'

Hazel nodded.

The hostess began to ask, 'Smoking or non—'

Jacko inclined his head in the direction in which Blewis had disappeared into the crowd. 'Next to him, if poss.'

'Luggage?'

Jacko held out both arms, as if submitting to a frisking. 'Not even an overnight bag.'

'If I hadn't heard that conversation, I'd have suspected you were fleeing the country and I would have called the law.' The hostess smiled as she pushed his documents at him.

'I am the law, madam,' he said, with play-acted pomposity.

She beamed now. 'You'll have to hurry, Lieutenant Columbo.'

Jacko did; so fast that he didn't say goodnight to Hazel or ask her to phone his wife to tell her where her wandering husband had gone to now.

'Ah.' Blewis lifted his blue coat from the seat next to him. 'We meet again. Thought we might.'

He handed up the coat for Jacko to stow with his brown mac in the cream cabinet above their heads. He sat down and belted up.

'Sorry about that,' said Blewis. 'I really do have an engagement.'

'Mmm.' Jacko was prepared to wait until they'd gone through the introductory pleasantries from the captain, the taxiing and the lifebelt drill, and they were airborne.

Blewis wasn't. 'Now you have me cornered...' He smiled invitingly.

'Spoken to Matthew, have you?' Jacko began.

A brisk nod. 'Briefly, on the phone.' A sad sigh. 'You left him in a right old state. Seen the good Captain Willis, too, I suppose?'

Jacko nodded.

'Still not satisfied?'

'About that aspect of the case, yes,' said Jacko.

A satisfied smile. 'He's not, you know.'

Jacko said nothing, thinking: Gays do know, must be able to recognize each other, spot the signs, in the same way that some men know when a woman fancies them. Not that either ever happened to him.

'What then?' asked Blewis, lowering himself, relaxing.

Jacko got some loose ends out of the way first. Yes, Blewis confirmed, he had seen that 1982 photo of the arms pile in the Falklands from Fine Focus files, but not Hamb or Matthew and it wasn't Summers who showed it to him.

'I've checked the paperwork again. It was ordered months before anyone could have dreamt that the Argies would invade. There's nothing in that, believe me.'

Jacko did. He dismissed it as a red herring.

Yes, Blewis said, he had been present when Summers produced the Gulf War arms pile photo in the offices of Midshires Munitions on his first visit. 'It caused great consternation until I found the papers in order.'

'How long did that take?'

'Only five minutes or so.'

Not long enough, Jacko reasoned, for Matthew to have negotiated Summers' silence there and then with an offer of free tips on the royals. That must have been set up in a later phone call. Matthew must have told me the truth about that. 'Why didn't you tell me all of this yesterday?'

'Sorry about that, old man.' A regretful face. 'Personally, I would have, but Matthew wanted clearance from his bastard of a pater.'

So absorbing was Blewis's rundown that followed on Lord Hamb that Jacko completely missed the usual tense minute or two as the plane picked up speed and the wait for the comforting clank of the wheels folding up into the wings. Even his ears escaped their usual waxed-up feeling.

'He's absolutely impossible. Pays his execs, even Matthew, very low basics, very high commission. "Hard work equals results" is one of his little homilies. Sermonizing shithouse.' It was as if flying off had freed his captive soul. 'I'll be pleased to be out of it.'

'How do you handle him then?'

'By staying out of the way as far as possible...'

Like me with Silent Knight, Jacko conceded.

'...and doing his bidding when you can't.'

Like me when Hamb hijacked me on the way back from hospital, Jacko concurred guiltily.

'I'll be out of it soon,' Blewis added with a pleasurable expression.

'You've landed a safe seat, I hear.'

A contented smile. 'Earned my spurs.'

He'd fought the two previous general elections in shipbuilding and coalfield constituencies, with rate-capped councils and heavy poll taxes, he said rather proudly, like a soldier who'd seen real action. Anyone who'd taken two hammerings at the polls like he must have done deserved a soft seat in a southern shire, Jacko acknowledged. 'Well done.'

Blewis clearly didn't regard Jacko's congratulations as premature and all but rubbed his hands. 'Roll on the election. Even the Commons can't be as much of a madhouse as working for him. It's been eight long years of hell, I can tell you.'

Bongs sounded for seat belts off and

cigarettes on. Jacko felt for his Bensons, then realized he was in a non-smoker's seat. 'What's his problem?'

'Ego. Haven't you noticed? Wouldn't be surprised if he wasn't photographed coming out of his mother's womb.'

Jacko wondered if Matthew had admitted to Blewis that on his publicity-crazed father's orders, he'd been tipping off Summers to royal photo opportunities at Rutland Water.

He suspected not; too hot for a future MP, soon to be freed from company loyalties. He decided against double-checking, another quest in mind: to find out if Matthew had told the truth about the cameraman who took those photos hanging on the wall at Midshires Munitions.

'Those photos in your boardroom—'

'Another bloody example,' Blewis broke in. 'Ordered sets to go up on all company premises last week. Cost a packet and then he complains about profits. His fizzog...' A local word for face, unusual when spoken with such a cultured accent. '...on all, you may have noticed.'

'Not the one with the white boat,' Jacko pointed out.

A shrug that said: Granted. 'Even he

310

wouldn't fly to the Philippines just for one snapshot.'

So it was having its funnel replaced in the Philippines, not Africa, thought Jacko, a touch shamed by his geography. 'It's a long way from home. What's it doing out there?'

'Ferrying foodstuffs. Matthew wants to diversity. Our normal trade is a bit...' He flicked a thumb downwards.

'I couldn't ID its flag. Not Cyprus, is it?'

'Cayman Islands. That's just its port of registration.' A sideways smile. 'Tax reasons. Matthew's quite cute.'

A chip off the old block, thought Jacko. 'The rest of those photos—the aerial shots of the string of barges, the water sports centre and so on—who took them?'

'Ah.' An understanding beam, seeing through the question. Blewis had commissioned them personally, he said, from a commercial photographer. He gave his name and address in Northampton. 'Not Summers. On the wrong track there, I'm afraid, Inspector.'

Jacko's anxiety returned as he wondered if he was running up a big travel bill for nothing.

The hostess came round with meals on plastic trays. Jacko took his. Blewis declined, apart from the white wine.

Jacko fiddled to unwrap his cutlery, concentrating on an always difficult manoeuvre, cramped for space. 'Normal trade's bad, then?'

A glum face, suddenly brightening. 'I'll say one thing in Hamb's favour. He runs a clean company in that respect. There's nothing dodgy about our arms deals, believe me.'

Jacko ate his way through melon and a lecture on the arms trade, much of it an expansion on Hamb's the night before.

'Iraq was very persona grata till the mid-eighties. "My enemy's enemy is my friend" and all that. And Iran was the big enemy then. Don't all want to be praying to the east with our women behind veils, now do we?' A low chuckle.

Then came the arms embargo and firms were not being paid by Baghdad the balance owed on goods earlier supplied. 'Lots of firms are in deep trouble.'

Jacko tried to bite off a cynical smile with a forkful of chicken breast, failed.

'I can see that amuses you,' said Blewis, evenly. 'Does most liberals.'

Got me pegged politically, anyway, Jacko admitted.

'See us as merchants of death, do you? What you don't see is that there has to be a balance of arms to maintain the stability of oil. You'd be the first to complain if your force's fleet of cars ran out of petrol.'

Jacko was biting on his chicken, nothing else, not wanting a philosophical debate.

'You're in no real position to criticize anyway. Would the police give up their arms unilaterally?'

Impossible, acknowledged Jacko acidly, but only because your trade keep churning them out for terrorists and robbers to get hold of.

'Quite apart from jobs, there's the intelligence aspect.' Blewis seemed to be trying to convince himself. 'By collating all the info we give them, the western powers know who is capable of waging what.'

Waging wars, he's talking about, Jacko knew. Marginally interesting that. 'Are you telling me that businessmen like you act as MI6 agents?'

He wasn't expecting a straight answer, so wasn't surprised by Blewis's evasive smile. 'They're not all James Bonds in espionage, you know.' Then, half an answer: 'And journalists, too, I think you'll find.'

Jacko tried not to gulp his too tart Muscadet. Never thought of that. Could Verne Summers have been a freelance government agent as well as a freelance cameraman, one set of pictures for Fine Focus to market, a secret, more revealing, second set for MI6?

Possible, you know, he told himself.

He was remembering a small incident that had stuck in his own photographic memory from the sixties. A uniformed constable then, he'd been on duty at a peace rally on a common in his home town.

Sitting on a fence, trying to look disinterested, had been a couple of CID officers and a man from Special Branch. A local newsman he knew walked up to them, bold as brass. A huddled conversation followed. The Special Branch man handed the journo a camera from under his raincoat.

He went off with it, into the crowd, and took photos of every one of the speakers and sections of the audience as they marched away behind CND banners.

Many he seemed to know and they smiled for his camera.

When they had gone, the journalist handed it back for Special Branch to develop, identify and file. Not for cash, Jacko was sure of that; for goodwill, future help.

Could Summers have operated on similar lines? How could he find out? Who could he ask? Not Blewis, certainly. He was probably in the spying business himself.

'Business still bad then?' asked Jacko idly.

'Been worse. A couple of years back. The shipping line almost went under. If it had, Matthew would have gone down with it.'

'Wasn't that about the time you lost a boat in—'

'Ship.' A pedantic little smile. 'Know about that, too, eh?'

'Hamb mentioned it last night.'

'That was partly the cause of it.'

'Of what?'

'Our financial difficulties.'

'Hamb told me the insurance was paid.'

'Took a long time, though. There was a big inquiry. They made us wait—and sweat.'

'Why?'

Well, said Blewis, there had been one or two cases of suspected scuttling in the past, insurance frauds.

'One ship went down off Beirut, the crew claiming they had hit a mine on the way in. Investigations showed they landed their cargo the day before. The cheeky buggers were claiming insurance for that as well as their old tub. Didn't get away with that one.'

Others had, though, he went on. He told another story, a rumour really, of a ship picking up a crew in a lifeboat whose own vessel had gone down. 'They'd completely rewritten the log. The skipper of the rescue boat found the original after they'd been put ashore. They were so blatant they didn't bother to destroy the evidence. Know what they'd done? Rendezvous-ed with a coaster, unloaded arms, scuttled their own ship and were claiming insurance for the loss of both cargo and vessel.'

'What happened?'

'Nothing. The skipper of the rescue boat wanted no part of it. Report something like that and you can find the Mafia after you in places like the Med.'

'In the case of the...what was its name?'

'*Froura Zo.*'

'What's that mean?'

'Greek. 'Fraid I don't know. Hamb changed them all when he took over. On his wife's say-so. She speaks it like a native. Not her old man or Matt, though.'

Jacko felt a spurt of acid gnawing at his stomach lining.

'Something to do with their wildlife work. Zo means animal in Greek. Something like that. At least he didn't name it after himself.' Blewis pulled a sardonic face.

Jacko put the gnawing down to the Muscadet. 'Hamb told me last night that he suspected Mossad.'

Blewis sneered into his plastic glass. 'Take no notice of him. If it's not Mossad it has to be the PLO or the Fundamentalists. There's always got to be drama for his cocktail and dinner parties.'

'What was it then?'

'A boiler, according to the one survivor who was washed up.'

'What happened to the rest?'

'Filipinos. Didn't make it to shore.'

'And the sole survivor?'

'Greek Cypriot. Went home to his family. Made another trip with us. Then, after surviving all of that, he got himself killed in a knife fight with a Brit over poker debts. Amazing, aren't they, seamen?'

So are some British soldiers, Jacko mused, sure now, beyond the slightest doubt, that the gnawing at his gut had nothing to do with the wine.

A handsome young man, a toy boy really, impeccably dressed, greeted Blewis with a smiling, two-handed grip in a long and narrow arrivals hall. They chatted briefly in French. Then, in English, Blewis introduced Jacko as an old acquaintance he had met by chance on the plane.

'Take the train to Central,' he said, flicking his head beyond a row of bank counters. 'Have a look at the Grand Place, all gothic and gilt,' he added, making it obvious that Jacko was not being invited to join them for supper. 'Goodnight.' With a perfunctory wave, he turned away.

Jacko stood for a second or so beneath a blue sign with a ring of golden stars which said: EC passengers. He'd never felt so European—or so unwanted.

He walked to a bank counter, changed thirty pounds, all he was carrying apart from loose change, into francs at roughly fifty to one. He took the steps down to a ticket office where he was promptly relieved of eighty-five of them. An escalator lowered him to a cold underground platform where a maroon two-coach train stood.

It was a twenty-five minute stop-go ride, comfortable in a soft grey seat, most of it at ground level, watching the yellow haze from street lights thicken as the city centre came closer.

He walked through a tiled foyer and out through a pillared entrance into a busy street. Instinct took him across the street and down a hill into a cobbled square where a fountain played a multitude of freezing sprays on to the bare backsides of water nymphs. He shivered.

Three modern, stylish hotels stood side-by-side. He picked one, not for its stepped gables, but because his credit card was advertised on its tinted glass windows along with the price of what was called 'a simple room'—close on a hundred and forty pounds.

Ah, well, he thought, the taxpayer will pay. He produced his passport and credit card, blamed an airline cock-up for the absence of luggage, and was directed to a lift which took him to his third floor room, clean and comfortable, but too modern for his taste, not at all like the Waldorf.

He picked up the cream bedside phone, followed the international code from a card, added the incident room number. He gave the overnight duty man his number and noted down the details of Velma's digs.

He drank a small but beautiful Belgian beer, priced on the menu at two pounds, from the fridge. He thought about phoning Little Velma, but realized he hadn't worked things out yet. So he drank another beer, stripped, bathed, dried himself, opened a third bottle, climbed into a single bed, smoked a cigarette, thumbing through a free guide which told him he was round the corner from the Grand Place. Sod it, he decided, he wasn't going to get up again. He wanted to rest here and think.

His mind didn't allow him to sleep well, hardly at all. So fast did his brain churn that he tossed and turned and sighed and scratched and never got round to snoring.

He was up before six, at the airport more than an hour ahead of take-off time, fretting as he envisaged, wrongly as it turned out, a long delay.

Having queued to check in, to go

through passport control and security, he decided against joining yet another queue at a duty-free supermarket. The ladies in his life—Jackie, Velma and, currently, Hazel—would have to do without chocolates or lace and he without fags and a bottle of booze.

Even after an incredibly long walk to his gate, further than he took his dog, there was plenty of time to use a round see-through booth, phone Velma's digs and talk to her at length.

He'd arrived and was leaving Brussels in darkness, saw none of its sights, not wanting to, too much on his mind. He had his breakfast, seated among the smokers this time, urging the plane to fly faster.

He was first down the ramp through Immigration and, without a bag to claim, first into Customs.

A peaked-capped officer in white short-sleeves called him across to his bench, eyeing his stubble suspiciously. 'Travelling alone and rather light, aren't you?'

Only his warrant card saved a strip search down to and beyond underpants that weren't his own and had been on for twenty-four hours now (less six for sleep, if you can call it that).

Strewth, he thought, stepping it out beneath ever-changing TV monitors in the arrivals hall, one floor down from Departures, arseholes to that for a job.

He was pleased he wasn't a Customs man, delighted to be a detective, felt tremendous.

The fact, the truth, was that he loved this lousy job on days like this when he knew he was getting somewhere.

19

Extra time

The usual crowd was all there in the incident room; plus Silent Knight, in his grey double-breasted suit. He, Hazel and Happy, the collator, hovered around Velma's desk next to the village hall stage.

He started the discussion without a good-morning. Or a welcome back, or kiss my arse, noted Jacko, no longer sure of himself, beset by doubts on the trip back that took well under two hours in a three-litre patrol car that had been waiting for him among the hotel courtesy coaches outside the arrivals hall.

'Any joy on the export certificates?' Knight used his demanding tone.

Velma answered, not looking up from a list of names Happy had placed before her. 'Give that end to Customs, if you like.' Now she did look up. 'Thanks, though, sir. We're now...well, fairly reasonably sure it isn't an arms scandal.' Pause. 'Or a sex scandal.'

'What then?' asked Silent with a bemused look.

Velma threw Jacko a glance that said: Over to you. He knew then she hadn't yet briefed Silent, not wanting to steal a subordinate's glory, typical of her, and he smiled down at her.

His briefing was very brief, full of obvious holes.

The bewildered look on Silent's face receded. 'Speculation,' he pronounced. 'You're a long way from any charges.'

Jacko noted the 'you'. Washing his hands of it, if it goes wrong, he thought.

Velma's pen was running through the collator's list of registered shot-firers and stopped three-quarters of the way down. 'Here's a good start,' she said enthusiastically.

Jacko looked over her shoulder. It was a name that had cropped up yesterday afternoon talking to Willis. 'Terrific,' he declared, delighted.

Knight looked over her other shoulder. 'How are you going to prove any link?'

'What did Verne Summers tell his lady over the phone in his last call?' Velma asked Jacko.

It was Hazel who answered. 'He intended to go back through the Fine Focus files to look at his old marine stuff.'

'And on Saturday morning he had been into Midshires Munitions and seen those new photos on the wall,' Jacko added.

'Yes, but...' Knight was confused again. '...where's the link?'

Jacko and Hazel moved to the nearest two desks, evicting their occupants. Over the first three days of the inquiry, they had not spent enough time in the incident room to command places of their own.

'Get on to...' Jacko stopped. He was going to give her Captain Willis, but decided, almost too late, that it was a man's job. '...McAllister or anybody at Fine Focus and get them to look out that shipping picture Summers borrowed in Cyprus.'

Before she dialled, she tapped her oval-faced gold wrist-watch, smiling mischievously, then mimed pulling a pint and drinking it. I win, she was telling him.

Jacko gave her what masqueraded as his poker face.

'Hallo.' A woman's voice, strained, not at all welcoming.

Jacko identified himself. 'Sorry to bother you, Mrs Willis.'

Her tone warmed. 'Thought you were one of them. The press is still camped outside, but at least they've stopped knocking or phoning every five minutes.'

'They could be busy elsewhere quite soon,' said Jacko, to make her feel less besieged.

'I suppose you want to speak to Simon.'

'Please.'

'Hang on. He's under the shower.'

A tepid one, I hope, thought Jacko.

Happy dialled a number, listened, said 'Shit' and noted down another number from an answering machine.

Velma phoned the Ministry of Defence and asked for the duty officer.

Silent Knight paced from desk to desk, doing what Jacko always knew he was good at—nothing.

Hazel cupped the mouthpiece. 'Just a junior on.' Like Verne Summers a dozen years ago, just starting out, thought Jacko, hanging on. 'What's he to look under?'

'Try Sea Disasters,' Jacko ventured.

'Hallo.' Captain Willis was on the line.

'First,' said Jacko, dispensing with all pleasantries, 'let me double-check the name of that Scots sapper who gave you grief in Cyprus.'

He wrote down the answer. 'Terrific,' he said.

'Now listen.' Velma lowered her voice. 'Piss me about on this query, you obstructive bastard, and I'll have you arrested for impeding our inquiries.'

Happy was noting down another number being given to him and didn't say 'Shit' this time.

Hazel hung on.

Silent paced.

'Now.' Jacko changed the topic. 'How's your Greek these days?'

'A bit rusty,' said Willis, modestly.

'Like that old tub you saw your two sappers boarding in Limassol, you mean? What was its name in English?'

'Animal Guard.'

'And what do guards stand?'

Only a moment's thought. 'Good lord,' said Willis, disbelievingly.

Hazel held the phone to her bosom, shapely in a tightish white polo-neck. 'No joy.'

'Try Shipwrecks,' said Jacko, not looking up from a phone book.

She passed on the message and the reply. 'Same.'

'How about Arms, Shipment of?'

A man's voice gave a longish number in a light Scots accent.

Jacko identified himself and stated the reason for his call. 'Tell me, what does it mean when a quarry manager like you—'

'Was...' a mournful voice interrupted.

'Not any more. Got canned yesterday. Gave up a good job in the Highlands for this. Now...'

Jacko offered brief commiserations. 'What does it mean when an ex-quarry manager like you says, "Not enough of the face was shifted."?'

'That the shot-firer hadn't dislodged enough rock. That's just what happened here...' He suddenly seemed to realize he was at home, not work, and corrected himself. '...there.'

'How's that come about?'

'Dynamite is used to bring down the amount of rock you require and if you haven't enough to fulfil your orders, then the shot-firer hasn't used enough dynamite. Happened here. Twice. He bungled it and I carry the can.'

'What was his excuse?'

'He's fucking incompetent, that's the truth. Claims he's got a bit of a gammy hand. Some war wound from the Gulf. Says it handicapped him when he was drilling. The hole. Right?'

'To put in the stick, right?' Jacko asked. 'Shaped like candlesticks you see in cowboy films. Like that?'

'They may come in that shape but

they're like plasticine. You can mould them to fit any hole or gap you like.'

'Did you believe him?'

'Never. I don't think he used enough, the right amount, for the job.'

Jacko asked for and got the shot-firer's name and who had recommended him and completed a hat-trick of 'Terrifics'.

'Try it in reverse, Shipment of Arms.' Only a frustrated Hazel remained on the phone.

Velma and Happy had replaced theirs. Both were smiling.

Jacko picked up his notebook from the borrowed desk and joined them, trailing a slow-moving Silent Knight.

'Well?' Knight demanded.

Velma's finger went to the name on the list which she'd highlighted in pale see-through green. 'Starling, Gordon.'

She pulled her notes towards her. 'Corby-born. Father a redundant steelworks semi-exec, native of Scotland. Joined the Royal Engineers at nineteen. Served in Captain Willis's squadron in Cyprus.'

Jacko broke in, uninvited, keen to knock the narrative into some form of chronology, the way he worked. 'Two years ago Willis sees Starling and a fellow squaddie boarding the...' He looked at his notes, making a fair stab at the pronunciation Blewis had used on the plane last night. '...*Froura Zo* in Limassol.'

He paused and raised his eyebrows to try to tell his audience: Cop this. 'Translated from Greek, that means *Animal Guard* which could be loosely interpreted into *Animal Vigil.*'

'You mean...' Bewilderment was back on Silent's face.

'Yep. No militant animal lib outfit was ever involved. That phone call to the press was just a piss-taker.'

'A mistake,' said Velma, grimly. 'Mercifully.'

Hazel joined them to hear Jacko continue, 'Within a week of that sighting by Willis of Starling and his mate, the *Froura Zo* is sunk at sea, all hands but one reportedly lost.'

Now Hazel came in, unable to contain herself. 'All but one were Filipinos. After the sinking Verne Summers got a commission from a paper in Manila to see if he could find a picture of

330

the crew. He borrowed it from the family of the sole survivor, sent it off via Fine Focus, who copied and filed it.'

Velma resumed from army records. 'Three months later Starling and a fellow soldier were involved in a knife fight, a bloodbath by the sounds of it, with a local seaman in Limassol. His mate died. So did the sailor.'

Jacko butted in. 'We know from Toby Blewis that it was the same sailor from *Animal Guard* who was washed up in the Lebanon and was shipped home to Cyprus.'

'And the MoD confirm that,' added Velma.

'You mean...' Silent was lost, barely comprehending. '...he was killed to silence him?'

Jacko shrugged, body language to tell him: Looks like it.

Velma went back to Starling. 'Invalided out with a hand injury which required micro-surgery and left him with diminished use. Demobbed to this address.' She tapped a number and the name of a road next to Starling's name.

Jacko again. 'Now works as a freelance

shot-firer. Got a licence and therefore access to dynamite. His contracts include Hamb's quarries. Matthew recommended him.'

Happy's turn. 'That photographer in Northampton took all but one in the collection on the walls. The odd one out came in by airmail on Hamb's instructions. On the back, he says, is the copyright stamp of a studio in Zamboanga.'

'Where's that?' asked Velma.

'The Philippines,' Happy replied. 'The pictures, six sets, all framed, were delivered last week.'

Jacko again, slower, thinking. 'On Saturday, Verne Summers pays his passing call on Midshires Munitions. It's only his third or fourth personal visit since he first confronted them with his Gulf War photo of that "Made in Corby" arms pile. He'd dropped by to see if there was another hunting job on for Monday. He browses like we did...' A nod at Hazel. '...at the framed pictures on the wall.'

'Any photographer would,' Hazel agreed.

'He sees the white boat, all spick and span and moored in the Philippines. Something catches his eye. His photographic memory recalls a rusting black tub tied up in Limassol. In his mind, he places one against the other, comparing them. A perfect match.'

'How?' Silent was asking such simple questions that Jacko wondered if he was playing the devil's advocate or was just plain thick; the latter, he decided. 'How's that possible?'

'The funnel,' Jacko speculated unsurely. 'Rakish, Hamb called it.' He warmed to the theory. 'It explains why Matthew's suddenly decided to have the funnel changed; so it won't be recognized ever again.'

Velma picked up the theory and improved on it. 'Summers either tackles Matthew there and then or Matthew realizes the game's up.'

'What game?' Silent was beginning to annoy Jacko, but he replied very patiently.

'The insurance company eventually paid out Hamb's company for the loss of the vessel. They got compensation for the cargo, too, though my guess is that found its way into hands other than its supposed destination. Add a repeat order from the Oman police and that pay-out got them out of considerable financial shit.

'But the fact is...well, the theory, anyway...must be that *Animal Guard* wasn't sunk at all. That · must follow, surely?' No one dissented. 'It was renamed, re-registered in the Cayman Islands and repainted.' He shook his head, hinting at grudging admiration. 'Then it was sold to Hamb's own company for half a million and set to work on the other side of the world. Matthew had to act. With his family's connections think of the *Sunday Times* headline.'

'So what's he do?' asked Silent, with a face that was fearing the worst.

'He hires Starling,' Jacko answered. 'He knows where to find him. He'd fixed him up with shot-firing work after his medical discharge, the same way his father had found a job for Captain Willis...'

'That's what I can't understand,' said Silent. 'Why did Hamb and Whitehall conspire to smear Willis?'

'Whitehall doesn't know it was an insurance scam. They thought it was an arms scandal; a potential one anyway. It was in the government's interest to keep the tin lid on and get Willis out of the way before he started babbling his suspicions to someone else.'

Silent just managed to stop himself nodding, brooding on it.

'So Matthew contacts Starling,' Jacko repeated. 'He'd already got rid, at the cost of his mate's life, of the one witness in Cyprus who could talk.

'The rest of the *Animal Guard* crew are back in the bosoms of their families, well paid, no doubt, for their work and silence. But Summers is over here, knowing, or, at least, suspecting, the truth. Maybe he couldn't be bought off again.'

'He wanted to be back at the sharp end of journalism,' Hazel added with a radiant smile, 'and the truth about what happened to *Animal Guard* was his way in.'

Silent went walkabout again, pacing round the desks, head down, hands behind his back, a sort of musing Prince Charles communing with nature walk, and was quiet for some time.

Jacko began to fear he was about to take charge, burst into frenzied activity, leap on to the stage that Noël Coward and Sir Malcolm Sargent had trod and cock up three days of hard work and hard travelling.

He was relieved when Velma spoke. 'So we must bring in Hamb, his son and Starling.'

'Why Lord Hamb?' asked Silent, the only officer to give him his title. 'What does he know about any insurance fraud or conspiracy to murder?'

'We don't know,' said Velma truthfully. 'Let's ask him. He's a crucial witness at the very least.'

And that's just about all, thought Jacko, a touch disgruntled. All they'd get him for was conspiracy to pervert the course of justice in stitching up Captain Willis with a bum rap and half Whitehall seemed to be in on that.

Velma turned to Happy, at her side, processing all her paperwork, for three days now. 'You're with me on Hamb.'

She was giving him a piece of the action as a thank you, nice touch, Jacko realized. Velma was looking at him: 'You and Hazel on Matthew.'

The easy end, he thought, contented. He knew exactly where Matthew would be. He was weak, Jacko was convinced of it. He would cave. He'd talk.

Silent was unbuttoning his double-breasted jacket, folding it across his stomach tighter, as if wrapping his insecurity in it, fastened it again and turned round. 'I'll take Starling.'

The hard end, Jacko acknowledged, and he's welcome to it. That's why he's on twice as much as me. Let him earn it.

'You appreciate,' said Velma, very quietly, 'that he could have stockpiled a bit of dynamite here and there from his shot-firing assignments.'

'That,' Hazel added, 'is how he got his hands on surplus in the army.'

Velma underscored the warning. 'It's his only way round the regulations on explosives.'

Without waiting for orders, Happy returned to his desk to call in a team of marksmen and alert the bomb squad.

They talked tactics for some while, Jacko not taking much part; guns and booby traps not his department.

Finally Silent fingered his watch which had more dials than a timekeeper at the Olympics. 'Let's take our targets at eleven thirty. Let's synchronize.'

Jacko looked at his cheapo and then at Hazel, fighting off a smile, bluffing, not yet ready to show his hand.

337

20

'Mrs Starling?'

'Aye.' She was wearing a woolly purple dress too tight for a big-boned frame, pink rubber gloves and the irritated look of a woman unused to having her housework routine disturbed by a knock on the clean white door of her neat semi in the old part of Corby, a place with a feel more of a village than a frontier town.

'Major Knight.' Silent raised a borrowed black trilby, smiling. 'RE Corps after-care officer. Gordon in?'

Her reply was a headshake, part sad, part suspicious.

'It's just that...well...you know...' On the radio linked to a mike under his white shirt, Silent was sounding slightly thrown. '...we like to pop in every so often to see our old boys, find out how they're settling down in civvy street and so on.'

'Not here.'

'Will he be here...'

'Not these eight months past. We hardly

saw him at Christmas and not at all for Hogmanay,' she said in a heavy Scots accent.

'I'd naturally like to see him while I'm in the area. Perhaps, to keep our records up to date, you might tell me where I could find him.'

She gave him an address even before he'd taken an envelope from a side pocket in his grey double-breasted that bulged slightly under his left armpit. 'Hope there's no money in it...'

'Depends,' said Silent, head down, noting the address, which, Mrs Starling added, was only five minutes away.

'...or she'll get her hands on it, if there is.'

'Married then, has he?'

She gave him a horrified look. 'God forbid.'

'Working, is he?'

'Now and then. Same line.'

'As?'

'As in the army. Demolition. Not many jobs about, though.'

'Will he be in now?'

'Most likely. You'll know if you see his van outside. An old Austin.'

Knight knew all about that already.

Happy, the collator, had given him, Little Velma and Jacko the colour and index number, too.

'In bed most like, with her,' she continued. 'Couch cabbage. Have a word with him, will you? Won't listen to his faaver.'

'I'll try.' He tipped his black trilby.

He strode down the street and round the corner to a plain blue transit van where he ordered a sergeant in civvies: 'Tell Control to delay Chief Superintendent Malloy and Inspector Jackson by five minutes.'

In the back of the van, six men, flak jackets beneath blue boilersuits, exchanged impatient looks, anything but calm, wanting to get on with it, to get it over and done with.

Jacko tapped his cheapo. Hazel glanced down at her gold watch, nodded, and started up his Vauxhall Cavalier. No car of her own, she'd got the driving bug again on her solo trip back from Heathrow airport last night and had pleaded with him to let her take the wheel.

She'd driven carefully up the peninsula road and south down the A6003 to a pot-holed lay-by where she pulled in when

Control rang on the portable to pass on the five-minute delay.

After a grey start that had blocked out any view of the North Sea from his window seat, a cold wind was beginning to break up the clouds and splashes of blue were appearing in the sky.

Within a mile or two of the lay-by, the crane-like tips of the sand dredgers popped into view above the straw-coloured grass bank that shielded the gravel pit from the road.

Crow didn't have to stop to think about which track to take at the Y-bend in the Land Rover, bench seat behind him neatly laden with packs, refolded tent and sleeping bag.

For almost half of the fourteen hours he'd kipped fitfully. The rubber cape he'd used as a groundsheet was now wrapped round him. He'd eaten before and after sleep, in strict accordance with the golden rule.

For three hours he'd kept watch from behind the overgrown grass bank, ideal cover, binoculars raised to his eyes in his left hand, working a black rubber ball in his right for physical and mental therapy.

Lorries fork right and stop on the weighbridge, check? he queried himself. Check.

Half an hour earlier, he'd seen the white Golf VW head left and park in front of brick-built buildings. Soon afterwards a bald, burly man had come out and had driven away in a fawn Metro. Getting rid of eyewitnesses, Crow had guessed.

His binoculars had followed the car all the way down the exit track and over the spot beyond the second weighbridge where he'd planted the mine just before dawn.

Cars fork left. Check? Check.

He tugged down the wheel slightly with his hundred per cent hand.

He'd seen no suspicious vehicles, no mystery callers, and was satisfied no hitman lay in wait. He'd collect and drive away; but not right away. He'd return to his hide and wait till the white Golf was half-way down the exit road.

Even if he wasn't springing an ambush, baiting a trap, he'd still have to die, Crow had decided.

Once he'd got the money he was of no further use to him, but he might be to the police. Tough, but there you go.

He pulled to a stop in the rough car-park.

Happy and Velma had stopped on the frost-crusted grass beside the crater in the dirt road beyond the plank bridge with its 'No Trespassing' notice that linked the peninsula to the island.

From here they got the view to their right that Verne Summers had seen, his last, across gradually rising land to the white stables where a girl groom was mucking out a horse-box with a two-pronged fork.

It was a vantage point with no line of vision to the front door of Island Lodge, only the black shutters of bedroom windows above overgrown shrubbery denuded of leaves.

The first they saw of the grey Rolls was when it purred noiselessly and very smoothly round a long curve by the copse of silver birch.

Lord Hamb, in a pin-striped three-piece suit and a black Afghan hat, was egalitarianly sitting alongside his all-purpose Filipino servant, who stopped short of Velma's maroon Ford. With the spreading willow tree opposite, there was no other way round the crater.

She took her warrant card from her shoulder bag. She and the collator got out.

The passenger window was activated, sliding silently down. Hamb beamed. 'Lads. Lads.' His oop north accent. 'Have you no home to go to?'

Velma realized they had been mistaken for press and showed him her card. 'My name is Detective Chief Superintendent Carole Malloy.'

'Well done, girl,' he said, condescendingly. 'That's the spirit, just what I like to hear.'

'We are going to arrest you—'

'Hahaha.' A hearty what-a-merry-jape laugh.

'You are not obliged to say anything but anything you do say may be given in evidence.' She'd met his glowing coal black eyes throughout the caution. 'Get out of the car, please, and come with us.'

His eyes went from best domestic to nutty slack. 'Now, see here, I think this has gone far enough.'

'Now, please, sir.'

'I have an appointment at one of my—'

'Now, please.'

With heaving effort, he rounded on his driver. 'Get me the Chief Constable.'

'No know number.' A panic-stricken tone and face.

'Fucking foreigner.'

Velma had pulled up the inside catch and opened the door. 'Now, please.'

Hamb snatched his car phone off its bracket, pressed a series of numbers. A screech jolted his head away from the earpiece. He threw the receiver into the driver's lap. 'Go ahead.'

'Them police.' An urgent peck towards Velma.

'Back up then.'

Velma touched his shoulder. 'Please, sir.'

'Get your fucking hand off me.'

She withdrew it. 'You've a right to a solicitor—'

'I don't want a fucking solicitor. I want your Chief and your job.'

'You can make any phone call you like from the police station.'

Hamb turned back to the driver. 'Go ahead, back up'—which, Velma was to say later, reminded her of an old Abbott and Costello scene when they were in a bus at the very end of a pier.

The driver gripped the wheel, did neither. Hamb leaned closer and shouted in his ear from less than a foot. 'You're fucking fired. Hear that? Fucking fired.'

The Filipino's face wore a hapless expression.

Behind them a dirty blue car rattled on the bridge and stopped just over it. Two photographers, a PA staffer and a woman freelance, who'd been driving aimlessly around, nothing better to do, short of ideas four days into the story, got out.

Hamb turned in his seat. 'The charge? What's the charge? I demand to know.' He shouted it.

'We're going to ask you questions about possible conspiracy to breach the arms embargo.'

'Rubbish. I've already explained that.'

'Plotting to defraud insurance.'

'Oh.' Shock filled his face.

'And possible conspiracy to murder.'

Defiant again. 'Complete cock. You're in big trouble. Hear me? Big trouble.'

'Get out, please.'

Hamb got out, slowly, clumsily. A rich smell that couldn't have come from the stables followed him out. Only then did he see the two photographers, who had

346

already shot half a roll each. 'Off. Off my fucking land.'

Velma took his arm at an elbow. He shook it free and marched towards the cameras, ranting obscenities. Nimbly, they backed away, ducking, like flyweight boxers, clicking all the time. 'If one word, one word, appears, you're for the high jump. Hear me? For it. You, your editors.' He jerked his thumb towards Velma and Happy. 'These two nincompoops. For it. All of you.'

Velma took a tight grip on his elbow, turning him away from them. His face was port-coloured. He was out of breath, gasping. He was wobbling with rage. She guided him towards her car where Happy had the back door open. She went on tiptoe, raising herself up, as close as she could, to whisper in his ear. 'Get in the car, you fat old fart, or you'll have a heart attack.'

Hazel took the left at the Y-fork, but Jacko's eyes stayed right, watching a giant lorry fast filling with pebbles, yellow liquid flooding from the tailgate, as if trying to make room for the more solid load coming from the hopper's chute above.

She parked on the roughly levelled ground in front of the brick-skinned buildings. Jacko got out. All this travelling merited a stretch and a stroll, he decided, while he finished the cigarette he'd lit after they pulled out of the lay-by.

Only four or five vehicles were parked, Matthew's white Golf among them. An oldish Land Rover, too, of no interest to him; certainly no old Austin van, with an index number that the collator had circulated, or he'd have retreated and called up reinforcements.

Hazel reached in the back for her long black raincoat. She clutched Jacko's brown one beneath it. Looking at him through the back window, she lifted it and offered it towards him.

He shook his head. Won't be here long, he was telling her. He dropped his cigarette end and trod on it.

'Yer.' She was dressed a bit like a cabbage in layers of green—grubby lime housecoat opened at the front to reveal a darker green cardigan and lighter green, long nightie.

Knight had stood for some time after a pasty-faced young girl, no more than ten, ricket-thin and thinly dressed, opened the door. She'd left it open while she went to rouse her mother.

He couldn't see inside the back room because the faded curtains were closed but he could hear a gun battle raging on TV via a white satellite dish on the roof.

A couple of minutes on the taped radio set in the transit van round the corner transmitted sound effects only, notably Silent's heavy breathing.

His eyes came away from dirty pots piled on the non-draining side of a sink next to a gas cooker with a greasy top to greet a worn face, fortyish, unmade like the bed she'd just left. 'Your daughter tells me Gordon isn't in. Would you be so...?'

'Who wants him?' Sleepy, not quite yawned.

'Knight's my name.' He doffed his trilby with a short flourish. 'Major Andy Knight. Engineers After-care.'

The sleep left her face. 'You had a breakdown then?'

'Yes,' said Silent, automatically. He hesitated. 'Of a sort, I suppose.'

'Where's Crow then?'

'Pardon?'

'Crow.'

Knight looked nonplussed.

'Gordon,' she explained.

'Oh, Sapper Starling. Sorry. That's what I was hoping you'd tell me. I see his van's still here.' Knight flicked his head in a direction through the house to the kerb outside.

'Silly sod. He...'

From behind the closed curtains came shrill quarrelling, then a boy's voice. 'Mum. Mum. She's turning off...'

'You've had it on all morning.' The girl's voice.

The woman turned her head away sharply, not ruffling dark, almost black hair, as greasy as the cooker top. 'Quiet.'

'But I want to finish this Arnie...' The boy again.

'My turn.' The girl now. 'It's my...'

'Shut it, I said, you little bastards.' The woman raised her voice. 'You deaf?'

'But...'

'Mum...'

'Fucking shut up.' The woman shrieked it. 'Or everything's off and you're both to school this afternoon.'

'Told you.' Soprano, softer, still unseen, so impossible this time to put a sex to it.

The woman held the back of a hand to her temple and groaned.

350

Silent smiled sympathy. 'You were telling me.'

'You going too?'

'Er...um...yes. When I've linked up with Gordon.'

'Never believed him, you know? Not really.' An immediate about-face. 'Suppose I did, though. Really.'

'No? Well, it is a little...you know...confidential, shall we say.'

A tight smile. 'Him and his manoeuvres. Thought he was...'

He heard the sound of a door opening behind him, flinched. She glared over his shoulder and called out, 'See? Crow's CO.'

She pointed proudly at him. Silent turned in time to tip his hat to a closing door in the next house.

'Bitch,' said the woman. 'Now she'd better believe us. Were you with him when he was wounded in the desert?'

'Back at base, I'm afraid.' Silent put on a modest face. 'Missed it.'

'Still got his medal in your museum, have you?'

'And very proud we are of it, too, madam. And him.'

'He's been in training, you know. Keeps

very fit. Hand's a lot better.'

'He's always been very keen.'

'Come in and wait for him.' She pulled the door wider open. 'He said he'd be back around midday if there was a breakdown. I'll get dressed. Terrible migraine, you know, but...' A soldiering-on smile, long-suffering.

Knight stepped into the cold kitchen and noticed a cracked mirror above a cracked sink. 'We need him rather urgently.'

'He went to meet you or, at least, somebody. Went last night for the exercises. A jeep picked him up.'

'There must be...'

'Then the convoy up north. That's right, isn't it?'

'Why yes, but there's been some cock-up ...pardon...misunderstanding...' He floundered for a second. '...about travel arrangements.'

'When it clicks that he's missed you he'll come here.'

'Where's he gone?' He looked at his timekeeper's watch. 'We're running a bit late.'

'To the training ground, of course. Told you.'

'Which training ground?'

A suspicious frown.

'We've several.'

'Muster was at nine last night, he said, and the convoy... What time is it?'

Knight had no need to look. 'Eleven thirty-five.'

'Leaves about now.'

'Ah, we've clearly a cross-wire here, I am sorry to say. Wrong rendezvous, by the sounds of it. Several of them, of course, and all special locations, of course.' A secretive smile. 'That's the way it is in...' A shrug. 'Well, you know. Where's he mustering?'

'That gravel pit on the Oakham road before Uppingham.'

Silent stepped swiftly back out of the kitchen. 'No bother. I'll nip round there and pick him up.'

21

Everything happened so fast, not quite altogether, but in such rapid succession, that Jacko heard him a fraction of a second before he saw him.

He'd rapped on the inner door, waited a moment or two. His portable phone began a muffled ring in his grey jacket pocket. Almost immediately, a bleep cheeped inside Hazel's shoulder bag.

Mechanically, he directed his right hand towards the pocket. Just as automatically, his eyes lowered to follow it and were down when the door was yanked open.

'Freeeeze.' It was bellowed in the voice of a barrack square drill instructor.

Only Jacko's eyes disobeyed.

They came up on a terrifying sight, as frightening as the deafening, stretched-out shout—a twisted face, sallowness accentuated by a head of black, spiky hair not much longer than the stubble on chin and cheeks. Wide eyes, steel grey, hot as a furnace, burnt into his.

He was too shocked, disorientated, scared, even to think: Fuck me, his first reaction to any surprise or emergency.

The rest of him did as he was told, too long in the job to take risks. His hand stayed outside the pocket, in view.

Unblinking, his eyes were photographing a tall, strong figure in a rubber khaki cape over sand-coloured battledress.

No hands were in sight until the cape

354

was parted from within. Now they were visible, dropping beyond his chest to clutch two grenades pegged either side of the buckle of a green webbing belt.

And now he did think: Oh fuck me.

If Hazel, just behind, moved, Jacko didn't sense it, but then all his senses were numb.

'Freeeeze.' The eyes shot a molten shaft over his shoulder towards her.

The phone inside the office began to ring, forming a strident trio with Jacko's pocket and Hazel's shoulder bag.

'Leave.' His eyes were back on Jacko and stayed there but he contorted his mouth sideways.

'In.' He backed away, yellow-stained calf-length boots making no sound on the thin carpet, the cape elbowed out. 'Both of you.'

With some effort—he'd felt frozen to the spot—Jacko unglued his shoes and walked in the inner office very slowly, just ahead of Hazel.

To his right, behind his desk, sat Matthew, face a portrait of abject terror; like mine, Jacko thought.

The phone on his desk rang incessantly.

Starling (not the slightest doubt in

Jacko's dazed mind who he was) high-stepped a backward circle, crouching, like an adagio dancer, the devil in the final death scene of a ridiculously choreographed ballet.

Jacko and Hazel shuffled round in the same slow rhythm, his hand feeling stitched to his noisy pocket, hers still holding the tag on the zip of her now-silent shoulder bag.

Starling had returned to the door and back-heeled it shut. He pulled himself erect. 'Answer.'

Jacko released his hand. 'Not you.' He screamed it, veins standing out at his temples. Jacko stilled his hand again, as much as he could, feeling it trembling. 'You.' He cricked his neck to shout to his right while still looking ahead.

Matthew lifted his phone, listened, stagnant black eyes on Starling. His Adam's apple grumbled to clear his throat. 'It's a woman. Asking for him.' He jerked his head towards Jacko. 'Jackson. Mrs Jackson. His wife, she says and—'

'That you, pally?' asked Starling, quieter.

Jacko nodded, not yet able to speak.

'A contact call,' Starling declared with the first trace of Scottishness. 'It's a contact call.'

He's right about that, Jacko judged, and I'll wager the message on the screen of Hazel's pager reads: 'Abort.' Too late. Knight's too fucking late. His gut gnawed with a mixture of anger and fear.

'Tell 'em this and no more,' said Starling, very deliberately. 'Answer no questions. I have Jackson and his woman. 'You?' He glared at Hazel. 'Who are you?'

Hazel couldn't move her mouth.

'Open and empty your bag.'

She couldn't move her fingers.

'No.' He countermanded himself. 'Police?' He shouted it. 'Are you police?'

She managed a tiny nod, a reflex, really.

He inclined his head right again, shouting. 'Tell 'em.'

Matthew repeated it, adding, begging, 'Please, just listen,' several times.

'If I see one more police officer, armed or not, they're dead.' Matthew relayed it, gabbling, hardly able to get his words in the proper order.

'Got that?' Matthew added that, too, then said, 'She wants to speak to you.'

'No negotiations. Say no negotiations. Tell 'em they'll hear my terms when I'm good and ready. Tell 'em no more calls.

Tell 'em that and then hang up.'

Matthew did as he was told.

'So...' His back was against the door, eyes on Matthew. '...you shopped me, you bastard.'

'Didn't. Didn't. I didn't.' It was machine-gunned. 'I swear, swear, swear it.'

'I warned you. In that message. Play fair or else.'

A doom-laden silence followed, Matthew clearly not comprehending, but too terrified to say so.

That message to the *Mirror*, he means, Jacko knew. But Matthew, a *Daily Telegraph* reader, hadn't seen it. He'd have missed its significance anyway, because he didn't speak Greek. He finally found voice, a weak one. 'He didn't shop you.'

'Shut it. Just shut it.'

'But...'Hazel's first word had a quiver in it. '...he didn't...'

'Shut it.' Barked.

Hazel shut it.

With a lopsided smirk, Starling pulled his shoulders back. 'Nobody speaks unless I tell 'em to.'

Nobody spoke for some time.

Oh shit. We've walked in on the pay-off,

Jacko was thinking, feeling so sick he was close to vomiting. Oh God. We've cornered a killer rat. Oh fuck me. He'd never felt so helpless, impotent; so nauseous.

One of the few courses he'd ever attended was to gain qualifications as a hostage negotiator. 'A good choice,' his wife had teased. 'You talk so much you'd bore them into surrender.'

Funny then; sick now.

Desperately he was trying to remember the basic dos and don'ts. 'Rule No 1 is to ensure that no one gets killed, especially No 1,' the instructor had said, only half joking.

Some hope here, he thought fatalistically. How can you negotiate, have a meaningful dialogue with a nutter, a military fantasist, a walking timebomb and—oh my God, yes, face up to it—a loose cannon who won't let you talk?

Keep quiet, he ordered himself; wait, watch, think.

'You shopped me,' Starling quieter.

'I didn't.' Matthew, quieter still. 'Didn't. Never. Why—'

'Why are they here then?' He flicked his head towards Jacko and Hazel.

'I can't... Don't... Just... I can't explain.'

Starling looked hard at Jacko. 'You.'

Jacko coughed twice. 'We'd come to arrest him.' He nodded at Matthew. 'Routine police work, elimination.' He managed an unconvincing shrug.

Starling threw back his cape, a Hollywood sword fighter's gesture. The front of it fell over his shoulders.

Jacko had a clear view of the grenades now, each side of a black balaclava tucked into the webbing belt at the stomach.

Both hung by steel grips. One was small and white, pear-shaped, with indentations. The other, bigger, a smooth black canister. Into this one's metal ring Starling hooked his right index finger. 'Talk.'

Jacko let his hand drop to his side. 'We worked out that Vernon Summers...the victim on Monday, you know?'

'I fucking know.' Snarled.

'...was killed to stop him blowing the whistle on him.' Jacko nodded at Matthew.

'Don't buy it.' Starling's expression was more dubious than dismissive. 'About what?'

The room went silent for a second or two until Starling started to scream. 'What? What about? Answer. What?'

'An insurance fraud over a ship,' Jacko answered, very quietly.

Matthew audibly groaned. The bags under his black eyes were puffed and just as black. He looked as if he hadn't slept for days.

'How?' Starling wasn't following. He flicked his head towards Matthew. 'If not him, how?'

'We found the link between you and his boat in Cyprus, the *Animal Guard.*'

Starling seemed impressed, ready to buy it now, 'Willis?'

A nod. 'Partly.'

'Lucky. That arsehole was lucky. Almost got him with the same shot.' A gloating grin was switched off as he rounded menacingly on Matthew. 'Why didn't you tell me?'

'About what?' Even in a sitting position Matthew's body was sagging, close to collapse.

'About Willis.'

'I just didn't...it never occured to me...'

Starling glowered at Jacko. He held out his left hand, flicking fingertips into its palm, like a beggar. 'Give then. How did you connect him...' His head moved towards Matthew. '...with me?'

361

'We traced the boat through photos to the Far East.'

'What boat?' A confused shadow crossed his face again.

'*Animal Guard.* Or *Vigil.*' Jacko shrugged to tell him: Call it what you like.

'Can't have done. How? Liar. How can there be pictures? It's at the bottom of...' He turned slowly to Matthew. 'Isn't it?'

A forlorn headshake.

'Why?'

'Change of plan. Last minute. Change of—'

'Why?'

As Jacko had suspected, Matthew caved right in, told all.

'My father's, my dad's, idea. Sorry. He vetoed my plan. Believe it. Me.' He was in such trauma he wasn't always finding the right word. 'Cash slow...sorry, flow. We were nearly...'

'So what happened to our dynamite? We took risks...'

'Don't know. I honestly don't know. Honestly. Overboard, I expect.'

Starling's eyes were steel hard. 'You mean... My...me and my mate... My mate...' He paused, trying to work something out. 'Knew it. Always knew. He got killed for a shared grand when you...' The answer didn't want to come. 'You told us it was to cut the wog's supply lines.'

'The ammo went to Israel,' said Matthew, matter-of-factly.

'What do I care about them? My mate got killed cutting up that seaman. For what?'

Matthew began talking fast, frantically. 'We had to. Don't you see? Had to. What happened to the ship made no difference. He was the only weak link. A security risk.'

Starling didn't appear to have heard him and answered his own question. 'A grand. A poxy grand.'

'It was...believe me...it was...it was my father's idea. We were going under, laying off.'

'How much did he make?'

Matthew couldn't bring himself to answer, so fearful of the consequences of the truth.

'How much? Come on.' Starling played with the ring on the grenade. 'How much did you make selling on the boat?'

'Two hundred.'

Starling's face registered total disbelief.

Matthew had divided the truth by two, small beer in his world of high finance, but a king's ransom to a drummed-out soldier. 'What, thousand?' A doom-laden pause. 'Right. Now you'll pay.'

Matthew lifted his hand from the desk, just fractionally.

'Keep those hands where they are.'

He touched the desk with his palm, hardly a pat. 'In the drawer there's...the rest...I've got the...in there.' A downward look.

'Fourteen thou? When you've made that much? Wipe your backside with it.'

Five more minutes agonizingly dragged by on Jacko's metal-plated cheapo, made all the longer by his frequent glances at it, wondering if it needed winding. Throughout them not one word did he or Hazel say, just standing there, very still.

Starling sidestepped from the door along the wall, back to it, in a sort of slither to behind the desk where Matthew sat. He seemed to be diminishing further, head and eyes rolling, like a drowning man, fast going under beneath a torrent of naked threats, hollered orders and endless obscenities that came from behind him.

On command, he pulled open the left-hand top drawer and Starling leant forward to lift out a thick brown envelope which he stuffed into a deep thigh pocket.

Jacko noticed for the first time a ball-shaped bulge in the twin pocket at the other thigh. Oh, Christ, he groaned inwardly, another grenade.

The words passing between them were shouted by Starling and whimpered by Matthew, who was never allowed to complete a sentence, so the conversation was disjointed and repetitive and echoed like Harold Pinter dialogue.

Jacko had to concentrate hard to follow, wondering for a brief moment if it was worth the effort, uncertain of his chances of surviving to recall it in evidence for judge and jury.

In his time he had often taken witness statements from cashiers in hold-ups and knew how armed robbers sought to overpower, humiliate and dominate and exercise complete control, like drill instructors and, let's be honest, a few bullying policemen during interrogations.

But this loopy was much worse than the worst of them. He revelled in it, loving it. It was as if the bitter grudges of a lifetime of being bossed and buggered about were being settled in this room.

Jacko listened, anyway; not so much out of a sense of duty, but because he was nosy. He didn't believe in heaven, though right now he dearly wanted to, so he never imagined himself on high, looking down, listening in, watching over his wife, kid and that handful of extra-special friends, willing things to turn out well for them.

The answers to all of life's great mysteries, he'd long since decided, were here on earth, so if he wanted to know, now might be his last chance of finding out.

'You got greedy. That's what. Greedy.' Back to the wall, Starling was breathing heavily, face twitching. His right hand lovingly cupped the black grenade, fingering it. Face and fingers working together reminded Jacko of Bogart playing with ball-bearings as the unhinged Captain Queeg in *The Caine Mutiny*.

Cracked, he told himself. He's completely crackers.

'Your old man a nut or something? Eh?' Starling stepped forward to shout, silver slaver at one corner of his mouth, into Matthew's ear. 'A fruitcake, eh?'

'Yes.' Matthew looked and sounded like a zombie, the living dead. Jacko felt a pang of pity for him.

'...having that fucking photo taken...'

'He thought—'

Starling wasn't listening. 'For bogeys, filth like him...' Eyes back on Jacko. '...to see.'

'He never believed, thought for one moment—'

Starling broke in again. 'That's his sodding trouble, sunshine. He never thought.'

Yeah, Jacko agreed, that was Hamb's trouble. He's every bit as much of a nut as Starling, but white, instead of blue or khaki, collared. He thought he was fireproof. He was taking the piss out of me, always getting my name wrong, offering me the bribe of a job, talking about *Animal Guard* in front of me on his squawk box, just managing to stop himself giggling. He'd volunteered that info, the stuff about the insurance payout, that bullshit about Mossad, to head me off, sure I'd accept his word and look no further.

Matthew was more or less confirming Jacko's private thoughts. 'He reckoned no one would put two and...' He half turned, to look behind him.

'Eyes front.' A barrack square bark, louder, much louder than Jacko's old army drill corporal who'd been credited with a voice that would give an aspirin headache.

'Sorry. He's got this ob...' Matthew went on tremulously. '...a mania for photos...'

'Maniac. That's right. Maniac. And you do his dirty work?'

'Everybody does...have to or...'

'How much did you make?'

'I'm trying to tell...'

'Try again.' A terrible tug at his throat. 'Harder.'

'Two hundred... Sold...' Matthew could barely speak. '...back to...company.'

Jacko let his eyes drop. He could understand, shared, in fact, Starling's hatred of Matthew. He'd been used, duped. But this was sadism.

Half a million, actually, plus the payout from the insurance for a ship that never sank, plus cash-in-the-hand for a cargo that was never lost, plus a repeat order for a couple of million pounds' worth of arms, Jacko calculated. The old fraud.

Hamb had kept his hands undirtied by weapons trafficking. He'd avoided the stigma of arms smuggling which would have had him shunned by his in-social set, the glossy house and gardens crowd.

Instead, he'd masterminded a massive insurance swindle, a white collar crime, often regarded in his world as no more than a sort of big business blood sport. And such was his vanity he couldn't resist having the fox's tail photographed after he'd made his killing and sticking it on the wall, like a big game trophy. That's what it was to him—a big game.

And the cool, clever, confident bastard tweaked my tail, too, Jacko was now more than every convinced, talking about it on that bloody squawk box, a joke at my expense, thinking I'd be too dim to see through what had gone on.

Heard about a score of 'em before, he thought, but never before come across one—celebrities and personalities who believe in their own publicity, their own invincibility, who think rules apply to ordinary mortals, not super-humans like them.

Jacko was suddenly filled to bursting with an overwhelming will to live, if only to see Hamb in court.

'His idea, was it?' Starling demanded. 'All his?'

'Yes.'

'All this, including Monday?'

Matthew stared into space.

'Yes, sir...' Starling was leaning forward, shouting again. '...or no, sir.'

Matthew's head dropped towards the desk.

Starling looked quickly at Jacko, who saw what Matthew couldn't—his right index finger hooking the ring of the black grenade. He freed his left index finger and in the same movement hooked the arm round Matthew's neck. 'Yes or no?'

'No.' Matthew gasped, more shocked than out of breath.

'Sir.'

'Sir.'

'Altogether.'

'No, sir.'

'Yours then. Give. Tell.'

'Mine.' An exhausted sigh. 'He...that Summers chap...he saw that picture...' He tried to nod towards Jacko, couldn't, too tight the hold. '...the one he saw. He recognized it as the *Guard*. More or less said so. Not in so many words. Just his look, the odd question about the fancy funnel. He was going to... I could tell, knew he was going... I had to, had to stop him or...'

'What was the panic, the rush to get it done Monday?'

'It was the only opportunity, the last chance. Told you that on Saturday night. He was about to be warned off. Dad had had enough of him. He wouldn't have come back again. It was then or never. Like I said. Honest.'

Starling tightened his elbow and cruelly yanked his head back.

Jacko felt no pity for Matthew now, just a loathing. All his life he'd been at his dad's beck and call, obeyed his every order. The first time he decided on something himself he'd ordered an execution, just like that. His dear old dad had ordered an end to Summers' because, with his royal sources of income dried up, he'd become an inconvenience, a witness.

Balls to him, Jacko decided. I'm not going to stick my neck out for him.

He began to worry how he'd fare, handle Starling's monsterings, the humiliations, when his turn came, as come it would. Not very well, he feared, and his stomach tightened.

'And me?' Starling demanded.

Matthew tried flattery. 'You did an excellent, first-rate...'

'Part of the plan is it, for me to end up like that seaman in Limassol? Or to walk into his trap?' Starling nodded at Jacko. 'Doing life? Or, better still, dead?'

'No.' Another gasp. 'Would I pay you if...'

'Because I'm the one person...'

'Only you and me knew. Honest. Not even dad. I wasn't going to tell Dad. I just wanted to end it, stop it all once and for all. It was getting out of... There was, would have been no risk. No...none, but for...'

He stopped at the sound of footsteps on the roof, then on the gravel path outside. The door in the room next door scraped open, followed by two pairs of footsteps.

'Quiet.' Starling whispered for the first time, into Matthew's ear. He unlocked his hold, eyes on Jacko, passing his left hand under his chin in a slicing motion. He stood with feet and cape apart, hands to his hip, posing. Both index fingers were threaded in the steel rings now.

From the other side of the door came foot-stamping and loud complaints about the cold and the sound of water being drawn and within a minute another set of footsteps, heavier, a louder voice jocularly accusing the first arrivals of skiving, then saying 'Not half' to an offer of tea.

On this side of the door such was the silence that Jacko thought he could hear the ticking of his cheapo.

Knight's undercover marksmen, he was thinking, pretending to be workers. When that door opens, he prayed, let them have guns in their hands. Don't let them try to talk, negotiate; just shoot. One bullet in the chest will do it and, dear God, let it find its target before any finger pulls the ring from either grenade.

I, he vowed, will take full responsibility, all the flak from the media, the complaints investigation and the inquest that's bound to follow.

When that door opens, he decided, he'd push Hazel down, but stand his own ground, point to Starling, shouting, 'He's armed. Shoot. Shoot. Shoot.'

Starling slithered, back against the wall, to and beyond the door, and stood next to the sand-filled fire bucket.

Jacko's eyes dwelt on it, then transferred themselves to the steel table on which the technical magazines stood. Depending

373

on where the unpinned grenade rolled one or other might come in handy to deaden the blast, he thought, without much real hope.

22

The door was pushed open. Jacko got a side-on view of the burly manager, hand on the knob, face turned away, grinning across his shoulder.

His hopes began to flow out of him like a slow puncture. He plugged the leak with a wild notion that he could have volunteered as the advance man who knew the layout; Knight's diversion.

The manager turned into the room. His ruddy, outdoor face filled with surprise when he saw Jacko and Hazel, steadied at the sight of Matthew slumped behind the desk—'Sorry, boss, I thought you'd be finished...'—and wobbled uncontrollably when a voice screamed, 'In. In. Face front.'

'Do as he says, mate.' Jacko motioned to him urgently with stiff fingers as if he was directing a driver into a tight parking spot. 'And keep quiet.'

'You out there.' Starling pressed himself closer to the wall. 'In here. Or they get it. In. Now.' He held the black grenade in his left hand, first finger of the other hooked into the ring.

The chatty controller and the balaclavaed driver Jacko had seen just twenty-four hours before, an age ago, walked slowly into the room. Their expressions were more perplexed then alarmed until they saw Starling. Then they registered something close to panic.

Jacko's hopes were no longer deflating. The slow puncture had become a blow-out. All this psyching-up and the wheel had come off his courage.

'What the...' said the controller, fingers beneath his maroon and white woolly hat, scratching his hair.

'Quiet.' In the next minute or so, Starling's screaming became almost hysterical, his questioning demented gabble. He wanted to know who the three men were, their jobs, what vehicles they had, where they were parked, where the keys were.

Standing in a huddle round Jacko and Hazel, as close as possible, for comfort's sake, they answered in mumbled monosyllables.

He's lost control, thought Jacko; he'd got far, far too many hostages; no plan at all. Surely, between the five of us, there's something we can do? If only I could think. Think, he urged himself.

'Right.' Starling shouted at the hunched Matthew, ignored for some time. 'On the phone to your old man. Now.'

Matthew's hands came to life, picking up the phone, dialling a number, slowly to make sure he got it right.

As he did so, Starling rapped out fresh orders. 'Tell him, all the ready cash about the place, all the jewellery, all the valuables to be collected up.'

Matthew started one sentence, stopped and asked a startled question, then: 'He's not there.'

'Where is he?'

'The police station.'

'We can confirm that, Gordon,' said Hazel with a beguiling smile, trying feminine wiles.

Starling totally ignored her, nodded at the phone. 'Who you talking to?'

'His secretary,' Matthew answered.

'Tell her.' He repeated his demands, adding, 'To be collected in half an hour.' He didn't even glance at his black waterproof watch. 'No police.'

Matthew passed it on with lots of pained 'Pleases' and a snapped, 'Don't ask questions,' but when he tried to add an explanatory phrase Starling barked at him to hang up. He did.

'Right.' Starling still. 'You.' He looked at Matthew. 'Take your car home to make the pick-up. Bring it to that church on the south side of the water.' He looked from him at the controller. 'Take him.' Then back again. 'Be there, both of you, in half an hour. No police. Or these all die; all four of 'em.'

He glared at Matthew who had made no attempt to move, too terrified to. 'Now.' A slow, sadistic smile spoked out from behind his short black beard. 'First.' He planted his feet a foot apart. 'Lick these.'

Matthew sat still.

'Come on.' That evil smile still. 'I'm giving you your life. More than my mate in Limassol got. Kiss 'em.' His smile disappeared. Loud: 'Now.' Louder still: 'I said now.'

Matthew stood groggily, fearful face not believing what he was hearing. He walked towards Starling like a drunk.

'Now.' Starling motioned downwards with the black grenade.

Matthew dropped to his knees, head down. Shoulders shaking, his head dropped further and he brushed both boots with his lips.

Jacko heard Hazel groan and guessed she'd looked away, the humiliation of it too much to view, but Jacko watched, thinking: That's right, you lickspittler. Kiss his bloody boots. You've been licking your old man's all your life. If you or his yes-men had told him to piss off, we wouldn't all be in this shit now. Everybody needs someone close enough, brave enough, to tell them: 'You're talking cock' now and then. The bigger they are, the more they need them.

Best place for you. On your knees. You're to blame for it, for not standing up to that fat fraud.

And did you, Jacko, in your car on Monday when you, a law officer, broke the law at his behest? Did you have the guts to stand up to him, to tell him to piss off?

378

And only then did Jacko turn his head away.

When he looked back, Matthew was pushing himself up. Sand smeared his mouth. He staggered, rubber-legged, to the door.

The controller followed him out, shrugging, all beyond him, at the manager and the driver.

Hazel was frowning so deeply at Jacko that her face had lost all trace of pity or fear. Doesn't make sense, she was telling him.

And it didn't, Jacko was agreeing. You don't let your number one hostage, son and heir to millions, go and keep two cops and two employees. He's the last card you play; your ace.

It didn't make sense, even as a diversion to send the police on a wild-goose chase. He's got no plan, no idea. He's off his rocker; gone.

'Right.' Starling slammed the door shut. 'All of you. Line up by that window.' He nodded sharply to a window at the end of the office.

All four gathered reluctantly in a

shambling line, shoulder to shoulder, backs to it, facing the now vacant desk. 'About turn.'

All four hesitated, a touch rebelliously. 'Now.'

They turned, staring sullenly across the lagoon to the banked-up road beyond.

Jacko felt Starling standing behind them and heard a hand rummaging in a pocket and something rattle like a box of matches. Going for his cigarettes, he thought. I'll burn one. Try to get some conversation going, open up communications, find out what's going on in this deranged mind.

It was only—what, fifteen minutes?—since he trod out his last cigarette, but it felt hours. He craved one, to settle his tattered nerves.

Matthew's white Golf VW came into view from the right, bouncing, going far too fast.

Right now, Jacko decided. He turned his head away from the window, just slightly. 'Give us a fag, mate.'

'Don't use the...'

Jacko didn't hear the tirade that followed.

In Starling's hand was a black box that Jacko assumed for half a second was a packet of John Player Special until he saw two black levers, the size of cocktail bar matchsticks.

In that next half-second he knew what it was. He'd seen one before. A neighbour's son used something similar to operate a whining model racing car up and down the driveway. He knew what it was, what it was for, what he was going to do, saw it all with absolute clarity in that second half-second.

Starling did have a plan. It wasn't a diversion or an extra pay-off. He was going to do what he'd done to Summers. He was going to get rid of Matthew and that little controller. And he was going to make an exhibition of it, to demonstrate just what he was capable of, his power.

Do something, he ordered himself, mentally barking much louder than his old army drill instructor. Act.

'Armed.' He shouted over his shoulder. 'He's armed. Shoot. Shoot.'

Hazel and the two men beside her dropped in a heap below the window into a huddle.

The black box fell with a tinkle on to the carpet. Starling's right hand joined his left on the black grenade. His right hand came away again. The ring was hooked to his index finger.

He was crouching, turning in one swift movement. The door was still shut.

He turned back swiftly, to Jacko, standing upright, shaking. 'Right, you tricky twat.' He caught his breath. 'Right. I'll teach you.' He retrieved the transmitter from the carpet and put it in a pocket.

Jacko glanced out of the window. A streak of off-white was going through the exit gate.

'Right.' He stepped to one side. 'Up.' Hazel and the two men unsteadily regained their feet.

'In the corner.' They walked in shuffling steps by him, eyes on him. The lorry driver reached the steel table first.

'Hurry it, you,' he said to the manager. 'Over there.' The manager joined the driver.

Starling looked at Hazel, following them. 'Not you. You, try that door.'

Clumsily, almost stumbling, Hazel moved to the door, turned the key and opened it slightly.

'Right.' He was looking at Jacko now. 'On your phone.' Jacko fished out his portable. 'Get on to your station.'

Jacko punched out the number, heard

the collator's voice, said nothing, just listening to the collator's repeated hallos.

'Tell 'em this. We're leaving now. You and me. That's all.' He flicked his head towards Hazel at the partly opened door. 'Not her. If I see one police car, they get this. Tell 'em I'm primed.' He held up the black grenade, grinning malevolently.

'Listen, Happy. Starling—'

'Mr Starling.'

'Mr Starling and me are leaving now. Just the two of us. Keep everyone well clear. Don't intercept. Make sure Knight knows that.'

'Destination?' asked Happy, softly, unruffled.

'Don't know.'

'Vehicle?'

'Don't know.'

'That's it,' screamed Starling.

'That's it,' said Jacko. He heard Happy say 'Good...' but thumbed off the 'luck.'

'Right.' Starling pulled the door wide open. 'You two, out.'

'Her, too?' Jacko queried, puzzled.

'Out, I said.' A snarl. 'Both of you.'

The cold hit Jacko as he stepped out on to the pea gravel path. Starling followed close behind Hazel.

He stood at the door, holding it open, looking from one pair of hostages to the other, appearing to think through his priorities, decided the first was Jacko and Hazel.

He stretched out the arm with the grenade in the hand. 'That lorry.'

Jacko looked down a set of wide, roughly constructed wooden steps to a lorry which stood in a sandy basin beneath a hopper less then thirty yards away. 'Half-way down the steps and wait.'

He started down, legs feeling as weak as in a flu bout. He heard Hazel get her orders: 'Stand on the top step. Both face front.'

Jacko came to a stop, heard the door slammed shut. 'Run,' screamed Starling. 'Run.'

Jacko looked over his shoulder. Hazel was stumbling, body pitched forward, two steps at a time towards him. Starling had almost caught up.

He turned to face the lorry and took another step down. From behind him, an ear-splitting explosion; a blast so fierce that it seemed to chase him down the steps, hurrying him.

With it came the sound of breaking glass and the acrid smell of a chemical's smoke. For a second the weak sunlight was magnified, then, in the next second, eclipsed by a thick black cloud. His ears deadened, as if he had just become airborne.

The cold-hearted bastard, Jacko thought, eyes front, stunned, horrified, rooted to the bottom step. Not daring to look back, he screwed his eyes shut, let his head hang.

He's blown them to bits; just blew them away. The ruthless, evil bastard.

Hazel was only a step away now, Starling one more behind. He was holding up the white grenade in his right hand. He wore its pin as a ring on his left second finger. The black grenade had gone. 'Go. Go. Go.'

Legs like lead, Jacko staggered to the lorry, brain dead, oblivious to Starling's shouts; drained and defeated; a coward, a failure, and very, very frightened.

23

'Open it.' Starling motioned with his hand, lethally loaded with the white grenade, to the passenger door of an eight-wheeled lorry backed into a hopper's loading bay beneath the silver chute. 'Get in.'

Jacko looked quickly around him, to the roof of the processing plant next door, at the three mountains of sand, the grass banks.

Heaven-sent for a stake-out, perfect visibility, he thought, but nothing in sight, apart from the gulls and crows that circled and cried in a sky of blues and whites and pale gold.

Where is Knight and his crack Anti-Terrorist Task Team? he asked himself angrily. Nowhere when you want him, the wanker.

'In,' Starling snapped.

Jacko climbed up slowly, pulled himself across the passenger seat and eased himself, stiffly (contradictory, true, but that's the way he was thinking) behind the wheel.

He felt high up, as if he was on the top

deck of the bus going to school, carefree, far-off days; safe days.

He looked at the clock on a wide dashboard with some dials he couldn't begin to fathom; just gone noon. God, I was in there less than half an hour.

For the first time he thought of his young son who'd be in the playground now, getting his shoes dirty playing football with his excitable mates, lovely kids, all of them.

He squeezed his temples with thumb and second finger, cold palm across hot forehead, to blank the vision out.

Think, he commanded himself.

The key was in the ignition. He'd never driven anything bigger than a hired van to help a workmate move house. He doubted if he could handle this. They'd all probably finish up in the lagoon.

Behind him, Hazel must have made some move to follow, for he heard Starling saying, quietly for him, 'Not you. Not yet.'

Jacko looked down on the heads of Hazel and Starling. He was stretching his neck forward, towards her as if he was about to give her a farewell kiss, a repulsive gesture. 'Unbutton.'

His left hand held up the white unpinned grenade in a sort of Black Power salute. 'Nothing rash.'

Hazel used both hands to undo the cape at his throat and he wriggled his shoulders free. She pulled it away from him, right-handed, with a flourish, like a matador executing a pass.

'Put it on.' She threw it around her. 'Fasten it.' Her fingers fumbled with the button.

Oh, Christ, he has got a plan, thought Jacko with a certainty not yet specified. 'Look, let her go. I'll not—'

'Shut it.'

'I'll do exactly as you say, but...'

Starling's eyes were close to Hazel, appraising her.

'...just let her go.'

Starling let go a meaningless, mirthless laugh.

'But—'

'Shut it. Hear me. Shut it.' He screamed it, then: 'Check?'

Jacko nodded.

'Check.' A barrack square bellow. 'Say check.'

'Check.'

'Sir. Say sir.'

Fuck that, thought Jacko, but he immediately changed his mind. 'Sir.' His head down, it came out as a short sigh, barely audible.

'Together and louder, you snot-gobbler.'

'Check, sir.'

'Better.' Starling switched his ghastly grin to Hazel. With his right hand, he withdrew the balaclava from the black belt on his fatigues, whose many bulging pockets were fully visible for the first time. 'Wear this.'

Hazel pulled it over her face, adjusting her hair beneath it, tidying it; just like a woman, thought Jacko. Like me, but I'm an old woman, a wanker, a failure.

'In.'

She climbed in and sat beside Jacko, not looking at him.

Starling climbed up on to the cab's foothold. 'Right. I'm travelling in the back. On the deck. Out of sight, but not out of mind, eh?' Another harsh laugh.

Oh God, Jacko thought, chilled. I've screwed this up. Utterly and completely. Missed my chance. I should have rushed him in there, when I'd got him off balance with that remote control in his hand. Whatever the risk I should have made my move then; shit or bust.

Starling swivelled his armed hand into a little wave. 'Plenty where this came from.'

In his pockets, Jacko guessed, with his black box of deathly tricks. He's going to make me drive down the exit road over the land mine he was going to detonate under Matthew. Without us seeing, he's going to bale out from the back as close as he dare and explode it right under us. 'Listen, Gordie—'

'Sir...'

Jacko ignored it this time. He flicked his head towards Hazel. 'There's no earthly need for her—'

'Oh, but there is.'

Shit. A fresh fear engulfed Jacko, just as chilling. Even if we make it over the mine, when I drive out of the exit gate, Knight and his sharpshooters will be waiting. We won't see them, but they'll be there. They'll already be in position. Out of vision, camouflaged, merging with the winter countryside.

And they're going to think Starling is my passenger and Hazel, dressed up to look like him, is going to be... Because of that phone call, my call, they're going to think she's... Oh God. Oh, no.

'Keep both windows down and start up.'

Jacko so desperately wanted to say: Piss off. He still couldn't find the courage. He wound down his window and turned the key. The engine burst into throbbing life.

'And wait for my command,' said Starling, lifting his left leg over the back.

Jacko waited. All he could do, he decided, was drive over the exit weighbridge, if he could manage that, then tell Hazel to yank open her door and jump. OK, she'd roll into the icy water. She'd be cold, but she'd survive.

And me? What happens to me? He didn't know, had no clue.

The Wages of Fear, he was telling himself, a real-life rerun.

What are the wages of fear?

Two grand a month for me; and, what, less than a grand and a half for her, and that's before tax. Is it worth it? Life or death, your life or death, in your hands. Is it bloody well worth it?

'Go.' A shout and then a tinny bang on the roof of the cab above his head.

Jacko tried to find first gear but the strange, springy lever resisted.

From behind him, a thud on the floor

as Starling slid down behind the cab and hit the metal deck.

From his right a roar like floodwater out of a mighty storm drain; all the more terrifying by its suddenness, its total unexpectedness.

A huge weight seemed to hit the lorry from above, rocking it violently, compressing it.

He cricked his neck back and up.

The silver chute was spewing a thick, round river of gold; a raging torrent of treacle, on and on, endless.

The chute was aimed behind him, at the back of the cab, but strayed from its target and hosed the roof and window. The noise was as deafening as that explosion, but an altogether different sound; thinner, flinty, non-stop.

Both ducked. Jacko's forehead rested on the wheel. Hazel got down much further into a ball in the ample leg space.

The roaring and the rocking went on and on. Can't be the fall-out from that white grenade, Jacko reasoned; can't be flying debris, not lasting this long.

He can't have lobbed it at some conveyor belt and set off some unintended chain reaction; pointless.

It was as if the heavens had opened in some form of biblical retribution, but this, he knew, was no natural disaster.

His spirits soared. Someone was operating the controls. Someone up there had got him; succeeded where I failed. But who? Couldn't be the controller. He'd gone with Matthew. Can't be the manager. He'll be dead. Who?

He raised his eyes towards the upper floor of the brick building, but couldn't see.

Liquid, thicker than curry sauce, yellow, not brown, was pouring through the opened window. Jacko's right cheek and ear felt sand-blasted. His back was wet and ice cold.

Down and down came a deluge that changed from rain to hailstones as big as pound coins from heaven.

Keep it coming, son, thought Jacko, winding up the window. The bigger the quantity, the greater the cushion against any blast from the back.

More and more glistening pebbles sheeted down the windscreen and Hazel's window now, so that he felt enclosed; in a yellow sea.

On and on, a gigantic pitter-patter. They

393

poured over and around and about them. Soon the sheets on the windscreen became thick sludge, oozing, and the impression he had was of being trapped on the seabed, and still submerging.

Still more stones rained down in a solid yellow monsoon. The lorry seemed to sink lower into the seabed.

He—whoever he is—must have let go a full load now, thought Jacko, anxious again.

That mad bastard behind will have drowned in it, if he hasn't let go and blown himself into more bits than Verne Summers and those two poor sods in the office.

Still they came, came, came, ceaselessly, on top and all around them. He began to wonder and worry about how long they could last for oxygen if they never stopped, and he felt the sands of time running out on him.

Waves of thick yellow molasses still slipped slowly over all three windows, but the roaring and the rocking had finally stopped.

Hazel pulled off the balaclava. Her face looked jaundiced in the cab's half-light.

Jacko tried to shoulder open the door, but couldn't budge it. It took both hands on the winder—and a long time and much sweating, cursing effort—to lower the window which seemed glued in its frame. It scratched, protestingly, glass on sand, all the way down.

Gratefully, eyes shut, he breathed in the sharp, fresh air.

His eyes opened on to a man he didn't at first recognize. 'You two all right?' Silent Knight's cultured, commanding voice.

His grey three-piece had become a tan-coloured two-piece with a blue flakjacket for a waistcoat. Three men in boilersuits, more brown than blue, stood behind him, looking as though they had been mud-wrestling.

'Fine,' both replied, one after the other, and Hazel added, 'Sir.'

'Hear anything go off?'

'Not in that row, no,' said Jacko. 'But I think he planted a mine on the exit road beyond the weighbridge.'

Knight turned to one of his men. 'Check that, will you?'

'His remote control is in a pocket,' Jacko added.

'Anything else?'

'More grenades on him, I think, but they shouldn't be primed.'

Knight turned to a second man. 'Alert the bomb squad.'

Jacko stuck his head out of the window and saw why the door wouldn't shift. Small pebbles had drifted in a big pile half-way up it. High heaps stood beneath all the other hoppers. 'Did Matthew and his passenger make it?'

'Oh yes,' Knight replied, very casually.

' 'Fraid you'll still need two body bags.'

'Why?' Startled.

'The bastard locked two of them up in the offices and lobbed a grenade in after them.'

Knight's face radiated relief as he shook his head. 'Stun grenade.'

'Are they all right?'

'They won't talk or hear much or see a lot for an hour or two, but they'll be OK.' Pause. 'You sure you're all right?'

'Yeah.' Not half, he thought. Relief overwhelmed him, running right through him. His indecision had cost no lives; except perhaps... 'What about...' He flicked his head backwards.

Knight shook his head again, this time rather sorrowfully. 'He got it in the back of the neck when he was kneeling. His head went straight under. I saw a hand come up out of the gravel once. Couldn't tell from the control room if he let go of anything, though. I didn't know which switch operated which hopper, so I let them all go. Sorry about that. Couldn't take chances, could I?' He smiled sheepishly. 'I couldn't find the off button either.'

Jacko shook his, smiling, thinking: Not bad, that, for a public school poofter. 'Thanks, guv.'

Knight nodded, smiling back. 'Bomb squad will dig you out. Sit tight for a few ticks.'

He turned to his third lieutenant. 'Total exclusion zone till it's swept clean.' And he walked away, not looking back.

Lots of ticks went by on Jacko's cheapo.

'What time is it?' asked Hazel.

'Ten after twelve,' he replied, not needing to look.

When he was happy, and he was close to delirium, Jacko was inclined to sing; normally the first tune that came into his head, often an old Lonnie Donegan. This time he selected his song deliberately, a come-on.

'Black gold, yellow gold, guess it's all the
   same,
Take my tip and give up the mining game,
Hey, hey, everybody drink on me.'

Hazel bit. 'Straight from here and into
a boozer, eh? On you.'
'Why?'
'I win. It's...' She stopped, working it
out. '...seventy-six hours.'
He put on his deepest frown. 'Aren't
you forgetting something? I didn't start
till quarter after midday on Monday.' He
looked at the clock on the dashboard. 'I
win with a couple of minutes to spare.
Easy.'
'Tightarse,' she said, good-humouredly.
Wet's a more accurate description, he
thought.
Now she had started talking, she hardly
stopped to draw breath. 'You can stuff this
for a game of soldiers. Sod CID. I'm going
back to PR. Handling the madhouse of the
media's got to be easier than this... God,
wasn't it scary? And you! Incredible, you
were. Waiting your chance. And so bloody
brave, the way you stopped him detonating
that mine.'

Jacko decided not to tell her he'd been silent because he could think of nothing useful to say. Besides, it would have been rude to interrupt her in full flow.

'What a risk you took! Couldn't bear the thought of losing Matthew, eh, our one witness against that old fraud Hamb? Was that it?'

Not really, he thought, enjoying himself, buoyed by her unquestioning faith in him, her failure to spot that, really, he was a bit of a failure. 'It was that Cobblers fan I wanted to save. Aren't many like us left in soccer's lower leagues.'

Hazel hadn't even heard his reply. 'Me?' She babbled on. 'Well, fuck me O'Riley. I've never been more terrified.' She slowed a little. 'I think I've wet my clean cotton clacks.' A cloud of shame passed over what had been a face never more beautiful, radiating joy, happy to be alive. Finally, she stopped talking.

'Well.' Jacko put on his confessional face. 'What with all this damp sand and all that happened back there...' A mournful sigh. '...well, I'm not too sure how your fella's underpants are faring either.'

'Never mind,' she said soothingly. 'We can always declare a no knickers day.'